GETTING DUNN

Text copyright © 2012 by Tom Schreck

Published by Thomas & Mercer
P.O. Box 400818
Las Vegas, NV 89140

ISBN-13: 9781612182810
ISBN-10: 161218281X

GETTING DUNN

TOM SCHRECK

THOMAS & MERCER

The muzzle flashed and TJ felt the bullets whiz just past her face.

She had caught sight of him, bearded and dressed in black, as he had come around the corner of the building. In the midst of the mortar fire, the yelling, and the chaos of the middle of the night, it seemed a miracle that she had spotted him.

"We're taking fire! Seven o'clock!" TJ yelled, ducking down the hatch of the Up-Armored HMMWV. Laser-like "pings" bounced all around TJ's M2 .50-caliber machine gun. The UAH was moving forward. TJ compensated with the rifle and fired at the guy in black. The movement had changed the man's positioning from seven o'clock to five o'clock and she missed shooting Alvarez, who was coming out of the air guard hatch, by inches.

"TJ, what the fuck!" screamed Alvarez, the platoon sergeant. TJ didn't have time to respond. Instead, she aimed again. A volley of bullets cascaded against the metal armor of the UAH and they sparked up. She felt the recoil of the .50 go through her.

TJ looked to her left. Alvarez was now sprawled out on the floor of the UAH beside her. He wasn't moving. Half his head was gone. In the chaos, she felt a chill and the taste of vomit in the back of her throat. Less than five seconds ago, Alvarez had been within two feet of TJ; it registered that he got hit with fire probably meant for her.

The UAH moved forward, into the bedlam of the firefight. A dilapidated building ahead erupted with gunfire. In the space where windows had been, dark figures appeared, lit up by their AK-47 fire. They were all over the place, shooting at TJ and the rest of the convoy. She continued to aim and fire almost mindlessly, working through the most intense fear she had ever felt. *I am going to die here*, she thought.

RPGs crisscrossed in front of TJ's line of sight, while several IEDs exploded at the same time. She felt her heart pound.

"They're all over the fucking place!" TJ screamed inside the UAH. The driver, Milford, helped by calling out targets, and TJ dropped the .50. The UAH directly in front of her got hit with an RPG. It caught fire and rolled over to its right.

Milford floored the UAH right into the heart of the ambush. The rounds kept pinging off the truck's armor, flashing past TJ's eyes. She fired into the building, pivoting off balance as the UAH accelerated. The roar of the firefight was deafening, and it was all physically exhausting. Milford kept the vehicle at full speed, and they blasted through the smoke and pings of incoming fire. The continual fire and explosions vibrated through TJ. She felt them as much as she saw them. Her body pulsated less as the UAH moved away from the action.

The UAH made it to Bridge 4. Milford pulled a U-turn so they were facing what they'd just been through and came to a stop. They were now a relatively safe distance from the firefight, so TJ took just a moment to catch her breath. Alvarez was dead, and the UAH was riddled with damage, but she was alive. TJ dismounted. She noticed she was bleeding from the shoulder, though she knew she hadn't been hit. A glob of something that looked like uncooked chicken breast was on her sleeve, covered in blood.

It was part of Alvarez's brain. She vomited reflexively. She didn't have time to process the horror of it, but she felt it physically and it went right through her. There was no time for it now. That would come later.

She scanned the sector in front of her and saw black smoke, fire, and a loud explosion coming from the factory just to the left of the intersection. It felt unreal and way too real all at once.

When they got the call to return to the ambush, TJ cursed to herself. She would go, no doubt, but she knew there was a good chance she would die there. The fact that they were heading back into fire with Alvarez's lifeless body didn't help the way she felt.

The squad headed back with TJ scanning out of the hatch. Up ahead at the intersection where the building had caught fire there were Iraqis running all through the streets, and it seemed like each had an AK-47 in his arms. The UAH was moving way too fast to get off any meaningful rounds so TJ held her fire. When the UAH slowed, it was a different story.

TJ fired the .50-caliber, and she kept 360ing as fast as she could, firing at everything that moved. Out of the back guard hatches, Murphy and Dobson manned their own M2 machine guns, like TJ, firing at everything. Kiowa helicopters were now overhead. Usually their presence comforted TJ, but not now, not in this mess.

Dangerously low on ammunition, TJ knew she would need to reload, and soon.

"Where's the ammo?" she yelled. She had no idea where the ammunition was kept because she had never come close to running out before.

"Strapped to the right side!" Marquason shouted back. No fucking way. She would have to crawl out of the hatch and into the line of fire to reload. TJ thought to herself about the fucking military genius that must've designed that bullshit and how far his head was up his ass.

With no alternative, she crawled out of the hatch and across the UAH to get the ammunition. Like everything of perceived value in the army, it was strapped down and sealed. Murphy did his best to cover her while she undid the straps and broke into the boxes of ammunition. She noticed her hands shaking as she tore through the cardboard and got her hands around the rounds. Bullets from the enemy's AK-47s started to ping around her. What the hell was Murphy doing?

When she turned to get back to the hatch, she got her answer.

Murphy was split open from chest to navel. His face, a twisted mask, was pressed against the UAH.

TJ crawled back into the hatch with as much speed as she could muster. She started to reload and realized she'd gotten the wrong caliber. She had picked up the 7.6 ammo meant for the 240 gunners.

Is this some sort of fucking joke? she thought. TJ crawled back out onto the UAH, this time without cover. She crawled as low and as fast as she possibly could while the whizzing rounds sparked up the metal of the vehicle. She grabbed the ammo, made sure it was .50, and hurried back to the hatch.

TJ felt a searing burn go through her bicep, and she knew she had been hit. She reached for the wound and lost her balance. She rolled off the UAH, trying and failing to grab at anything to hold her weight.

The thud to the ground sent pain through her shoulder. But it didn't come close to her panicked reaction to being alone, off the UAH, and unarmed.

"I'm off the vehicle!" she screamed. Through the din of the fire-fight and the black smoke it was impossible for her to be noticed. She dropped to her belly to crawl around the UAH for cover from the right side, which was only marginally safer than where she had been. She was near the rear axle when the UAH lurched forward. Milford must've floored it on orders to get out of the ambush.

That left TJ alone and in the open. She knew she was about to die.

She screamed as loudly as she could, but it was useless. Watching the UAH pull away from her, she waited for the inevitable.

Then she watched in horror as an RPG struck her UAH and exploded, obliterating it.

"Lieutenant Dunn, I'm sorry to have to be the one—" Father Rivest started to say.

TJ, sedated and loaded with painkillers, looked up from her hospital bed. Her affect remained flat.

The chaplain lowered his head. David Strickland, TJ's college classmate and the best friend of her fiancé, Trent Halle, was there too. He stood next to the chaplain.

"David?" TJ asked, ignoring the chaplain.

The chaplain's eyes darted to Strickland and then back to TJ. He seemed thrown off, as though his routine had been interrupted.

"Father, I know. They're dead, right?" TJ asked.

"Well, I'm sorry to say, yes, Lieutenant."

TJ closed her eyes. She knew, but hearing confirmation made it real. She let the narcotics and the tranquilizers wash over her. She kept her eyes closed, trying to make the world go away. Then, the vision of the RPG exploding came back to her and that weird feeling of pins-and-needles anxiety washed over her. Even through the fog of the drugs she felt it. The pharmaceuticals didn't take it away; they just muffled it. She finally opened her eyes.

"I'm sorry to say that's not the only reason I'm here, Lieutenant," the priest said.

"What? What are you talking about?" She shifted her gaze to Strickland, who looked down at his boots.

"David?"

Strickland looked up for an instant without making eye contact and then looked down.

"It's Captain Halle," the priest said.

Oh no, no. TJ closed her eyes again.

"Lieutenant Dunn," the priest began. "Lieutenant, I'm so sorry."

She began to cry, knowing what she was about to hear.

"Captain Halle is gone. I'm so sorry," the priest said.

TJ kept her eyes closed while she shook. Tears streamed down both cheeks. The realization went right through her and she could do nothing about the feelings it brought. After a long moment, she opened her eyes. Her stomach felt sick. She felt nothing was real.

She opened her eyes and looked again at Strickland.

"How, where, David?" she asked.

Strickland looked at the priest for help, then back down at his boots.

"Lieutenant—"

TJ didn't let the priest finish. "David! How?"

Strickland finally looked up. Tears filled his eyes. His mouth opened, but nothing came out.

"David! Tell me."

Tears now covered Strickland's face.

"He killed himself, TJ, in the barracks. In Kabul," Strickland said.

• CHAPTER ONE

"You can't touch me there," Tommie reminded him. But she said it playfully, with a flirt in her eyes. Working the floor brought in most of her cash.

"Tommie Gunn, you know you want it," Roy said. The forty-something construction foreman was dressed in dusty Carhartts. He was a regular on Tommie's shifts.

With an exaggerated forlorn look, he slid the ten-dollar bill over her shoulder and down her arm, where it dragged over the scar on her bicep. From there he tickled her side with the bill until he slid it in the space between her G-string and hip. He let the palm of his hand linger while he raised his eyebrows to her. Tommie winked and kissed him on the cheek.

A ten was a lot, but Roy was consistent with it. He tipped the other dancers a single but the girls knew Tommie was his favorite. They all had regulars too.

"How many crunches you do in a day, Tommie?" Roy asked. "You're shredded." He tilted his head and watched as Tommie shimmied between his legs to rub up against his midsection. Every customer who nodded got a lap dance with the expectation of a big

1

tip. With a half dozen trips to the stage and by working the room, the best girls could bring in three hundred to five hundred a night during the week, and twice that on weekends.

Tommie Gunn was one of the best.

She hit every single customer and did her best to flirt just the right amount to titillate a tip out of each of them. She finished the room, took the wad of bills from both sides of her black leather thong, and headed to the green room. The absurdity of calling the space off the greasy kitchen at Belle's Taco Stand the "green room," like it was the *Tonight Show*, wasn't lost on Tommie.

Tequila Sheila went on right after Tommie. If she lived up to her nickname, there was a good chance that she'd take a spill right out of her Lucite platforms. In the green room with the other girls, Tommie rifled through her bills, placing them all right side up and ordering by denomination with the dexterity of a bank teller.

"Fucking razor burn. I should've done the laser," Maureen "Whitey" O'Hara said. "Whitey" was a pale redhead. "Fucking bumps, damn!" She was standing topless in front of the floor-to-ceiling mirror, pulling down the sides of her G-string. She dabbed Noxzema around her shaved pubic area.

"Girl, what you thinking, goin' all Brazilian and shit? You weren't meant to be hairless. Besides, they all be getting off on that little red tumbleweed," Kaneesha said. Kaneesha went by the stage name "Dee-lish," and she didn't ever hold back.

Whitey rolled her eyes and winced at the Noxzema sting. The group was startled by a loud thump followed by, "Aww, shit!"

"Bitch fell on her ass *again!*" Kaneesha said.

The three of them looked through the curtain that separated the green room from the stage platform. Tequila, on her back, topless and rolling from side to side, kept repeating, "Fuck, it hurts."

The door that connected the office and the green room flew open. Maria Belle, the club owner, was not pleased.

"She fall again?" Maria asked them. Her pursed lips and furrowed brow let everyone know that this wasn't an evening to mess with Maria. An even five feet and a shade under two hundred pounds, she was built like a Mexican sumo wrestler.

The girls didn't answer, not wanting to throw Tequila in.

"Dumb bitch," Maria said to herself, her accent heavier with the anger. "Kaneesha, get out there."

Maria stood with her hands on her hips, shaking her head. The girls knew to stay away from her when she was like this. They had all been on the wrong end of her tantrums and, at times, hated her. Tequila came limping into the green room, plopped herself down on the couch, and slid into an impossible slouching position, eyes closed. Maria rolled her eyes while the girls suppressed laughter. The tension eased.

"TJ, you want to pick up an extra shift Sunday night?" Maria asked Tommie. "We got a bachelor party requesting a girl-girl." TJ Dunn went by "Tommie Gunn" when she danced.

"I don't think I can, sorry," TJ said. "If I can, I'll call." She had finished her last shift of the night and was changing into her street clothes.

"You in a hurry or something?" Maria said. She watched Tommie get out of her thong and top. She was naked only for an instant and then threw on a baggy pair of camo pants, her Fighting Irish hoodie, and Yankees cap. Her dirty blond hair was short and spiky. She just ran her hand through it, and then put on her hat.

Maria watched TJ while she finished dressing and threw the canvas knapsack over her shoulder.

TJ felt her stare.

"What?" TJ asked.

"Hey, don't let the regulars see you on the way out. It's bad for the image," Maria said.

TJ smirked, put the $311 in a zippered case, threw her knapsack over her shoulder, and went out the kitchen exit to the parking lot. With the brim of the ball cap pulled slightly down, she walked right past Roy, who was smoking a Marlboro at the back of the building. He didn't notice her.

She started the Suzuki, let it rev just for a moment to get it warm, and put it into gear. She headed downtown on the motorcycle the hardcore bikers referred to as a "Rice Rocket." TJ didn't care; it was simply a mode of transportation for her, not a lifestyle statement. It got her where she wanted to go, and got her there fast.

The bike's power was wasted on Central Avenue's stop-and-go traffic, and TJ felt the engine wanting to let loose. Instead, it revved, then stopped, then revved again every quarter mile. The stop-and-go bullshit got worse as she got downtown, to the small stretch of the city that catered to the bohemians.

Albany liked to call it the "Village in the City" a not-so-subtle reference to Greenwich Village. A few gay bars, cheap Chinese takeout, and tattoo places didn't exactly equal Delancey Street, but the street had a certain feel to it. She pulled up in front of the storefront with the small "Aquarius Switchboard" sign in the window, killed the engine, and walked the bike in the front door.

"You *do* have things to live for!" Heather said into the phone while acknowledging TJ with a quick wave. Heather was a social work student from Westchester County.

"There's the hope for the future. There's a chance to see a sunrise. There's baseball. You said you liked baseball," Heather said into the receiver.

TJ winced. If she called a suicide hotline and got a perky grad student looking to cheer up the world, it might just be enough to make her end it, even if she'd just called for directions to City Hall.

"Hello? Hello? Hel—He hung up," Heather said and slumped her shoulders. TJ noticed her tan today was a bit more intense, a bit redder. She must've stayed underneath the bulbs a tad too long.

"What was his issue?" TJ asked.

"He's only twenty-three and his girlfriend broke up with him because of performance issues. He can't deal."

"Carlos, right?" TJ asked.

"Yeah. How'd you know?"

"He's been calling every Wednesday night for nine months."

"Has he made any attempts?"

"Not that I know of. I think he just likes to vent. Last time I told him to get some Viagra."

"I thought we weren't supposed to give advice. Aren't we supposed to just do active listening?" Heather asked, and then got distracted by her own impossibly perfect French manicure.

"Technically, but I think Carlos needs to move on. I get tired of hearing—"

The phone on TJ's desk rang. She grabbed it, nodded at Heather, and turned away. Heather went to write her call summary.

"Aquarius Switchboard. I'm TJ. Can I help?" TJ said it the same way she did every time she picked up the phone.

"Hello…I've never called something like this…" the male voice said. It was timidity as much as it was weariness. You didn't have to work on the switchboard long to recognize the emotion.

"Go ahead," TJ said gently.

"It just, I don't know…it isn't worth it. I don't want to live like this…" the voice trailed off.

"Can I ask you your name? My name is TJ." In her training TJ had learned this was about establishing rapport.

"Jamal. Hi, TJ."

"Tell me more about 'it isn't worth it.'" TJ deliberately used his expression as a way to let him know she listened.

"My fiancée died six months ago." Jamal's voice caught in his throat. TJ could hear the shallow gasps of air that went along with crying. She felt the hairs on her neck stand up and got a hollow feeling in her stomach.

"My God, that had to hurt a lot," TJ said. It was a technique called validation, but for TJ the words came quite naturally.

"Yeah…" He sniffled up his tears with a deep inhale.

"I bet it's been very difficult since then."

"It hurts so much. Everything is an effort. Everything seems like utter bullshit."

TJ let the silence hang. Therapeutically, because silence encouraged a client to continue, but also because, right now, she wasn't confident that she wasn't going to cry herself.

"Are you feeling suicidal?" TJ asked. It was the policy to ask that question of all callers.

"I feel like life isn't worth living. I feel like I wish I was gone."

"Do you have any intention of harming yourself?"

There was a pause. The caller stayed silent.

"Jamal?"

"I don't think so. I don't feel it's right to commit suicide. I know that sounds corny and stupid, but I don't feel I can because of God."

"That doesn't sound stupid to me," TJ said. She meant it. She could identify.

They talked for another ten minutes. Jamal was able to speak without crying. He got through the moment and he didn't feel desperate. That was the point of the switchboard.

TJ made Jamal promise to call again if he felt like he needed it. He agreed.

TJ hung up and got up for coffee before she began her notes. She did her best not to let thoughts of Trent enter her head. She poured the coffee into a Styrofoam cup and brought it back to her desk. Thankfully, Heather was on her cell phone talking to a friend about someone on Facebook whom she had friended but now thought was stalking her.

TJ entered the "Notes" part of the computer screen and began to fill in the blanks about the call. She had just clicked on "new caller" and "depression" when the phone rang.

"Aquarius Switchboard, this is TJ, how can I help?"

"I'm going to say this once. Listen close and don't bother putting a trace on this because I won't be on long enough," the muffled voice said. TJ recognized the voice-altering device she had learned about during her military days.

"You'll start getting suicide calls from ex-GIs. It's all over the news that it's reaching epidemic levels. It's not what it appears."

He hung up.

• CHAPTER TWO

"What happened?" Heather asked. TJ hadn't let go of the phone. It just dangled in her hand, away from her ear.

"TJ? What happened?"

TJ looked through the storefront window and thought about Trent. The familiar sickish feeling in her stomach and the rancid feeling it brought came back. Her mouth went dry and she felt disconnected.

"TJ!"

TJ blinked a couple of times and turned to Heather. The wide whites of Heather's eyes contrasted with her ridiculously tan face. It was enough to bring TJ back into the moment.

"Huh?" TJ said.

"What is it? You got all weird for a second."

"Oh, ah, it was a prank. Usual bullshit."

Heather squinted in disbelief and shook her head but she didn't press. TJ had trained her to know when was enough during their nine months sharing a shift.

TJ went to the kitchen to put on a fresh pot of coffee just to be doing something. The call had drained her and she had started to feel her shift at the Taco in her ankles and thighs. If she could do that bullshit in her Nikes it wouldn't hurt. Maria, however, didn't want anyone dancing in running shoes.

Her mind went back to when the chaplain had given her the news, and she did what she could to suppress it. She cracked her neck, twisted her torso, and heard the pop in her spine while she watched the coffee brew.

"Oooh, that sound grosses me out," Heather said. TJ didn't know she was behind her, and she got startled out of her thoughts again.

"Is that from, like, working out?" Heather asked.

"Yeah."

"I've been doing this modified Pilates stuff that's supposed to work my core and it's, like, intense. What do you do?"

"I do a lot of core, try to work in aerobic stuff, maybe some kickboxing," TJ said.

"Which gym?"

"I don't go to the gym. I use my place." TJ knew Heather didn't listen all that well, despite her volunteer job on the switchboard. She could never go too long without talking about herself.

"I did cardio-kickboxing for a while. It's hard, but this one guy in the class was semi stalking me so I got away from it. Is that what you do?"

"Yeah." TJ thought about her hand-to-hand MP training. She thought about the full-contact sparring she had done with the men in her unit. She thought about the ribs she had cracked and her broken nose that, due to her good luck, had healed perfectly.

"I have the Tae Bo DVDs but I hate working out at home. That Billy Blanks has an awesome body," Heather said.

The phone rang. TJ had never been so grateful to hear from someone contemplating suicide. She made sure she got to it before Heather.

"Aquarius Switchboard, I'm TJ. How can I help?"

"Look, I'm not calling to have someone talk me out of anything." The man's voice was calm and measured. "I'm calling so someone will come clean up and find me before my parents do."

"Why don't you tell me a bit about what's going on," TJ said. The goal was to engage callers in conversation. Get them to talk as a first step, and then gradually help them see options.

"The address is six twenty Madison Avenue, Apartment A. It's a brownstone walk-up, and I'm on the first floor." His voice didn't waver.

"There's no rush. Could you tell me—"

The piercing explosion of a gunshot echoed through TJ's head.

• CHAPTER THREE

"He was twenty-five years old," TJ told Dr. LaMontagne. "He had been back for seventeen days. I mean, I don't get it. Why when you get back? You've been through all the shit and then you kill yourself when you're home?" TJ could feel the rage.

Dr. LaMontagne looked at TJ calmly. TJ marveled at her sense of control. She never seemed surprised, never seemed off guard, and never lacked for a cogent comment.

"Many times people don't feel the strength to commit suicide until they are out of the traumatic situation. They can't escape while it's happening, but when they step back from it and the acute reaction to the trauma lifts, they have more of a sense of self-control to take action," Dr. LaMontagne said. She had a mocha complexion and spoke with the slight British accent of her Bahamian roots. In terms of therapy, she was no-nonsense, and in TJ's mind, about as practical as a shrink could be.

"What kind of bullshit is that? Someone goes through hell and then kills himself when it's over?" TJ did her best to let her words flow freely while in therapy. She had gotten used to it even though it was in conflict with what she had practiced most of her life.

Dr. LaMontagne nodded. She was attractive, TJ thought, in a very businessy way. Her hair was pulled back tight off her face and gathered in a bun. She wore a sharp, tan business suit. She needed no makeup, and a short string of pearls around her neck was her only jewelry. Everything about her reflected discipline and communicated to TJ that this woman had it together. TJ envied LaMontagne's poise and confidence, which worked to accentuate her physical beauty. She respected LaMontagne like no other woman because of how she carried herself. That, and the way she stayed away from the usual psychobabble Freudian shit.

"In some ways you're right, it is counterintuitive. But think it through. Killing yourself takes some courage; maybe courage isn't the right word, but it takes nerve at least. You have to have some sense of power. When you're being traumatized you don't have that."

TJ shook her head and brushed at a coffee stain on her old camouflage pants.

"What about Trent?" Dr. LaMontagne asked. TJ could feel Dr. LaMontagne's eyes. TJ refused to make eye contact.

Dr. LaMontagne waited for her response. TJ had been coming to sessions long enough to know that LaMontagne could let silence hang for eternity. It was one of the very clear ways that therapy differed from casual conversation. Most people hated the discomfort of silence. Dr. LaMontagne could wait with uncomfortable silence in the air forever.

"What do you mean?" TJ asked by way of delay.

Dr. LaMontagne didn't fall for it. She waited.

TJ brushed again at the coffee stain and looked at the bookshelf in the office. Dr. LaMontagne's office was just two blocks down on Central Avenue from the hotline's office.

Finally, tears ran down TJ's face. She didn't rub them away; she refused to sniff or cough to acknowledge them. They ran down her cheeks as though detached from her. Inside, emotion boiled.

Dr. LaMontagne waited.

TJ swallowed, her first tacit acknowledgement of the tears.

"He's a fucking asshole for doing it. I am so fucking pissed at him," TJ said. She felt betrayal even as she vented. She did her best to follow what she had learned in therapy, but it left her emotionally confused.

The psychologist didn't respond.

"He fucking did this to me. Now *I'm* a fucking head case. He doesn't have to deal with it. I do."

Her face was a mess from the tears and she realized it was ridiculous to ignore them. She began to wipe them, and then the rush of the emotion came. TJ held her hands to her face and doubled over. With her elbows resting on her thighs, she sobbed. Then she folded her arms across her knees and buried her head.

She cried so hard, she gagged and coughed.

Dr. LaMontagne looked on.

TJ let go of it as it came out of her. It hurt physically. Release came, but with it a sense that the pain would continue.

"TJ, I will tell you again. Working a suicide hotline right now doesn't make sense for you." LaMontagne said it clearly and a bit louder than she had spoken during the rest of the conversation. The tentativeness that was sometimes in her voice for therapeutic rapport was absent.

TJ sat up and sniffled. She wiped her eyes on the Notre Dame hoodie.

"I have to."

LaMontagne allowed silence for a long moment.

"Does this compulsion to face what you fear always work for you? It served you as a soldier. But does it serve you now?" Dr. LaMontagne asked.

TJ didn't have an answer. She knew better than to rationalize, make excuses, or bullshit her way through an answer. LaMontagne understood and guided her to places she didn't want to go.

"Doing what I fear makes it go away," TJ said.

"Is fear what you're experiencing?" LaMontagne asked.

TJ didn't like the topic.

"Yeah, it's fear. I hate being cowed into doing something or maybe, better put, *not* doing something."

LaMontagne waited for her to continue.

"If I face it, go after it, I can…" TJ struggled for the word.

LaMontagne waited a moment and then spoke.

"Conquer it?" LaMontagne asked.

"Conquer sounds too strong."

LaMontagne gave a half smile. "Give it a better word."

TJ thought for a minute. The only thing she could come up with was "conquer," but she didn't want to say it.

LaMontagne went on. "TJ, do you think we are meant to 'conquer' every painful emotion?"

"I don't like feeling trapped by something." TJ felt sad behind her eyes. It set off a touch of panic.

"Of course you don't like it. Must we like everything we experience?" LaMontagne asked her. She didn't accuse or patronize.

"So I should just sit in my shit and mope? I can't spend my life crying." TJ felt her eyes well.

"Is acceptance sitting and moping?"

TJ hated the conversation. She wanted to get away from it. She wanted to go work out, run or hit a heavy bag. She didn't want to do this shit.

"You left it, didn't you?" LaMontagne asked.

TJ didn't understand. "Left it? Left what?"

"The feeling."

TJ got quiet again. LaMontagne had her. She didn't have an answer. She didn't have a response.

"I think I want to get going," TJ said.

"You can, but isn't that really running away from this? Doesn't that go against what you truly value?"

TJ pursed her lips. A solitary tear ran down her face and she felt her right hand turn into a fist.

"I gotta go," TJ said.

"Before you go, tell me something. You got close to the emotion. You felt the sadness, the grief, and then it left you. Now your hands are balled up in fists and you look like you're suppressing rage. How does that happen?"

"How does it happen?"

"Yes, inside of you, how do you convert grief to rage?"

TJ never had been asked a question like that. She didn't know how to answer. She thought hard.

"I guess it's easier for me to feel pissed off than it is to feel hurt."

LaMontagne leaned forward and lowered her voice.

"Easier..." She paused. "But which emotion is more authentic?"

"Authentic?"

"Yes, you know what I mean. And you know the answer," LaMontagne said with confidence.

"I don't like to feel hurt," TJ said.

"Because..." LaMontagne started a sentence that she wanted her client to finish.

TJ exhaled. She thought of how to answer but found it difficult to stay with what she was experiencing. Maybe because she had grown tired, or maybe it had something to do with the denial that LaMontagne sometimes talked about.

"I...I don't know..."

"You lost it, didn't you? You got close and then you let it go away. You try to conquer things in your life, but at this level you run because of fear."

TJ felt overwhelmed. She didn't understand emotionally or maybe even logically if she got what LaMontagne was saying. She never liked to feel that she feared anything.

"You need to think about this a lot," LaMontagne said with a comforting nod.

The session ended on that note. TJ felt drained, spent, and a little like a failure, though she knew that probably wasn't the case. Therapy often didn't feel good. It lacked the concrete finality of the other things TJ did when her emotions became too much. If she worked out, she knew relief would come and she'd get a different outlook. This was a completely different feeling, and she didn't like where it left her.

She left LaMontagne's office in a daze, heading toward the Suzuki.

As she walked through the parking lot, she cried so hard she couldn't see.

• CHAPTER FOUR

TJ had never gotten used to sleeping later than 5:00 a.m. Sleep hadn't come all that easily anyway since Iraq and all that had happened. But even on nights when she stared at the ceiling, praying for sleep to come for hours, she was still awake for the day by five or earlier.

She ran most mornings, taking the first ten minutes to jog until her joints loosened up, her head cleared, and she came alive. Then she began her interval work. Running wasn't a slow, meditative process for TJ, it was a balls-out attempt to rocket her heart rate to new levels. Jogging was aerobic, meaning she used her lung capacity to propel her. Anaerobic sprinting called on completely different energy stores and commanded that the cardiovascular system step into overdrive.

That all meant her morning runs were intense and explosive. TJ wore a heart rate monitor. She liked to see how close she could get to her calculated maximum heart rate and how long she could keep it there. Over the years, this was the type of competition she had gravitated to, the kind that was entirely internal. Watching her heart rate climb over two hundred while her chest heaved and her head pounded was a game for TJ.

The workout also exhausted her and in doing so kept emotions at bay. This morning was a full-out sprint up State Street, starting at Broadway and not stopping until Lark. Her heart peaked at 207. She could feel her eyeballs throbbing from the workout. She cooled down with a half-mile walk before she finished the workout as she had begun it, with a ten-minute jog back to her apartment.

By the time the coffee was made and she had thrown on her old robe, her pulse was back in the sixties. Later in the day, when she was fully resting, it would fall into the high thirties. She read the paper and sipped the black instant coffee. She skimmed the paper, not finding much of it worthy to linger on until she came to a piece that caught her attention.

The *Union Times* ran a feature on the suicide.

The national concern for military suicide has become a local issue. Sgt. David Collins, who returned from 14 months in Iraq six weeks ago, took his own life yesterday. Collins, who lived in Albany, was 26 years old. Originally from Venice, Florida, Collins's reasons for living in the area are unclear.

As of late, there has been an extremely high rate of suicide in the military, even for war periods.

"We are doing everything we can to address it," said Col. Edward Kasper, head of the army suicide prevention program.

The army normally releases figures on suicide annually, but due to the large number of deaths related to the conflicts in Iraq and Afghanistan, officials decided to announce monthly figures to focus attention on the problem and on the prevention programs available.

Kasper spoke of bolstered efforts in the military to combat the rise in suicides.

"We've increased the number of mental health counselors in country and we are doing everything we can in the prevention department."

The military reports adding mental health staff, military suicide hotlines, and battlefield stress management programs. Kasper reports that there have been close to 200 suicides in 2009 with more still under investigation.

David Collins was in combat in Fallujah for nine straight months. He was wounded with six others when an IED exploded near his convoy. He sustained minor injuries, and was treated at an army hospital and returned to duty.

No one who lives in the apartment building where Collins was found claims to know him or that he was in the military. Collins apparently rarely left his apartment. He was not employed or seeking employment. The Veterans Administration claims they are unable to confirm or deny if he was receiving mental health treatment at the Stratton VA hospital due to confidentiality concerns.

TJ exhaled hard, put the paper down, and took a sip of coffee. She looked out the window and felt it come over her. She wondered if she would ever feel normal again.

• CHAPTER FIVE

"Don't you want to have a fella?" Billy asked. He looked up at TJ as he took a loud slurp of his coffee. He scrunched up his forehead so he had even more wrinkles than usual. Billy was seventy, so that was a lot. They were sitting in Billy's preferred rendezvous spot—the Gateway Diner. It was always noisy, busy, and bright.

"C'mon, Billy, you're the only man for me," TJ said. She laughed.

"I'm serious, honey. You've been in town awhile and you're a good-looking girl. You should have a man to be complete."

"Yeah, well…" If Billy wasn't old enough to be her grandfather she'd have taken the time to straighten out his sexist views, but there was no point. Billy was TJ's other shift partner at the hotline. TJ worked two or three times what most volunteers did so she had different partners. She worked with Heather and Billy and some- times other volunteers, but Billy was the only friend—as casual a friendship as it was—she had. Heather and TJ had so little in com- mon that there really wasn't any place for a friendship to develop outside of the hotline. Realistically, she wouldn't have gotten close to Billy if he hadn't been so persistent.

"How come you don't work anyplace?" Billy asked. Billy didn't know any boundaries.

"I don't know. After the service I just wanted to take a break."

"You got enough money? If you don't, I can help you out, you know."

"You gonna be my sugar daddy?" TJ laughed and sipped her coffee.

"What am I gonna do with money? Mary Anne's gone, the two kids are in California making millions, at least as far as I know. They don't call. So, what the hell am I going to do with my money?"

"Why don't you travel, see things, go to the beach?" TJ asked.

"Ahhhh…" Billy waved her off with a swipe of his arm. He made a crabby face and folded both arms on the Formica table in front of them.

There was a rare moment of silence between the two of them just in time for the waitress to drop off Billy's order: a sausage, bacon, cheese, and tomato omelet with home fries and a double order of toast. The waitress slid TJ's Egg Beaters omelet in front of her.

"No wonder you're so skinny."

"It's a wonder you have any blood at all flowing to your heart. Could you possibly put any more cholesterol on a plate?" TJ asked.

"Ahhh…" another wave. "I had the bypass. It's like an interstate of veins in there. I'll be hooked up to some machine, brain-dead, and the ticker will keep firing."

"Nice." TJ shook her head.

"Do me a favor, though, TJ. When they're not looking, kick the plug out for me. I don't want to be lying there for eternity with a pantload of shit."

TJ put her fork down and swallowed hard. Billy plowed right through attempting to get the right combination of sausage, bacon, and home fries on each forkful. TJ's affected disgust with the pant-load comment went ignored.

"How about mom and dad? You never mention them." He said it with a mouthful of toast and in between slurps of coffee. TJ hid the chill that went over her.

"Dad's dead six years. Mom is in Michigan. I owe her a phone call."

"Sorry about your dad. He couldn't have been too old?"

TJ needed to get off this topic, but wanted to do it gracefully so as not to draw attention to it.

"He died when I was in college. He was fifty-seven." She focused on keeping any feeling out of her voice. It wasn't easy.

"Fifty-seven! Geez, what got him?" Billy was just making conversation, seemingly completely unaware of what he was bringing up. TJ swallowed.

"He was in the army. There was an accident." She said it as clearly and as matter-of-factly as she could so that it didn't encourage further inquiry.

"Hmm, during peacetime?" Billy asked.

"No, he was in Afghanistan." TJ braced.

"Geez, TJ, I'm sorry. How's your mom doing?"

TJ was relieved that Billy got off Dad. She let Billy know that Mom had good days and bad days. TJ told him that she felt bad that she didn't call her mom as often as she should. She let Billy know that her mom was fine, financially.

She didn't go in to details about her dad. She didn't want to, not with Billy. It wasn't that Billy had *poor* boundaries, it was that he had no boundaries at all. He was harmless, TJ had to admit. His heart was in the right place and he was a cool seventy-year-old, but that didn't mean TJ wanted to open the front door of her life to him.

"What do you make of the calls we get?" Billy asked her, thankfully changing the subject. A squish of home fries mixed with sausage oozed into the corners of his mouth as he spoke.

"What do you mean?"

"I don't know. Don't you think sometimes that it's a bunch of losers bellyachin'?"

"Geez, Billy…"

"C'mon, you know what I mean. There's people who get all jammed up and need someone to talk to. Life screwed 'em and it wasn't fair and all that. I don't mind those folks. It's the ones that make a shitload of stupid decisions then they call us and whine about it." Billy stabbed at a fat sausage that was spilling out of its casing.

"Yeah, I know what you mean, I guess. But the way I look at it, even if their crisis is their fault, that doesn't mean they don't deserve help. I think of screwy things I've done in my life, and those were the times that I needed the most help."

Billy had his mouth wide open and was up to the second knuckle of his index finger, digging at something in what had to be a wisdom tooth it was so far back in his mouth. Whatever it was, he got it. He pulled it out of his mouth, looked at it, and then ate it again.

"How about the nut jobs who call three times a day to tell us they're making dinner? I mean, is that really a damn crisis?"

"I think those folks just need someone to talk to." TJ sipped her coffee even though it had lost almost all of its heat.

"In my day, those people hung around the church and the priest had to talk to them. 'Course, there were a hell of a lot more priests back then. That was when they weren't diddlin' little boys all the time and had time to talk to the neighborhood's nuts." Billy punctuated his sentence by a loud sucking of his teeth.

"Being mentally ill has to be awful. The people who call us every day are really tedious to listen to, but I wouldn't trade places with them."

"Are they mentally ill or just weak and lazy?"

"Honestly, I think some are mentally ill *and* weak and lazy. Somehow, I think it's easier to be weak and lazy when you're mentally ill. I think people can do things to make their situations better, but it's harder with the mental illness." TJ looked down at her half-eaten omelet.

"Like they don't have what it takes to get over it and that makes it worse."

"Something like that. I mean, they may do a lot of self-defeating stuff like the rest of us, but it's easier for them to make mistakes and have sloppy habits than it is for us."

Billy rubbed the bridge of his nose back and forth with his index finger. He squinted like he was going to sneeze, but didn't.

"So we listen to them because maybe no one else will and because it makes them feel better even if they'll have to call us again the next day?" Billy asked.

TJ shrugged.

"Shit. It gets me out of the house. I feel a little useful. I get to talk to people. I get to hang out with pretty chicks like you." Billy winked and made a clacking sound like a gunshot while he shot TJ with his thumb and forefinger.

TJ winked back and couldn't keep herself from giggling.

• CHAPTER SIX

TJ got called into the Taco to sub. Angelina, who had been hired earlier that week, had disappeared and no one had any idea when or if she'd be back. Dancers dropped out of sight all the time. Sometimes they got out of the business, sometimes they got high, and sometimes they had boyfriend trouble.

Getting called in for an extra shift was part of the business. TJ was happy that Dr. LaMontagne had left the discussion of dancing out of their last session. Dancing brought in a lot of fast cash without TJ having to think. TJ just couldn't see working a legit gig and dealing with the boredom, with the office politics, and the daily grind. For now, she could make men drool, take their cash, and channel her energies into the hotline work.

"Hey, TJ," Gloria said when TJ came in the dressing room. "I thought you were off."

"Angelina didn't show again, so Maria called me," TJ said.

"I hope she doesn't call me in for tomorrow. I got a paper to write for Monday." Gloria went to the local community college.

"What's the paper on?"

"Not sure yet. I'm supposed to write about the psychologist Jung and his contribution to psychology." Gloria pronounced the *J* in Jung.

"He's kind of interesting. Sort of like Freud but a little different," TJ said. She consciously didn't correct Gloria's pronunciation.

"Do you think all that bullshit about sex that Freud talked about is true?" Gloria balanced a cigarette in the corner of her mouth while she pulled up the exaggerated cheerleading skirt. She wore a tiny matching blue thong that showed off her butt cheeks. Without taking the cigarette out of her mouth, she pulled on the contrasting sweater that covered three-quarters of her breasts and hung off them revealing a good portion of skin. The sweater had "I Love a Team!" scrawled across the front in script.

"Freud freaks me out. He did a lot of cocaine, you know." TJ was ready for her set too. She wore a men's business suit and Poindexter glasses. The suit, made with Velcro fasteners, would pull right off her, three-quarters through her act.

"What about that shit about boys wanting to have sex with their mothers? That Pull guy was messed up." Gloria laced up her saddle shoes.

"Pull guy?"

"Eddie Pull theory. That bullshit about little boys wanting to do their moms." Gloria stuck her thumbs in the elastic of the thong to release the itch pressure and swung her hips back to reposition the G-string on her skin.

TJ didn't want to insult Gloria but couldn't resist. "Yeah, the Oe-di-pal shit is fucked up." TJ said it slowly and pronounced it carefully.

Gloria's face went blank for an instant. Then she spoke.

"The whole Oedipal thing seems perverted, you know." Gloria reapplied a candy apple lip gloss, stabbed out her cig, and got ready to go on.

"Hey, good luck with the Jung paper." TJ pronounced it properly, like "young."

Gloria paused, and then she seemed to get it.

"Yeah, Jung is cool. I can get into Jung." She didn't pronounce the *J* this time, either.

TJ knew she'd be on stage in twelve minutes, right after Gloria finished. She began to loosen up, first by shadowboxing for three minutes and then by stretching. The other dancers had a good time with the shadowboxing. It had earned her the nickname "Rocky." TJ laughed along with the girls, but never once considered stopping. Since she had been a high school freshman studying kickboxing, she had warmed up with the same routine.

Before slipping into her four-inch patent leather heels, TJ bent over and put her palms flat on the floor. She felt the pop in her back as the right collection of joints and bones limbered. She locked her legs to get that extra pull in the hamstrings, came up slowly, and then went back down, this time going farther.

She heard the fade out of Mötley Crüe's "Girls, Girls, Girls" and knew she was due on stage. She pulled on the suit coat and checked the Velcro to make sure it was fastened. She pulled the fedora over her eyes. With the bass line from the *Mission: Impossible* theme blaring, TJ strutted on stage.

She put one foot in front of the other and exaggerated her shoulder movements with the strut. She projected power first, femininity second. When she approached the pole, she grabbed it with her right hand and felt her triceps flex. Her left arm went to her hip as she looked at her suitors with defiance. Pivoting on her right leg with her left bent up, she whipped her body around the pole twice with force.

She let the fedora fly off and she left the pole, landing in front of it with her shoulders straight and her legs wide apart. Her hair was greased and parted like a businessman's circa 1965. She made a show of taking off the black glasses and placing them in her breast pocket. With the double-breasted, pinstriped suit still on, she slid slowly into a sideways split, the whole time almost glaring at the audience. As her legs slid steadily down, the room went quiet. Years of advanced martial arts training, she thought, put to use to titillate horny, desperate men.

TJ rolled over, sprang to her feet, and in one motion pulled at her outfit. It came off in her hands and she threw it with anger to the back of the stage. She was topless in heels, with a thong pulled high on her hips. The triangle of fabric covered less than four square inches. Unlike her peers, TJ's breasts were small and looked even smaller in contrast to her developed pectorals. The scar on her bicep, the three and half inches of twisted flesh left to remind her of Iraq, reflected the stage lights.

The bar erupted on the move, and now they hooted and hollered. The atypical hush in the strip club was gone, but TJ knew she had made an unusual impact. That was her solace as she moved into more typical dancer fare. She turned, grabbed her ankles, and ground her ass into the air, coming up slowly from the stretch. She liked doing the Wall Street bit to start the set, but she knew what she had to do to get the dollars when she toured the floor. She had no illusions when it came to that.

Sinatra's "Fly Me to the Moon" from his Sands concert came on, and that meant TJ was should start to wind down. Feeling a bit winded, she mellowed a bit on stage and mostly strutted and stretched, taking time to reposition the fedora at an angle on her head. She moved to the front of the stage and cocked her hands on her hips. As she looked directly out into the crowd, she caught a glimpse of something that threw her.

She was surprised enough that it threw off her rhythm, and she stutter-stepped a little as she looked hard at the figure at the corner of the bar. The low stage lights made it more difficult, but she strained to see.

Unless her mind was playing tricks on her, the man in the corner was David Strickland, Trent's best friend from the service and the man who had told her of her fiancé's suicide.

"Whoa, Gunns, getting a little rude?" Roy asked as TJ blew past him. As a strip club regular, he knew the procedure. He didn't get why TJ would skip working the room, especially after a set that had set the place on fire.

TJ ignored him and hurried to the corner of the bar where she'd seen Strickland. Or, at least, where she thought she'd seen Strickland.

"A big black guy was just standing here," TJ said to a group of three twenty-somethings drinking Coors Light. "Where did he go?" she demanded.

They ignored her. TJ had forgotten for a moment where she was and who she was to the customers. She was a stripper. If she wasn't being overtly sexual or at least flirtatious, she didn't exist in the consciousness of the customers.

"Leon, a big black guy just left. Did you see him?" TJ asked the tattooed doorman. Leon, usually under the influence, had a disposition and intellect that made him well suited to a career that consisted of sitting on a barstool, showing his tats, and acting menacing. TJ guessed his SAT scores probably hadn't reached triple figures. The expression he usually wore on his face was more reminiscent a bovine than a human nature.

Leon shrugged an indifferent response.

"What the hell are you doing?" Maria asked from behind TJ. "You skipped the floor." She looked pissed off.

"Sorry, Maria. I—"

"I don't care what it is. The floor." Maria's eyes directed TJ to the customers.

TJ knew the rules. Neglecting the customers bred bad blood. It also hurt tips, not just for that dancer, but for all the dancers. TJ put on her slut smile, got her mind right, and started to work the bar.

Inside, though, her mind raced. It was hard to put anything into working the floor. Even as the men took turns sliding the bills under her thong, she couldn't stop thinking about David Strickland and what possibly could have brought him here.

* * *

"I want to talk about the dancing," Dr. LaMontagne said. Today she wore a navy blue pinstriped business suit with conservative pumps and a cream-colored silk chemise. A diamond tennis bracelet sparkled in the room's light as it dangled from her wrist. To TJ, she embodied an adult, having her life together. She was confident and self-assured but not afraid to be feminine at the same time.

"Again?" TJ asked. They had gone over it before.

"Yes."

"Like I've said. I average almost a thousand a week, cash. I work two or three nights. I enjoy the exercise and the other shit doesn't affect me."

"What's the 'other shit'?"

"C'mon. I have a college degree. I went to a Catholic, conservative college and I'm aware enough of women's issues. I don't need to go over this."

"Humor me." LaMontagne didn't smile.

TJ sighed.

"Dancing objectifies women, no doubt. But I believe if I do it to make money while I'm aware that I am the one with the power, I won't lose myself. I am using my body, my, uh, sexuality, to exploit men for a profit."

LaMontagne waited.

TJ tried to outlast her. Quickly she realized she knew better.

"*I'm* in charge. I don't get used."

"I believe you. Does that make it healthy?"

TJ considered her point. This was an entirely new angle. TJ had rationalized dancing as being OK if she wasn't being victimized or exploited. She had read the feminist literature and had armed herself with the understanding that using sex and being in control of her sexuality was feminist. LaMontagne was going someplace else.

LaMontagne waited for her to continue.

"Who the hell knows what's healthy?" TJ knew she was copping out. LaMontagne had this way, without ever saying anything, of getting her to realize when she was being real and when she was bullshitting.

LaMontagne finally spoke.

"Do you think dancing nude in front of men brings you closer to where you want to be?"

"Financially."

LaMontagne frowned.

"What are you getting at?" TJ asked.

"You tell me," LaMontagne said.

TJ thought a moment, then shook her head in confusion and looked at LaMontagne.

"You say you remain angry at Trent," LaMontagne said.

"Yeah, that's not hard to grasp, is it?"

"And now you seem OK with, and even proud of, exploiting men with your sexuality."

"So?"

"You objectify them. You take their money while you control them."

"Yeah."

"They become something to get something from, something less than human."

TJ remained quiet.

"Can you think of an angrier expression?" LaMontagne asked.

The psychologist's words hit TJ like a punch in the stomach. She knew on an emotional level that LaMontagne was right. But she didn't want to accept it.

"I don't know. That's a little Freudian, isn't it? I mean, I dance, I get paid, and I go home. I don't weep out of my superego and dream of Daddy not holding me enough."

LaMontagne ignored the sarcasm. TJ marveled at her ability to do it. It must be exhausting to spend every waking moment tuned into the feelings of others.

"Daddy..." LaMontagne said; nothing else.

"What?" TJ eventually asked.

"You've said very little about your father. On intake you said he was dead and that he died while in the service but not in combat."

TJ felt a burn start in the left side of her chest. She became aware of her face reddening and tried her best to show no reaction, which, she knew, was a reaction itself.

LaMontagne stayed quiet.

"Not sure what you're looking for here, Doctor." TJ rarely got this formal.

"Tell me about your father."

"Look, I spent a lot of time reading up on therapy. I deliberately chose your practice because you're a cognitive behaviorist. I know what that means. I know we're supposed to focus on the here and now and not get into whether I was hugged enough by my daddy." TJ became aware of her voice's volume.

"Past relationships can interfere with current emotions, functioning, and present relationships if you are somehow following old rules or scripts. That doesn't have to be psychoanalytical," LaMontagne said. TJ knew LaMontagne was right. She hated it.

TJ exhaled hard and crossed her leg, placing her right ankle on her left knee. She slouched back and looked up at the ceiling while she folded her hands. As she spoke, she was aware the words didn't sound like her own. She spoke slowly, in a measured cadence, keeping her eyes on the ceiling all the while.

"My father jumped off a bridge six and half years ago while in Afghanistan."

It was the first time she had ever said it out loud. Immediately, she felt it, physically. It was as if a bolt of electricity had just shot into her. Sweat began to form on her back and she felt her hands begin to shake.

TJ had never seen LaMontagne look shocked before. She also felt it deep inside her. Something had just been let out that she would never be able to put back.

"You've never mentioned it." LaMontagne sat back in her chair, still with a surprised look to her. "I think we need to talk about this."

TJ felt panic. She wished she had kept her mouth shut. "I think I need to go," TJ said, deliberately not making eye contact.

"I think we need to talk about this," LaMontagne said firmly.

TJ felt too much to think straight. She sensed herself get up from the chair and walk toward the door, but it felt like something she observed, something she wasn't really a part of. She felt herself swallow hard, and she felt her hand on the doorknob.

She walked to the parking lot, trying not to feel at all.

• CHAPTER SEVEN

Going to Aquarius right after therapy sucked.

TJ wondered how much easier life could be if she didn't have to spend every waking hour wondering about her motives. She thought of Roy and the other mindless Taco patrons and envied the way they moved through life. Get a beer, look at naked women, say stupid shit, and jack off. Effortless, compared to her life.

"Can you speak louder? I'm hard of hearing," Billy said. "What? Huh?" Billy winced into the receiver. "Goddamn it, this phone is screwed up." Billy looked at the phone like he expected it to argue with him. "What? I can't hear you! Huh?"

Then he slammed it down, hanging up on the caller.

"Damn thing," he said. "Mornin', TJ."

"Morning, Billy." TJ had seen Billy's phone tantrums before. Knowing it wouldn't do any good, she resisted the urge to say something despite the fact that he had just hung up on a potentially suicidal person.

"Do you know what's wrong with this phone?" Billy asked rhetorically.

TJ shrugged while she looked through the call log. She scanned through the brief notes about depressed lovers, a sad note about an elderly woman, a thwarted sex call, and then came upon a call that chilled her.

Abraham, the overnight counselor from Guyana, had left this:

Caller said the army is making murders look like suicides and there will be another very soon. Refused to elaborate and abruptly terminated the call.

TJ studied the two sentences, rereading them at least ten times. She raised her head and stared out the window. The feeling from the day with the chaplain came back to her. Not thoughts, just a visceral emotional reaction that she had no control over. It weakened her.

"Says here they're looking to drill for more oil in Alaska. I miss that cutie governor they had there. She was a looker! As a woman, you gotta love her, TJ, huh?" Billy paused for just a moment. "TJ, you ain't listening. Earth to TJ," Billy increased the volume enough that TJ came back.

"What?"

"You ought to get yourself a pair of them leather boots she used to wear. Nice and shiny—hooha!" Billy liked to punctuate sentences with "Hooha!"

"Who are you talking about?" TJ asked, unable to contain her annoyance.

"That woman who was governor of Alaska. She's all woman!"

"She's an idiot," TJ said.

"No she ain't. She—"

The phone rang and TJ beat Billy to it.

"Aquarius, how can I help?" TJ asked.

TJ heard breathing but no voice. She waited.

"I don't even know why I called," a raspy voice said. TJ heard choked-back tears.

"Tell me about it," TJ said.

"It's not worth it. It's not worth it…"

"What isn't?" TJ tried to remain calm, unpanicked, and soft.

She heard a deep inhalation, the collapse into tears, followed by a wail of pain.

"Put words to it, if you can," TJ said.

More pained wailing. "Oh God…" Wailing.

"Please, let me know," TJ said.

Sobs and an almost unintelligible, "No more…no more…"

"Please, let me hear. Let me know. Let me help."

Dial tone.

TJ looked at the phone. A sick twist knotted her gut.

"Another hang-up? I hate that stuff. Why call a suicide hotline and not—"

TJ couldn't listen to Billy's bullshit, not now. Sometimes the calls got to her when she didn't expect it. She didn't get it, because there were plenty of times when it just didn't faze her. Not like she didn't care, but that she was in control emotionally. You had to be to work the hotline.

"Was it a hang-up?" Billy barked. He didn't like being ignored.

"Yeah…sort of. He started to talk and then hung up."

"Weirdo."

TJ couldn't help but break a smile. Billy was a curious suicide hotline operator. TJ had given up wondering why he did it. He hung up when he couldn't hear the caller, sometimes he told callers to get over it, and half the time he read the *New York Post* while someone was speaking to him. Despite that, he was the only social contact she had.

Though she didn't even like to admit it to herself, she cherished their breakfast meetings, during which Billy offered his view on life and tips for TJ to improve hers. TJ didn't mind when he was over-the-top because his heart was in the right place. She didn't pay any attention to his advice anyway. She simply enjoyed his companionship.

And maybe something else; maybe she liked that he cared.

TJ poured another cup of coffee. Getting coffee, whether it was during a shift with Heather or Billy, got her out of the phone room and gave her a legitimate excuse to get away. Both of them liked to hear their own voices, and sometimes TJ just had to remove herself. Right now, she could also take the time to wipe her eyes and compose herself.

After a deep breath, she was back at her desk, and when the phone rang she was the first to pick up.

"I have this problem," the male voice said softly.

"Can you tell me about it?" TJ asked.

"Well, it's kind of weird."

"Go ahead, it's OK," TJ said after pausing to keep the conversation slow and comfortable.

"I like to wear women's panties. I have them on right now. They're red and satiny and I'm touching—"

TJ hung up and shook her head. Sex calls were common on the hotline. Common, that is, if you were a woman.

"What was that about?" Billy asked. He had the *Post* open to the centerfold, reading an article about an ex-governor's mistress who was back in the news. He sucked his back teeth while he read, his glasses balanced on his nose.

"Sex call," TJ said.

Billy's head snapped around.

"Pervert?"

"I don't think we're supposed to call them that."

"Yeah, sure. What he'd want?"

TJ exhaled. "You don't want to know." She smiled.

"Yeah, I do."

"Never mind."

"C'mon, what'd he say?"

TJ feigned annoyance and shook her head.

"He was wearing red panties. Then he started telling me he was touching himself. That's when I hung up." TJ raised her eyebrows to say "case closed."

"How come I don't get calls like that?" Billy sounded disappointed.

"You get hang-ups, don't you?"

"Of course, all the time."

"They're probably sex callers who hang up when they get you. They want a woman."

Billy made a face.

"How come women don't call me and talk about their panties and touching themselves?"

"Women are wired differently. Why, Billy, do you really want women to call you about wearing men's underwear?" TJ raised her eyebrows and tilted her head.

"Hell yeah, I do!"

The phone rang again. TJ picked up first again.

"It's Rhonda," a frail, female voice said. Rhonda called several times a day. Mostly, she told whoever would listen about what she had planned for the day.

"I'm thinking about making a meatloaf. I'm trying to decide if I should put egg in it," Rhonda said after TJ greeted her.

"Do you usually put egg in it?" TJ asked.

"Sometimes. I'm trying to watch my cholesterol. I'm a large person. I don't like to say 'fat' or 'obese.' I think words like that are hurtful. I'm large. That's part of my identity." Rhonda said these same words in the same order with the same inflection every time she called.

"Good for you," TJ said.

"I'm three hundred twenty-four pounds and I love myself."

"You should love yourself," TJ said. She doodled with her right hand, doing her best to draw that one-line image of a dog that Picasso did. Picasso's looked artful. TJ's looked like it was done by an inattentive kindergartener.

"The egg probably won't make a difference. I'm trying to take small steps toward wellness. Small steps are important because over time they lead to significant changes."

TJ had long ago stopped wondering how Rhonda had gotten so Oprahfied. The next dog looked particularly odd and TJ couldn't tell if the ear was too long or if it was the way it connected to the rest of the head that was off.

"Pudding is a good dessert. It's easy. I put chocolate syrup in it to make it special. It's important to be good to yourself."

TJ's fourth dog looked really deformed and she realized her interpretation of Picasso was deteriorating, not improving.

"I think my plans are set. I'm going to go now. Thanks for listening." Rhonda ended the call, to TJ's relief.

"Was that Rhonda?" Billy asked with his eyebrows up.

"Yeah."

"She's a pain in the ass. Talk about a boring son of a bitch."

"Billy!" TJ pursed her lips in mock condemnation, and Billy chuckled.

He went back to the *Post*, sucked his teeth, and let out a sigh that ended with a slight burp.

"S-cuse," Billy said. The two of them sat in silence with the phones quiet for what seemed like a long time. By the fifth hour of the shift, TJ was bored and her mind drifted. She thought again of seeing Strickland at the Taco.

Maybe her mind had just played tricks on her. After therapy, maybe her thoughts got scrambled and then they just spun around randomly until they fell on something, flavored it, and misinterpreted it. Where did emotions go? Were they tangible in the brain?

Could you spot them with a CAT scan? If they had a physical component to them, did that make them real? Was Strickland really there or were memories from her tour spinning around, making some random big black dude in the bar into Strickland?

The guy had moved like Strickland. He was the same size and he was the only black guy in a place that didn't get a lot of black customers. TJ wasn't entirely comfortable dismissing the possibility that she'd seen him, nor did she feel comfortable believing he was there. The whole thing made her feel a little nuts, like she wasn't totally in touch with reality.

That scared her more than anything.

TJ took a deep breath and decided not to fight the feelings about Trent that came over her. Sometimes she just didn't want to spend the energy.

"Billy, I'm going to get some air," she said and went out the front door. She turned right, walked to the corner, and leaned on the stop sign. She felt herself start to cry.

• CHAPTER EIGHT

David Strickland knew he didn't blend in well. At six foot five and with a dark chocolate complexion, picking him out of an Albany crowd didn't present a challenge. Still, his training had taught him how to become invisible.

TJ's new life bewildered him. Drifting to upstate New York, going from combat to topless dancing and working at a suicide hotline—none of it made sense. TJ had lived like an elite MP as long as Strickland had known her. Her body, shredded with functional muscle and built for combat, seemed out of place in heels and a thong. Even so, he acknowledged to himself that she looked damned good, her body like Demi Moore's in *Striptease* but even harder, a combination of *GI Jane* and *Striptease*.

Strickland remembered sparring with her. They had both trained in Tae Kwon Do and she had asked him for some work. He hadn't taken it seriously at first, but a minute into the sparring her speed had confused him. She'd feinted, shuffled and stepped in, and when she'd planted a side kick with her heel into his ribs it had hurt for a week. She could *fight*, and not just for a woman. Of course, they had just been sparring, so David hadn't unleashed his power even if he had gone full speed. You couldn't take sheer power out of the equation.

He and Trent were in ROTC at Notre Dame together. Notre Dame had very few black students who weren't scholarship athletes, but Strickland had grown up in a white world. Not to say he had become white, but he was comfortable around both races. Still, the rich, suburban Catholic white boys kept him a little bit at a distance.

He did well with the women at ND. Liberal Irish Catholic girls liked dating black men as a statement or to let Mom and Dad know that their little girl was on her own. Strickland sensed it and used it to his advantage. There was no use pretending it was something it wasn't. When Trent, his best friend from the dorm, met TJ, Strickland was happy for him and jealous at the same time. TJ was not just hot; she didn't carry with her a lot of the pretense that the other princesses at school carried. Strickland even thought she got a little argumentative at times and he kidded Trent about taking shit from her.

He liked the way she moved, no doubt, and on more than one occasion, he'd thought she was flirting with him. Not to the point where she was going to act on it right there and then, but instead planting the seed, as women often did. A kind of insurance thing, like, "if this doesn't work out, maybe we could have some fun."

There was no question he had feelings for her. Some of them were complicated. He was genuinely concerned about her and he shared her grief over losing Trent. There was also something else, but Strickland moved on, not ready to admit the truth to himself. Lastly, there was Jordan, the money, and the threat TJ brought to his entire way of life.

He also didn't trust what TJ knew or didn't know. The plan called for ignoring her after she got out, and Jordan had said that TJ would buy the explanations, be overwhelmed with grief, and disappear into civilian life. She had done just that, but Strickland still couldn't let it go. He didn't know exactly why he went to the club where TJ danced. No doubt curiosity, plain and simple, factored in, but he didn't know where it fit strategically. He thought he might have gotten out of there before she had seen him. If not, he hoped it wouldn't come back to haunt him.

He hoped.

Strickland, the ideal soldier, always followed orders. That was how things got done—with efficiency and economy. His actions lately didn't make sense even to him because they went against what had been ingrained in him. He couldn't help himself.

Too much at stake to leave it to chance.

He watched TJ closely as she came out the front door. He could see she was crying and wondered what had gotten to her. Unstable, she clearly presented trouble if her emotions got channeled in the wrong direction. That was precisely what brought him here. However, it wasn't just the business of soldiering right now that had him interested. As he watched her, he thought of holding her, comforting her, and being there for her. Jordan wouldn't like that. Strickland wasn't sure he liked it either. Sometimes the military mind-set and its systematic dismissal of anything emotional were welcome.

He wouldn't let how he felt interfere with what he had to do. That pass from acting on emotions was nice to have, especially when his emotions were complex and difficult to name.

He kept his eyes on her, and as he did, he felt something in his gut. There was queasiness, anxiety, and honestly, a bit of a longing.

He had watched her cry; maybe the hotline bullshit got to her. He had watched her leave her shrink's office overcome with emotion to the point that she seemed almost to stagger. Her life had clearly become a mess: stripping, volunteer work with a collection of weirdos, and complete isolation outside of those two activities.

He didn't get it, except to acknowledge that Trent's death had rocked her world even more than he had imagined that it had. For that, he felt sad and more than a little guilty.

That was his emotional side.

He watched her take a deep breath, leave the stop sign, and head back toward the entrance. Strickland waited until he saw the door close behind her before he walked away. There was no question the woman was unstable, and unstable meant unpredictable. Unpredictability brought uncertainty, and in the world where Strickland lived, uncertainty was not a good thing.

He had to make a phone call.

That was his soldiering side.

• CHAPTER NINE

TJ slept hard on the musty twin bed. The studio apartment she rented above a garage in the lower-middle-class neighborhood was dark and damp and had a bit of a moldy smell. After living in barracks, TJ didn't really need a lot from where she lived. Her apartment had something to sleep on, a place to keep food, a place for gear, and even a thirteen-inch black-and-white television. Having any more belongings wouldn't have fit with where she was in life; she didn't want anything that would suggest anything other than transiency.

She wanted to be alone. She needed it. It had been two years without a man in her life, but she felt that any kind of dating bullshit somehow would trivialize the memory of Trent. She didn't know how to reconcile that. Tonight, all alone, she felt it.

But she did need people, and pretending not to didn't work. She never talked about her emotions, and except for her time with LaMontagne, she really didn't have a vehicle to get it all out. The dancers weren't an option. She was careful never to be patronizing; some of them were a mess, but she still never entertained sharing with any of them on a peer level. At Aquarius, Heather, focused on the depth of her tan and on her French manicure, didn't present an option. Billy was grandfatherly, a buddy, but not a man she could really confide in.

Tonight, alone and exhausted, it hurt. She tried to deny it. She tried not to give it respect with the flip "fuck-the-world" attitude she had learned in Iraq. She tried to stay busy with activities that called for her attention and kept her from boredom. She worked out hard, part of her motivation to exhaust herself and numb her feelings. But after midnight, alone, before sleep came, she couldn't deny how bad it felt. Tears ran down her cheeks, and though she pretended to ignore them, she knew everything she tried failed to work.

Sleep came eventually. It, too, brought more pain and memories.

Naked on top of Trent, he's inside her and she's riding him. He's incredibly hard and she's grinding into him with everything she has. Covered in sweat, the two bodies move together; he's going in and out of her rapidly. She braces her hands against his chest as she concentrates on him.

Now she is circling her hips on top of him. He's so rigid that she can't get enough of it. His six-pack abs and tight pectoral muscles flex as she grinds into him. His breath quickens, her chest heaves, and she feels him come. She escalates her grind until she feels it well up inside her. The orgasm cascades, rippling through every nerve ending in her, and she cries out in ecstasy. He quakes as she rides everything out of the experience, not wanting to stop, not wanting it to be over.

TJ awoke with her hand between her legs. She was dripping wet and spent. When her mind cleared, she realized she'd had another sex dream. She felt the orgasm that just shook her and she knew she had come hard. She was alone, but still embarrassed that she only got off unconsciously while she slept.

She couldn't allow herself this pleasure while awake. She knew it was ridiculous, but sex, even masturbation, without Trent seemed like a violation. That didn't feel like it would ever change. The dreams felt like a betrayal, her body's revolt against how she lived her life now. The dreams made her feel like even more of a freak, a woman out of touch and hopelessly drifting.

She had no idea what the dreams meant, but they disturbed her. She had never had sex dreams until Trent died. She felt guilty, as if that side of her had no right to live on. It simply didn't feel right, and she didn't want it to be a part of her despite making money dancing for men who were fueling their own sexual desires. Not now, and not in the foreseeable future.

She stared at the ceiling, embarrassed even in her solitude. Why was she so out of touch and disconnected with the world around her? She had no one to call and no one to share this with. She thought about how the only human she shared things with was Dr. LaMontagne. TJ felt embarrassed that she had to pay LaMontagne to listen to her.

Pathetic.

Her thoughts drifted to her father. She did her best not to think about him; she simply closed him out. He didn't deserve her thoughts. He didn't deserve to be missed. He had just checked out and left her and her mother alone without a decent explanation. No matter what stress he had been under, no matter how bad things could've gotten, he had cowardly exited without any thought toward the impact on those remaining. No, she wasn't going to pay tribute to him with "I miss Daddy" thoughts and longing. She was adamant that she wouldn't do that.

She avoided thinking about her mother too, but for different reasons. Since her discharge, she had visited her mom once, for just a weekend. It was too much. She couldn't bring herself to stay in touch. TJ knew she couldn't deal with her mom's sadness, not on top of her own. She couldn't face the sick thing they shared in common. She didn't want to look her mother in the eye and have them both know what they would always have to live with.

She couldn't think about Mom at all.

It was a long time before sleep came again.

• CHAPTER TEN

Strickland wondered how much she knew.

She had been stationed in Iraq while Trent was in Kabul, thousands of miles apart with different assignments, duties, and peers. They were allowed to see each other only occasionally on leave but stayed in contact by sharing e-mails almost daily. Strickland wasn't stupid; people often believed that telling a spouse or a fiancée was the same as not telling anyone. TJ and Trent were very close and, military or not, Trent could have made that kind of mistake. It wouldn't have seemed like a mistake to him. TJ was going to be his wife and he didn't keep secrets from her. Strickland hoped for TJ's sake that Trent had made an exception when it came to what was going on in Afghanistan.

Either way, Strickland didn't feel like chancing it.

Back at the Residence Inn, Strickland toyed with his laptop, watched ESPN, and ate pizza straight from the box. The pizza box made him smile. He remembered the neatly stacked and taped hundreds delivered in these same generic pizza boxes in Iraq, the kind that weren't printed with a store name or logo, just the word "Pizza."

Over there, it had seemed ridiculously simple. Several hundred thousand dollars of untraceable cash delivered in pizza boxes. Fucking ridiculous.

Except Strickland knew his life and his future rode on secrets kept. His old friend, the new stripper, his best friend's fiancée, might know his secrets. Strickland found that unacceptable. He had learned as a soldier to minimize risk, to cover all angles and to leave as little as possible to chance. That was burned into him by the military and he lived his life with that in mind at all times.

He had liked the military and even liked Afghanistan. He knew it sounded stupid, but he knew he wasn't the only one. The military offered the comfort of not having to think. You did what you were told, you did time, and you got rank. As your rank went up, so did your quality of life. He had been in long enough to know how things worked, how to get what he needed and how to have a little fun. Life was consistent and predictable. He knew how to leverage his own influence and skills to his advantage.

The soldiers who got in trouble were the ones who thought too much. They questioned procedure, mission, or ethics. Strickland saw that as just plain stupid. The military was going to be the way it was, regardless of anyone's complaining. He didn't see his acceptance of the bullshit as cowardly. He saw it as utilitarian. He measured what the stakes were at all times and he made choices based on what would benefit him the most.

Now, on the outside, in semi civilian life, the rules had changed on him. He had gravitated toward this life with Jordan because it gave him an approximation of the life he had mastered. It was only an approximation, though, and he often got confused about being a civilian. There were too many gray areas, too many choices for each individual to take. That meant variables, lots of variables. Strickland hated variables he couldn't account for.

TJ was a variable. In the military, she could be contained and controlled easily. Out here, she was free to be as crazy as she wanted to be. And she was doing just that. Stripping at night, counseling nut jobs for no money at all, and…seemingly nothing else. Who knew what she was capable of?

He wondered about her and Trent. Had he told her or not? He also didn't like to admit to himself how much he thought about TJ. No doubt, he was attracted to her, but he had always been respectful of that safe distance friends kept from each other's girlfriends. That wouldn't be necessary any longer. He thought again of the playful exchanges between him and TJ and he knew she was interested. The tilt of her head, the lingering of a look, the soft laugh— they were all the type of coy flirtation that Strickland knew women were capable of.

There was something else now. The stripping made Strickland think. Almost all questions he'd ever had about her sexual inhibitions had been erased. A woman just didn't choose to dance nude in front of men unless she at least thought about sex and about what excited men. Strickland got excited by the thought of how that could get translated in the bedroom.

The image of her topless, grinding, and working the pole, was burned into his brain. She was hot, but in a much different way than the other dancers. No silicone, no ridiculous six-inch heels; no, TJ's body was functional like a fighter's but unmistakably feminine. It was exactly the combination that appealed to Strickland. She was hard and soft at the same time.

He caught himself thinking of her and consciously tried to think of something else. Jordan. He had an odd relationship with the man. He was a pain-in-the-ass high-ranking military type. Though Jordan was tedious in his procedural bullshit and an ultra-control freak, Strickland still found himself wanting to please the man. Maybe it was because Jordan drove himself hard to do what he wanted done. Why was it important to him to impress Jordan? He wasn't sure, but even alone he felt a little embarrassed by the needy feeling of wanting Jordan's approval. Strickland thought for a moment that whatever quality Jordan had, it was exactly what you wanted in a commanding officer.

Strickland had done things he hadn't wanted to do in the past because of orders. He had done things that he hadn't believed were right and he had done things that had gone against his own moral code. These things didn't bother him much because he could partition them off in his thinking and chalk them up to just following orders.

Strickland gulped the rest of his beer and stared blankly at *Sports Center*. He thought of Trent, the best friend he ever had, and he ran over in his mind what had happened. He thought of Jordan and how he blindly followed his CO's orders. And he thought of TJ and how she looked at the Taco.

He wondered what the future held. What would Jordan decide to do about TJ?

Strickland wondered if would have to kill her.

• CHAPTER ELEVEN

TJ hadn't thrown a punch or a kick since she left Iraq except in her warm-up routine before dancing. She thought getting back into a routine might help her. Help her with stress, anger, grief—all of the demons that swam inside her.

She looked in the phone book for a gym and decided that she didn't want to train anyplace where a Taco customer might drop in or where someone familiar with Aquarius might stop by. She didn't want to answer questions about the paradox of balancing the helping arts and the martial arts. She didn't always understand herself her attraction to both wanting to help people and to knowing how to kick someone's ass. She found it tedious to try to explain it to someone else.

And she certainly didn't want to get into her motivation for dancing almost nude in front of men for a living.

The YMCA in nearby Crawford had a boxing gym and it only cost the usual Y guest fee to use. She didn't see any boxing or kickboxing classes listed, which was a good sign because that meant it was probably an old-school fight gym, not a hangout for wannabe yuppies who, like suburban guys with Harleys, played make-believe.

Going to a boxing gym for the first time brought TJ anxiety. Each one had its different rules and expectations. They weren't the formal rules spelled out for members, they were the real rules, the ones that the people who gathered there followed. There was always a rank system, not unlike the belt system in the martial arts but less regimented. In some ways, the ranking system in an old-school boxing gym was truer to Old World karate than the current over-marketed karate businesses that flourished in modern society.

TJ knew that when karate had originated there had been no belt system. The black belt became what it was because those who trained the longest had the oldest, most tattered sashes that closed their traditional robes. Over time, the sashes frayed and got discolored, but you could tell by looking at the older practitioners that they had been around for a while. Those with experience were also kind and patient with beginners because they had a sense of honor and reverence for the art. In a boxing gym, all you had to do was look at who had the older, worn equipment, who carried themselves without trying to impress, and who had a sense of respect for others. They were easy to spot and, though almost all of these identifying criteria were unspoken and left unidentified by most, they were definitely there.

TJ took the Suzuki to Crawford, paid her pass fee, got directions to the gym, and headed upstairs. She peeked through a door window on her way up the stairs at a formal karate glass going on in an auxiliary gym. She thought of the formal ranking system and how Americanized and profit-oriented karate had become. She wondered if bad karate still helped people or actually made them worse off. The classes would lead them to believe that they could defend themselves when they would undoubtedly get their asses kicked in a street encounter. Fortunately, most would never have to find out. Maybe inside that made people feel better even if what they were spending their time doing wasn't practicing a true martial art.

She went down a hallway and found the boxing gym. Small, damp, and stinky, it was all business and carried the very air of authenticity she had been looking for. She dropped her small bag and began wrapping her hands. Only three other fighters were working out, and they all appeared to be boxers and not kickboxers. A fat but hard-hitting guy hit a duct-taped heavy bag; a small Latin guy made the speed bag whistle; and a white left-handed heavyweight hit the coach's pads in the ring. The coach, an older black guy, kept scolding the lefty for not turning over his hook. The fighter exhaled in frustration and kept throwing the hooks on command. He wore scuffed bag gloves and his cutoff sweatshirt was soaked through, sticking to his back.

TJ loosened up in front of the floor-to-ceiling mirror with a giant crack that ran its length. She worked her hands for the first round, mixed in some half-extended kicks in the second, and put them together for the third round. She paced herself with the timing of the round bell that everyone in the gym obeyed. She was aware that she was new and a woman to boot and she felt fleeting glances from the four men she shared the room with. Their eyes darted in her direction during the one-minute rest between rounds but moved on when the bell commanded the gym back to work. She was glad when the evaluation part of her visit was over and she was able to focus on her warm-up, the movement of her body, and her technique.

In rounds four, five, and six, TJ stepped up her work rate, putting together a full-out shadowboxing routine. This wasn't the Taco dance warm-up, this was simulating the work that would go on during sparring. Full speed, full snap, and full power combined with the footwork brought sweat over her entire body. Her heart rate went up and she could feel her chest begin to heave as she strained in the third round of this part of her workout.

In between rounds six and seven, she paused for a sip from the old porcelain water fountain near the coaches' office.

"Tae kwon do?" the left-handed white guy asked. TJ hadn't seen him watching her and he startled her just for a second as she straightened up by the fountain. "But some boxing too, right?"

TJ nodded and blew off the drop of sweat that collected on her nose.

"Your stuff looks good," he said

TJ nodded, knowing that was boxing gym parlance for "You can stay."

"Duffy," he said and extended his glove.

"TJ," she said and bumped gloves with him.

In the unspoken code of the boxing gym, that interaction carried the weight of a country club acceptance letter. That sort of approval didn't always come, often never did for a woman, and TJ did her best to hide how good it made her feel.

The bell sounded the call to return to work. TJ moved over to the heavy bag while Duffy unwrapped his hands. TJ threw a jab, right hand and back leg roundhouse kick combination in rapid succession. Pleased and surprised with the height of the kick, she snickered to herself that doing exotic dancing for a living had its advantages. After three rounds on the heavy bag, she moved to three rounds on the speed bag and then finished up with three rounds of lighter shadowboxing in the ring.

As the workout went on, she felt the "ring rust," as fighters called it, melt off her, and she felt good moving and simulating fighting. This had been her release over the last ten years and she hadn't been conscious of how much she missed it. While she moved, feinted, punched, and kicked, her mind stayed focused on just those movements. It was the curative nature of fighting. Some people didn't understand how meditative it was; it took the day-to-day crap away for the time being. She was pleased with not only how her body responded but also with how her body performed. It was a mistake to have left this part of her life alone for as long as she had.

She unwrapped her hands and toweled off. As her heart rate slowed and the adrenaline cleared her veins, her exhilaration was tempered by the memory of her workouts with Trent. She felt the pang of loneliness that came with doing something solo that she used to share with the man she loved. She and Trent had shared workouts, even sparred together, an activity that most other couples would never understand. It wasn't about pain or even one-upmanship. It was about sharing and moving together in much the same way that couples danced. She missed it; she missed him, and moments like this brought it home and reminded her exactly why she had stopped training.

She wondered when, if, it would be right again.

"First time here?" Duffy asked. He had started to do some light stretching at the end of his workout. The comment jarred TJ out of her thoughts.

"Yeah." It took her a second to respond. "It's been awhile," TJ said.

"You got some shit."

TJ nodded and gave a half smile. That was about as demonstrative as folks got in a gym.

"You've probably noticed that no one's going to mistake this place for Gold's Gym," Duffy said.

"Yeah. That's good," she said. "I miss the days when people stayed out of boxing gyms. These 'boxercise' classes have screwed things up."

Duffy laughed. "You got that right." He had his hands on his hips and he was rotating his back in slow, measured circles. "Hey, if you're looking for someone to move around with in there, I'd be happy to get some work." Duffy nodded toward the old floor ring.

"I'm not sure I'm in your weight division."

"And I know I'm not as fast as you. I'm just talking about moving around, you know, letting punches go. You can kick if you want."

"Do you kick?"

He laughed. "I got into this as a kid after getting my black belt downstairs. One day I tried boxing, thinking it would be easy. I got my ass kicked by a novice boxer. So, I used to be a kicker but if I threw a kick now I think my hamstrings would rip like old twine."

"You still fight?"

"Yeah, I'm a bad pro."

TJ looked at him quizzically.

"I don't mean it to be self-effacing. I've got over thirty fights and a fair share of losses. I beat the guys that suck and almost always lose to the guys with talent."

"Almost?" TJ noted he used the words "self-effacing." Not just your average pug.

"A couple of years ago I beat an Olympic champ in the Garden. That was kind of the highlight."

"In Madison Square Garden?"

"Yeah, Smitty's got a picture of it by the door to his office. I knew the guy cut easy and I cuffed him." TJ was flattered that he didn't explain "cuffed." He gave her cred for knowing that dragging the taped cuff of a glove over skin could tear scar tissue.

"Nice…"

Duffy shrugged.

TJ threw her wraps into her knapsack while Duffy stretched his neck to both sides.

"Hey, I gotta split. See you around," TJ said.

"Nice meeting you. Keep in mind my offer." Duffy smiled at her.

She returned it.

• CHAPTER TWELVE

Monday nights at the Taco were the slowest of the week.

It didn't mean money couldn't be made. In fact, in some cases the slow nights produced the best take, at least for the dancers. The ultra regulars came out on Mondays, the breed of man who somehow imagined he had a deeper relationship with the girls.

These guys would get booths by themselves by the stage; they'd even dress up and inevitably douse themselves in buckets of cologne, usually Polo or Aramis. If the scent didn't induce the gagging reflex, the gold chains and slicked-back hair would. They were the most pathetic thing about stripping, the lowest in a world that had no shortage of shame. The men themselves were sometimes likable but always, without exception, creepy in one way or another.

TJ had Roy, actually low on the creep scale because he didn't seem to pretend that much. His wife, at least according to him, hated sex almost as much as she hated him. With an air of tragedy and self-defeat, Roy had a certain charm in his complete lack of charm. In that way he didn't quite fit the category. Ironic as it seemed, Roy's willingness to accept his own pathos gave him more integrity and made him far easier to like. Of course, the bar in this arena wasn't set terribly high.

Unlike Roy, Giovanni, another of TJ's followers, presented with no charm at all. A bodybuilder and *Sopranos* extra wannabe, Gio acted every bit the stereotyped role of Italian American circa 1975. Part *Saturday Night Fever*, part *Rambo*, Gio had clearly created an illusion in his head that TJ wanted him, and he acted the role of provocateur. He teased her with twenties like he was just tipping her to help her out and to give her a taste of his cool. TJ despised his obnoxious air, but the idiot stayed from eight to midnight on Mondays, and when she worked the floor that meant between $100 and $140 just from Gio.

That made it easy to work him.

TJ half smiled when she thought of the money Gio came up with and his willingness to drop hundreds of dollars a night on her. Then her session with LaMontagne about the angry nature of her dancing crept into her consciousness. Was LaMontagne right? TJ was taking pleasure in exploiting a loser guy with a macho image for her own benefit. Was that really hostile or was it simply the absurdity of the situation? TJ tried but couldn't quite shake off the nagging sense that her therapist was right. More than that, she realized that therapy took the mindlessness out of just about everything, and TJ wasn't at all that convinced that that was a good thing.

"There's hardly anyone out there," Shanekwa said to TJ in the dressing room. "This is gonna suck."

"Monday," TJ said.

Shanekwa, a light-skinned black woman, played up a well-developed butt in her routines, and she had become famous for showing it off. She would face away from the audience and violently shimmy so her ass shook, almost vibrated. The men loved it and Neeki had made it her signature move. She also loved to run her tongue around her lips or flit it back and forth on a beer bottle she'd grab from a customer. She appealed to the lowest common denominator in the audience. TJ didn't like going on after her because in many ways the ignorant patrons then expected every other dancer to act like a whore. Shanekwa got them in the mood for something that TJ wasn't interested in giving.

Besides making her ass quake, Shanekwa had some other signature moves. She didn't hide her crack addiction well, and more than a few customers and dancers suggested that she brought some of her other skills out to the parking lot at the end of the night. She had to have known that turning tricks would get her fired if Maria found out because that type of extracurricular activity could cost Maria her liquor license. It also cast a sordid light on the whole place and, in a way, on every dancer working the Taco. Stereotypes came with the gig and there was no use complaining about that. But being mistaken for a prostitute was something else entirely, and Neeki was resented by just about everyone who did any amount of thinking at all.

TJ loosened up and watched a little bit of Neeki's butt routine. With no one looking, TJ tried it by herself. She couldn't get the right combination—the looseness to make her stuff jiggle and the right timing to contract her muscles for the shimmy. Even though no one saw her do it, TJ felt embarrassed for even trying.

Neeki didn't seem to tire of the move, and for that matter, neither did the audience. She did it over and over again while they gawked, hooted, and hollered.

Neeki then grabbed an empty Bud bottle from the front table and slowly put her mouth around it, then paused to flick her tongue on the end. She grabbed it with her fist and pumped rapidly up and down with a wide-eyed smile for the audience. She then went down on the bottle, taking her cue from the cheering crowd to take all of it down her throat. When she pulled off it, she arched her eyebrows and let the strings of saliva connect her to her prop.

TJ hadn't been much in the mood tonight before seeing Shanekwa dance, but now her desire to work was almost nonexistent. Tonight, she went through the motions.

Unfortunately, it showed in the tips. Roy kicked in his ten without enthusiasm, and Gio went for three rounds of twenties but acted as if his disappointment should bother TJ. The rest of the room just seemed disinterested. A few even turned away when she worked for her dollar dance. Like it or not, TJ had flopped and the lack of tips provided direct feedback that her act didn't bring the right amount of fire.

It left TJ wondering how women sustained this gig over a significant period of time, sometimes years. She also wondered what it would do to her psyche if she did this for any length of time. Would the dysfunctional need to please men get ingrained in her? Damn, she hated when LaMontagne seeped into her day-to-day life.

The Taco activity slowed down to a crawl. Maria decided to close down at one thirty. With two drunks at the bar and no one else, she couldn't justify keeping the neon on. Maria was pragmatic. She was all about the money.

Relieved, TJ dressed quickly and headed out to her bike. She was the last dancer left in the green room, which just made everything seem that much darker. She wanted a beer and she wanted to go to sleep.

The Yankees cap covered her forehead and, as usual, she walked with her head down through the parking lot to the bike. She'd just mounted the bike, ready for a quick getaway, when a yell startled her.

"C'mon, bitch. Take it, take all of it." A drunken voice echoed from between two of the remaining cars in the lot. TJ looked up and saw one of the customers leaning against a Ford Explorer. He looked down as he yelled.

"C'mon, be a good 'ho."

TJ got off the bike and walked over. From a distance, she could see Neeki going down on the guy. The guy kept up the disparaging commentary.

"Dirty bitch."

TJ knew some guys liked it like that. Degrading a woman added to their experience, even if they were the ones paying for the attention. It made her sick but she knew, even in that moment, that Neeki made her own choices.

"Take it, whore."

TJ started to walk away, disgusted at the situation and disgusted with Neeki. She heard a crack and, turning back around, saw Neeki sprawled between the cars on the pavement. The prick wound up and kicked her with his work boots. Neeki yelped.

TJ went into automatic mode. She crossed the lot and was between the cars in an instant. She grabbed a handful of the guy's hair, reached for his chin, and violently jerked his head to the left. He went down, hitting the right side of his face against the Explorer's front fender. He landed with TJ on top of him. She had her hand around his throat.

Breathing hard, she had that focused intensity that she'd had when she had worked as an MP. If he moved, if he went to hit her, she could snap her wrist and the man would die. That simple. The guy on the ground, feeling the vulnerable position his Adam's apple was in, seemed to sense it too.

He stirred in the way people did after head trauma, letting out a soft moan, and he blinked like a man trying to figure out what the hell had just happened. As TJ waited for her breathing to slow, she heard the sound of a lock and load, then the voice.

"TJ, get the fuck off him," Maria said. She held a handgun pointed at TJ from a ten-foot distance. "Now."

TJ got off the man, backed away from him, and faced Maria. She brushed at the gravel on her sweatshirt and slowly let her awareness of the world outside her confrontation come into focus. She headed toward Neeki but was startled by Maria's voice.

"You, get your sorry ass up and get out," Maria said to the guy flat on his back. "Don't ever let me see you in my club again." He looked ridiculous lying there with his jeans and tighty-whiteys around his ankles.

The guy shook his head when he got to all fours and said some shit under his breath. He got to his feet, pulled up his pants, and walked with his head bowed to the driver side of his car.

Maria wasn't finished.

"Neeki, don't come back. You're done here." She took a breath and looked at TJ. "TJ, I don't know what kind of shit you just pulled, but never again. Never again."

She turned and went back in through the kitchen door.

"Fuck's the matter with you, crazy bitch? I needed this job!" Neeki glared at TJ. "Fuckin' crazy-ass bitch." Through the glare, TJ could see her left eye was already swelling shut from the punch she'd taken.

Neeki grabbed her purse and turned away, heading to her beat-up Sentra parked in the back.

"Neeki..."

She just kept walking, leaving TJ behind.

• CHAPTER THIRTEEN

"I've followed her for five days, sir," Strickland said. His relation-ship with Jordan was one that was hard to categorize. He was Strickland's superior officer, yes, but also part friend and part father figure.

"What's your impression?" Jordan asked. Strickland was per-fect for his operation: obedient, in need of approval, and not bur-dened with ethical dilemmas.

"Ah...it's very odd, sir," Strickland hesitated. "I don't mean to sound unclear, but she leads far from a typical life. Certainly not like the others."

Strickland knew Jordan valued clarity above all else, and giv-ing a muddy response would be met with disapproval.

"Tell me."

"First off, she works as an exotic dancer. Seems to do pretty well too. Not a high-end place, but not the gutter either. No VIP room and no evidence of anything further on her part in terms of prostitution. No evidence of her using drugs or anything illegal." Strickland knew Jordan would be surprised by the information.

"A topless place?" It sounded like it didn't quite register with Jordan.

"Yes, sir. And she looks good, more muscular than the others and no breast augmentation, but she has her own fan base, if you will." Strickland felt a little out of line describing her appearance, but his relationship with Jordan had become somewhat less formal since they both left active duty. Strickland knew he was in the subordinate position but he still sometimes attempted conversation that was more congenial.

Strickland continued.

"She's done two shifts since I got here. The rest of her time, typical work hours anyway, she volunteers at a suicide hotline."

"You're shittin' me." Jordan half laughed.

"No, sir." Strickland didn't allow himself to laugh. "It's a place distraught people call in to talk to someone. She works with various partners, an odd collection."

"She does that all week?"

"I estimated forty to fifty hours last week." Strickland searched for the right words. "Sir, several times I've witnessed her leaving the storefront where the hotline is located to go for a walk or get some air. Then, she breaks down in tears." Strickland knew that Jordan would sense that as significant.

"Hmmm, I don't like the sound of that," Jordan said.

"She goes to psychotherapy weekly. I've seen her leave a session and it appeared she had been crying there, as well."

"Clearly, she's unstable," Jordan stated matter-of-factly.

"Yes, sir," Strickland said.

"That's exactly what we were afraid of."

Strickland stayed silent.

"Stay close to her. Do what you have to do assess where her head is," Jordan said.

"Should I make contact with her?" Strickland asked.

Jordan took time to think. He wasn't sure. Originally, he had planned on just keeping an eye on everyone involved. If and only if they presented a problem, he would simply eliminate them according to protocol. Jordan hadn't counted on Strickland making contact. That is, except to kill someone when the situation called for it.

"Do you think you could talk to her without her getting suspicious?" Jordan asked.

"Sir, I was very close with Trent. It wouldn't be strange for me to look her up. You know, old friends, closure, that stuff."

"I don't like it. It seems like unnecessary risk."

"If I presented it like I was having trouble with Trent's death and that I came to her for support, it wouldn't draw suspicion."

"And what if she doesn't buy your story? What if she continues to behave in an unstable manner?"

Strickland got quiet.

"Strickland—did you hear me?"

"Yes, sir."

"What if she seems to be a danger?" Jordan raised his voice.

"Then, sir, I will eliminate her according to protocol," Strickland said.

* * *

Strickland thought about Trent. He thought about how Trent had been the best friend he had ever had and how things got in the way. And Jordan. He'd do anything for Jordan, without really being certain as to why he felt such loyalty. He thought about TJ and how she must feel.

Things were complicated. Missing his best friend didn't mean he had to forfeit making a living, a living he deserved after all the military shit he had had to put up with. He could separate the two.

One was emotional and the other was practical, simple, about getting what he needed.

Strickland leaned back on the hotel bed and let his mind go to TJ. His best friend's girl, a cliché he was uncomfortable with, went through his head. But seeing her dance topless had created conflicting emotions in him. He was both excited and revolted by it. She'd looked hot up there. It had fostered an image of her that he had never allowed himself to visualize before. At the same time, she seemed less the woman he'd wanted all these years and more a slut doing it for money.

Strickland didn't spend a lot of time getting in touch with his feelings. He had learned long ago that it got in the way of doing what was necessary. He was still a soldier; he had to keep his actions sharp and clear.

There were times, though, that he tired of not permitting himself to feel.

• CHAPTER FOURTEEN

"Let's go over your dreams," LaMontagne said. TJ immediately felt a sense of panic.

"I thought dream analysis was Freudian bullshit and you followed cognitive-behavioral theory," TJ said.

TJ had entered into therapy only after learning as much as she could about the process. Like everything else TJ did, she had carefully evaluated her decision to get therapy. She researched various schools of psychotherapy and methods and found that cognitive-behavioral therapy yielded the most consistent results in the shortest time. Since she hated the idea of being in therapy, she wanted it to be as efficient as possible.

Dream analysis was outdated Freudian crap. Everything she had read said most evaluation studies found it useless. And she didn't want to talk about the sex dreams she'd been having.

"I do practice cognitive-behavioral psychotherapy, but that doesn't mean I don't occasionally borrow techniques from other disciplines. Sometimes dreams make for good discussion," LaMontagne replied without hesitation.

"I don't come to therapy for lively banter."

"Trust me. Why do you want to avoid a dream discussion?"

TJ didn't have a good answer. She didn't really want to say "embarrassment." But she knew LaMontagne wouldn't let this go.

"My dreams are all about sex. They're almost pornographic," TJ said, and looked down at her Nikes. "I'm embarrassed by them when I'm alone, let alone discussing them with another woman."

"Another woman or another *person*?" LaMontagne asked. She leaned forward and put her elbows on her knees, trying to look TJ in the eye.

"What's with all the Freudian bullshit? Christ..."

LaMontagne let it get silent.

TJ looked out the window and watched rain drizzle down the office window. She looked back at her shoes. She knew LaMontagne would let the silence go and eventually TJ would break. Since coming to therapy, she had learned that silence was LaMontagne's favorite tool to get her to talk. Sitting in close proximity to another person in silence inspired one to speak. Otherwise, it felt like being on an endless elevator ride. Taking a deep breath, she began.

"I'm usually having sex with Trent. He's inside of me and we're fucking. We're covered in sweat. I can see him hard, I can see his face when he gets off, the details are all there. It's really explicit. It makes me feel weird when they're over."

TJ took LaMontagne's silence as a signal to keep talking. She didn't want to, but knew she'd have to.

"When I wake up I'm masturbating or just finishing," TJ felt flushed.

"To orgasm?" LaMontagne asked.

"Yeah."

LaMontagne nodded and sat back.

"Then can you sleep?"

"Yeah." TJ felt like squirming but resisted. She felt that anxiety that accompanied sharing something that she'd never wanted another human to know. She felt her face flush and the tension in her muscles throughout her body.

"Do you masturbate any other times?"

"No." Could she not let this go? TJ wanted to be anywhere else.

LaMontagne went quiet. She waited.

TJ continued to fight the urge to squirm. She wanted to demonstrate to the doctor that this topic didn't shake her. She became conscious of the fact that she was keeping perfectly still and wondered if that gave away her level of anxiety. Becoming acutely aware of one's body language had to communicate something.

"It doesn't feel right. But that has nothing to do with my feelings about masturbation. I have no problem with that, never have. It..."

LaMontagne waited.

TJ felt tears well.

"It doesn't feel right with him gone. Like it's too, I don't know, superficial. Too self-centered—hell, is there anything in the world more self-centered?" TJ tried a laugh but felt sick in her stomach.

"You don't feel it's right to have any pleasure since his death," LaMontagne said.

TJ sat back. She looked out the window. The rain came down hard now. She tried hard to suppress tears but they ran down her cheeks like the rain outside on the window. Inside, she felt completely out of control. She tried too hard to keep her system of checks and balances, to live life in a calculated way. Her system had failed to work properly, and it left her overwhelmed.

"It hurts a lot, doesn't it? LaMontagne said.

TJ held off the tears as best she could. It seemed like the one point of control to focus on. They ran down her face just the same. TJ sniffled when she physically had to. When she had to inhale, the crying choked her. That was enough to make the tears come harder. She put her face in her hands and bawled.

"It's OK to cry," LaMontagne said softly.

TJ's stomach clenched and the hurt ran through her. Now, she didn't care what she looked like or sounded like. It went beyond that, and she let it out because she had no choice. There was a point where emotion couldn't be contained. TJ had reached her breaking point.

"I don't understand why he did it. It was such a bullshit, cowardly thing!" She cried hard, and the sadness melded with anger, almost rage. Her hands became tight fists.

"There's no question suicide is a selfish act, maybe the most selfish act there is," LaMontagne said firmly. The softness had left her voice and was replaced by an affirming tone.

"Every time I feel that, though, I hate myself."

LaMontagne didn't say anything. Instead, she looked directly at TJ.

"He must've been fucked up, I mean really fucked up and hurting. But why…" TJ's crying kicked in again and she couldn't speak.

LaMontagne leaned forward, folding her arms on her knees. She waited for a moment before encouraging.

"Finish that."

TJ swallowed and tried to catch up with her breathing.

"Why didn't he reach out to me? Why didn't he let me know? Didn't I matter? Didn't—God damn him. He was just like my father."

LaMontagne let TJ's crying slow before she spoke. She spoke very carefully.

"The two most important men in your life killed themselves. They ended their lives without a word to you and left you alone." It was a statement, not a question.

"Yeah, that's exactly what they fuckin' did." TJ's face was red from the weeping and she wiped her nose with a wadded tissue.

"And you're left with a feeling that you don't deserve pleasure. Why is that?"

TJ found it difficult to think clearly.

"Huh? I'm not sure I understand."

LaMontagne leaned forward.

"You," LaMontagne pointed at TJ for emphasis. "You don't feel like you deserve pleasure. They killed themselves. And *you* don't deserve to feel good."

TJ squinted. She thought hard. LaMontagne remained quiet.

"You're saying that they did something to themselves. They acted selfishly without concern for me. Now, I'm the one feeling like shit." TJ looked out the window. The rain had let up.

"Do you need to be punished for the choices the two men in your life made? Choices they made without consulting you?" LaMontagne asked. She spoke deliberately.

TJ sat silently. "But I still don't feel like I should feel good about anything," TJ said.

"Because you were somehow responsible for their choices?" LaMontagne asked.

TJ let it sink in. She had to admit there were some ah-ha moments in therapy, when she conceived something in a new way that was completely out of sync with everything she had believed, consciously or unconsciously. She had read that suicide survivors often felt responsible for the deaths of their loved ones but she had dismissed the notion that she felt that way.

Until now.

• CHAPTER FIFTEEN

"One of them shit shoes," Billy explained. "Those little yippy-yappy dogs."

"Shih tzu," TJ said.

"Right, pain in the ass." Billy thumbed through the *New York Post*. He stopped, folded the paper, and held it up to TJ.

"Speaking of shit shoes, or, in this case, shit heels!" He held up a centerfold feature. The left side had a headline, "Passing the Bucks: Over $18 Billion Unaccounted For In Iraq and Afghanistan."

"What's that all about?" TJ asked. She was curious even as she silently cursed herself for engaging Billy. Billy explained while TJ regretfully wished she had made a pot of coffee or pretended to do paperwork.

"Someone is getting rich off of the war. Your tax dollars are making some unethical military men richer than, well, maybe Saddam Hussein." He read aloud:

"*Auditors admitted today that a wire transfer for $500 million slated for Iraqi reconstruction is unaccounted for. The payment is yet another example of the corruption uncovered in the Iraq rebuilding efforts.*"

Billy went to go on but TJ excused herself to the bathroom. She didn't have to go, but she didn't want Billy reading the whole article to her. When she got out of the bathroom, she went and made coffee, straightened up the loose files on top of the file cabinet, and went back to her desk.

Unfazed, Billy continued.

"Check this part out:

"US dollars have disappeared without a trace, confounding Pentagon auditors who are now trying to trace where the money went…and what exactly, if anything, the US got in return." Billy paused for a second. "That shit is unbelievable."

"Billy, I got to do some notes," TJ said.

"*Tsk, tsk, tsk.* War makes strange bedfellows," Billy said. His glasses were down to the very tip of his nose. He stopped reading aloud but continued to suck his teeth and click his tongue for emphasis when he came across something interesting in the article.

The phone rang, answering TJ's prayers.

"Aquarius, can I help you?" she asked.

The other end remained silent. TJ had been doing this long enough to be patient. She didn't need to keep asking if the caller needed to be helped.

"Hello…" a female voice finally said.

"Yes, my name is TJ. Would you like to tell me your name?"

"Joanne."

"Hi, Joanne."

TJ heard her exhale and then heard something that sounded like the caller wetting her lips.

"I hear voices sometimes," the caller said.

TJ waited to see if she was going to say more. She didn't.

"Would you like to tell me about the voices?" TJ asked. It was an open-ended question focused on repeating what the caller said, designed to get her to speak.

"They're angry voices. They call me names. They tell me to hurt myself."

"That sounds like something that would be really hard to deal with," TJ said softly, trying to validate her feelings.

"Today, the medication isn't helping. So I started to drink. Now the voices are worse. I thought they'd get better. They didn't."

"Joanne, are you thinking about suicide right now?" It was a direct question, and one that the Aquarius procedure called for.

"I have lots of pills. I have a razor…"

Her words were slurred. There was a chance she could fall asleep. There was also a chance that she had already taken the pills or drank enough to kill herself without taking any more action. TJ shifted in her chair and leaned forward, alert.

"Joanne, have you taken more pills than you're prescribed today?" TJ concentrated on not being judgmental. She wanted to sound like she was gathering information, not making an accusation.

"I took the Risperdal. I also have been drinking vodka, about half a bottle so far."

That could be dangerous, but probably not fatal. Very much cause for concern, but in her experience on the hotline, TJ had learned about the fine demarcations of suicide fatality possibilities.

"Tell me about the voices," TJ said.

"They tell me I'm a dirty whore, that I'm a slut for fucking black men. They tell me I deserved to have been raped and beaten. They tell me to kill myself." She slurred her words badly now, and TJ heard it worsen as the caller's crying intensified.

TJ swallowed.

"That's really hard. It must be difficult to live hearing voices." Aquarius directed the volunteers to use strictly active listening and not to give advice. Sometimes TJ felt foolish and wanted to be more encouraging. Sometimes she felt mentally ill people needed more reassurance.

"I hate myself. I hate the voices. They are right. I am no fucking good." Joanne started to cry.

"Joanne, were you raped?" TJ felt like it was an important question.

"Yes, three years ago."

"You didn't deserve to be raped. No matter what, you didn't deserve to be raped." TJ began to feel anxious. She wasn't confident that she was helping.

"My father said I deserved it for being a nigger-fucking whore." The slurring had gotten to the point where it was hard to understand her.

"Joanne, that must've really hurt."

Joanne cried into the phone.

"I just want the voices to stop. I don't want to hear it. I want it to be over forever."

"Joanne, are you going to commit suicide?"

TJ just heard crying.

"Joanne! Talk to me!"

She continued to cry.

"Joanne, where are your pills?" TJ said.

"They're right here."

"That makes me really nervous, Joanne. Can you do me a favor and put them in another room while we talk?" It was a technique TJ had learned to bargain with a suicidal caller. At first, it had seemed absurd, but her experience had taught her that some very practical things lessened the chance of a person going through with the act. Simply making the access to the means more difficult often bought the caller more time to talk through it.

"Put them in the other room? Why?"

"I'd feel better if you couldn't just take them quickly. Could you do that for me?"

"Where should I put them?"

"Can you put them in the medicine cabinet?"

"OK." TJ heard footsteps on a hard floor, a door open, a door close, and then footsteps back to the phone.

"I did it," Joanne said.

"Thank you, Joanne," TJ said.

"I still want to kill myself."

"Please don't."

"Why not? I feel like shit all day every day. Always have. My father…"

TJ let the silence hang to see if Joanne would finish. She heard breathing and the sound of the type of crying that came without much sound. TJ let her feel her emotion.

"My father made me have sex with him starting at age six, and he never stopped. He still makes me. Then he calls me a no-good whore," the woman said. She now could talk more clearly, summoning an almost matter-of-fact tone. TJ recognized it as a defense mechanism that callers often lapsed into as they spoke about their most trying issues.

"He did the same thing to my mother. My mother got addicted to heroin to get high instead of living life. She died when I was eight. He beat her in front of me most every night."

TJ swallowed hard and tried to concentrate. She wanted to say the right thing and resisted the urge simply to say, "that must've been hard," or, "how terrible!" She tried to get in touch with a response that was real. A genuine response that wasn't canned or full of social work contrivance.

"God, I feel hurt just hearing what you're saying," TJ said. It felt better than anything else she could think of.

She heard Joanne cry. Now the tears had sound to them, and TJ could tell she was crying hard and letting the tears come.

"I don't want to feel anymore. I don't want this. I'd rather not feel anything. If it was over, I wouldn't feel."

She wasn't talking to TJ. She was talking to herself. It sounded like she was convincing herself. TJ noticed that her slurring had become more pronounced. The combination of her emotional experience and the loosening of her inhibitions and judgment frightened TJ. She heard the receiver land roughly, perhaps on a table.

"Joanne! Joanne! Talk to me!" TJ didn't get a response.

Panic surged through TJ, but like a good soldier, she reverted to procedure.

"Billy," TJ's voice had volume and intensity but it was measured and without panic. "I need a trace, immediately."

Billy's head turned. He hesitated only for a moment, the put down the *Post* and went to the blue binder that was on each desk. The front page had the directions for a suicide in progress.

He called the police. "My name is Billy. I am a hotline counselor at Aquarius. We need an immediate trace on a phone line for a caller who is imminently suicidal," he read from bolded print on the page.

TJ checked off that procedural box in her head. She talked calmly and firmly into the receiver. She still didn't get any response and she couldn't pick up any sound from Joanne's side at all.

Billy handed TJ a note. *The police and rescue teams are on the way.* Billy, for all his quirks, executed the procedure by the book. He took his seat and watched TJ to see if she needed assistance.

TJ looked toward Billy and shook her head. She heard nothing and felt a sick sensation in her throat. TJ and Billy sat in silence as the time crawled by. They had both had suicidal callers. They had both heard the awful experiences life could deal people, but neither one of them had had an active suicide on the line in progress before. They both sat, chilled, and waited.

Then, through the receiver, TJ heard muffled voices and then the splintering of wood.

"She's in the bathroom!" a voice yelled. In another moment, "She's unconscious."

Per procedure, TJ stayed on the phone while she heard the voices shout instructions back and forth to each other. Finally, she heard the receiver being picked up.

"Officer McVeigh, Albany Police," the voice said.

"Officer, this is TJ, from the Aquarius switchboard. The caller had mentioned taking pills and having more pills available to her. She mentioned taking Risperdal and drinking vodka. I got the impression she had other medications available. The call began at nine oh nine p.m."

"Thank you. We'll take it from here."

"Uh, officer, is she, uh, OK?"

"She's breathing. She's unconscious but she's breathing. I have to go." He hung up.

TJ kept the phone in her hand for a long moment while she mentally went through her checklist again. Billy just looked at her. TJ finally placed the receiver in the cradle. They both sat silently.

"Nice job," Billy said softly.

TJ nodded without looking at him and exhaled hard.

That's how it could go at Aquarius. Crisis, crisis de-escalated, sometimes a hang-up, sometimes tears, but rarely resolution. Unlike in a professional counseling job, they didn't get to find out how the stories ended. They did what they could, hopefully patched people up, and then they were left with the silence of a disconnection. That is, until the next call came. And they could go from a true life-threatening emergency to a mental health caller checking in to let them know they were cooking dinner, or some perverted sex caller who wanted to hear a female voice while he cranked his business.

Sometimes TJ found it difficult to adjust, to go back to normal without feeling things after an intense call. She felt wrung out and often confused. On the phone, she was connected to a flesh-and-blood person, but strangely distant at the same time.

Mostly, she did her best to keep Trent off her mind. This whole suicide hotline gig was originally meant to confront the roles suicide played in her life, to learn about it and in doing so to take the power away from it. But, with time, it had morphed into something else. Now she liked doing it, or at least felt like doing it was something important. The longer she did it, the more she resisted thinking about Trent. The irony of that wasn't lost on her.

Of course, having Billy around helped.

"You know, I watched this show on *National Geographic* last night." Billy had waited five minutes since Joanne's call, which, in his mind, was the proper transition time to get to something he was interested in. "It said that we never landed on the moon. It said it was all filmed in the desert. You could tell because there was wind on that flag that Neil Armstead placed in the lunar landscape," Billy said.

"Strong," TJ said.

"Yeah, well, he had to be to be an astronaut. That was part of the qualifications."

"No, his last name was Arm*strong*. Not Armstead."

"Who?"

After the last call, TJ didn't feel like playing Costello to Billy's Abbott, so she left it alone.

"Billy, the movement of the flag wasn't wind. It was the sway from the movement of pushing it into the moon's soil. It moved like wind but it wasn't. It was just the continued movement in the low gravity."

"Bullshit. That's what they want you to believe," Billy said.

TJ looked at Billy and didn't know how to respond.

"Then how come you can't see any stars? Huh? How you gonna answer that, college girl?" Billy felt like he had her in a corner.

TJ knew from watching the same show that the stars weren't present because of camera angle or the flash or some totally reasonable explanation, but she couldn't quite remember.

"Geez, that's right, Billy. Now that you mention it, there were no stars. Hmm…that's weird."

Billy gave a self-satisfied nod, winked, and sucked his teeth. He folded his arms and leaned back in his office chair, plopping his feet up on the desk. He wore cheap sports sandals, and his toenails were long enough to hook salmon out of a stream.

"Hey, TJ, you got a fella?" Again.

"Huh?"

"A boyfriend?"

"Oh, nah."

"Why not?"

"C'mon, Billy, I don't know."

Billy hesitated.

"Can I give you a little constructive criticism?"

TJ knew he was going to no matter what she answered. She raised her eyebrows instead of answering.

"You oughta wear some more feminine outfits. You know, show some leg, wear a nice pink golf shirt. Get some pumps. You look kind of…"

"Kind of what, Billy?" She was starting to enjoy this.

"I don't know…guyish."

"Guyish? You're saying I look like a man?" TJ smiled to herself and wondered what Billy would think if he caught her act at the Taco.

"Not like a man, God no, but the army pants, ball cap, and sweatshirt don't emphasize your finer qualities."

TJ smirked and put her hands on her hips in mock outrage.

"Billy, you're sexist."

"No, I'm trying to be helpful. You should—" The phone interrupted.

TJ's reaction time was faster, and she got to the receiver before Billy.

"Aquarius, can I help you?"

"Keep your eyes and ears open. The suicides will keep coming till all threats are eliminated. Follow the war money." The digitally altered voice made it impossible to identify.

"What the hell—" He hung up before TJ got it out.

She slammed the phone down and cursed.

"Hey! What's that all about?" Billy shouted, clearly startled.

"Goddamn it, mind your own business for once!" TJ said.

TJ ignored Billy and just exhaled and walked out the front door. It was just too weird, especially after Joanne's call, and too close to her. She didn't want to play games. Not with idle threats, not with conspiracy theories; she simply didn't want any of it.

She certainly didn't want the storm of memories it stirred.

TJ leaned against her favorite stop sign again. Moments like this made her wish she smoked. Instead, she breathed hard and fought Trent's memory. It never really worked. Her fights with his memory and everything around his death just made her stomach tighten. She could suppress some of the feeling, or at least put it off. It meant tension, anger, and depression channeled in other directions. She knew her reaction to Billy, though understandable, wasn't fair.

After one more deep breath, she returned to the office.

"I'm sorry, Billy. I didn't mean to react like I did," she said.

"Don't worry about it," Billy said, but he didn't make eye contact.

She had hurt his feelings and that bothered her. Billy, undeniably a bug, still didn't deserve that.

TJ picked up the part of the paper that Billy had finished and read silently, mostly to kill the awkward silence that had developed. Her eyes fell to the story Billy had referenced.

The investigator general's audit showed that $2 billion in seized Iraqi assets were given away without any clear directive as to where the money would be spent. No notes have been found related to the money's destination and many believe it fell into the hands of army officers who found ways of hiding and laundering the money. It is unclear how the funds were transferred, to whom and for what purposes.

Today's report sets the new total of Iraq defense funds possibly lost or stolen at almost $20 billion.

• CHAPTER SIXTEEN

Jordan looked at the list. Of the fourteen, eight had been eliminated, four more were identified, and two couldn't be found. So much for VA records.

Suicides in the military remained a media focus. *Newsweek* and *Time* ran reports about the prevalence and how no other war, not even Vietnam, had as many. Lack of support, the age of the soldiers, and the guerilla nature of the enemy all made the list for explanations.

Two on the list had actually committed suicide. That was how the idea had come to him. Spread out across the country, some out of the country, it had developed into a perfect plan. Strickland did a good job. He was skilled, with no conscience, and his greed equaled Jordan's own, Jordan thought.

But now, Dunn presented problems. She appeared unstable and she wasn't assimilating back into civilian life easily. She was a loose end.

Jordan hated loose ends.

The others weren't difficult. They were typical vets with typical issues. Some went back to old jobs, drank too much, and slowly drove away friends and spouses. That was predictable. Some got addicted, some committed crimes, and some even found God.

The combination of stripping, therapy, and suicide hotline counseling wasn't typical.

Jordan worried about what she told her shrink or, God forbid, if she talked to any of the other dancers. Those whores couldn't keep their mouths shut and would do anything for money. There were too many variables.

Of course, there was always the chance that she didn't know anything. She hadn't had much physical contact with Trent in the service, plus he'd seemed like he could keep secrets. But they were getting married. For Christ's sake, they probably told each other every time they went to the bathroom.

He thought about cutting her in, but quickly dismissed it. Anyone liberal enough to listen to depressed people whine on the phone all week probably has no interest in easy money.

There was no question she was a problem.

Jordan didn't have patience for these kinds of problems.

Strickland was close to her, best friends with Trent once upon a time. Jordan knew how greedy Strickland was, but could he do his best friend's surviving fiancée?

Probably.

He didn't like it, though. Maybe it was time to get someone else on the assignment, or at least to give an unbiased assessment. It would have to be someone cold-blooded, who could kill without hesitation.

It would also have to be someone who could do a little thinking. Strategy, Jordan thought, not philosophy. He'd have to be almost invisible, a man who could go in and out under the radar. The kind of soldier you could pass on the streets three times in a day and not notice.

Jordan didn't have a lot of personnel like that. There was only one individual he thought of who could pull it off, be precise, almost surgical, and do it all without being noticed. The perfect candidate was different from Strickland in many important ways.

CHAPTER SEVENTEEN

"Can we talk about Trent today?" Dr. LaMontagne asked. There was a tentative gentleness to her voice.

TJ got quiet.

Finally, she spoke. "Yeah, sure, I mean, that's why I come here, I guess." TJ verbally agreed but her body language communicated reluctance.

LaMontagne let TJ's response hang for a moment. It underlined TJ's hesitancy. She gave TJ a chance to change her mind without saying anything. After the pause, she spoke.

"When you think of him now, what do you experience?"

TJ didn't expect the question.

"What do I experience?" she asked. LaMontagne nodded.

"Uh, it's strange, actually. When I catch myself thinking of him I shut it off. It's like I start to think of him, I don't know, *accidently*. You know, like I wasn't aware of it. Then something automatically shuts it down. Even when I try to think of him then, I can't. I can't get it back."

"And when that happens, how would you describe what happens to you emotionally?"

"Anxiety." TJ didn't have to think long.

"Say more..."

"Uh, it's like one part of me wants to think about Trent, feel the hurt, and let it come over me no matter what it feels like. Then the other part shuts it down. Almost like a computer that can't find a file or won't grant you access to a part of the hard drive." TJ had never consciously thought of the process before.

"You can't get to the feeling," LaMontagne said. She had sat up and rested her elbows on her knees, intently looking at TJ.

"No, it's like it is there, but below the surface. I want to but I can't get there."

"And the feeling you can reach instead is anxiety?" LaMontagne asked.

"Yes."

"Talk about the anxiety."

"Phew..." TJ exhaled as she gave it thought. "It feels like a barrier. Like there's some protective firewall that won't allow me access to the feeling around Trent. It instead creates a discomfort, a nervousness in place of what the emotion would be."

LaMontagne nodded but didn't say anything. She then raised her eyebrows and tilted her head. TJ had been coming long enough to know that that was a signal to keep speaking. She had learned at the hotline that it was called a "minimal encourager."

"I want to feel it. I want to, I swear I do, even if it's painful. I'd rather face it and feel it instead of fearing it. It's like I want to..." TJ couldn't find the words.

"Fight it? But it's an opponent that doesn't show up for a fight," LaMontagne said. Her metaphor was intentional.

"Yes."

"It's not a fair fight, is it?" LaMontagne asked.

"No. Not when you put it that way."

LaMontagne sat back and let out a bit of a sigh. She crossed her legs, let out a breath, and tilted her head, looking at TJ. She pursed her lips and wrinkled her brow before speaking.

"TJ, is it a fight?" She said it softly.

TJ felt what she said before she understood it. She waited and tried to let it sink in.

"You mean, like everything else in my life, I'm trying to conquer something. In this case, trying to fight it. The problem is it's not an opponent who wants to do battle. I'm, like, the only one in the fight." TJ said it slowly. The truth was dawning on her as she sounded it out.

"TJ, you go to war with what you don't understand. You fight everything in life that presents a challenge to you. You are in a constant state of battle," LaMontagne said with emphasis.

"When I was young I learned not to avoid things. I learned to go through things, not around them."

LaMontagne's breathing was slow and measured.

"You're going to tell me that I can't fight everything. That there are some things that can't, or maybe aren't best, handled by going straight in. That some things aren't meant to be battled," TJ said.

"Well, what do you think?" LaMontagne asked.

The two of them sat in silence for a long moment.

"And with Trent's memory, that means what?"

"You tell me," LaMontagne said.

TJ exhaled hard. She felt her eyes well and she had to strain to talk.

"It means not doing battle. Not trying to conquer. Not trying to go straight at it and fight." TJ's voice trembled and she continued. "How the fuck do I do that?"

Tears streamed down her face and the hurt was in her voice.

"I have no idea how to do that. Can you please tell me how to not fight something like that?" TJ swallowed hard and did her best to ignore the tears.

LaMontagne sat up and looked at TJ. "It is something you'll have to learn and experience for yourself."

TJ just looked at her. Panic mixed with hurt.

"I...I...I don't know what to do," TJ said. She felt the helplessness of a child.

"It may, quite possibly, be the hardest thing you've ever attempted. You will feel vulnerable, maybe defenseless and afraid. Your temptation will be to fight through it. I don't think that's what you need right now." LaMontagne raised her eyebrows in a way that demonstrated compassion.

"I can't fight everything," TJ said, almost to herself.

"You can if you want to experience life the way you've been experiencing it," LaMontagne said.

TJ looked out the window at the gray day. Her mind flashed back to the UAH and her crawling across the front of it to get the ammunition without anyone to cover her. She thought of what that had felt like to her. She realized that what she was experiencing right now in LaMontagne's office was an entirely different kind of fear.

It was a type of fear she felt less able to handle.

• CHAPTER EIGHTEEN

The session stayed with TJ. Often, she could throw herself into a workout, go for a run, or even mindlessly watch TV and let the intensity of the session fade away from her consciousness. This one remained no matter what she did.

Sleep barely came at all, and when it did, it was uneven and tense. It was a dreamless sleep during which TJ kept going over in her head what had been said at the session.

I can't fight everything.

Nothing had ever felt so foreign.

She was grateful when daylight came. The lack of sleep made the morning run unpleasant. It took forever to get warm, and even when she did she got very little of the high she looked for in her exercise. After a breakfast of coffee and a plain whole wheat bagel, a meal as bland as her life, she thought, she was happy to have a shift at the hotline first thing this morning.

Morning shifts meant working alone, and they were different in other ways, as well. The morning hours tended toward check-in calls from mental health patients who just needed to share something with another warm being. TJ often got bored doing this but inside knew that, though they weren't necessarily in crisis, the check-in callers needed Aquarius as much as anyone, maybe more than anyone else. TJ did her best to pay attention when the regulars called, but still found herself doodling when the calls got tedious.

This morning was unusually quiet, and it was a full two hours before the phone rang.

The sound startled TJ. She gave the usual greeting and could barely hear breathing on the other end.

"Since he left..." The caller's voice trailed. She sounded faint, like she was barely there.

"Please tell me more," TJ said. It was a simple technique called an "encourager."

"Uh, I don't know, it's like, why bother? I got nothing going on in my life. Nothing worth anything."

"You sound very sad." Another technique, this one called "reflection of feeling," designed to let the caller know she understood. Supposedly, it gave them validation. TJ relied on the fundamentals when she didn't know what else to say.

"Yeah, it's more than sad. It's left me with nothing. There's nothing to live for. I know that sounds overdramatic, but there really isn't," the caller said.

"I need to ask you if you're feeling suicidal now." TJ, required to assess the level of suicidal ideation, always felt uncomfortable just blurting that statement out.

The caller remained silent.

A moment passed, and TJ felt uncomfortable.

"Please, are you feeling suicidal now?" The procedure required a "now" statement.

"Yes..."

"Do you have a plan for how you would kill yourself?" Again, the directness of such an intimate question seemed out of place. But the procedures required it and TJ remained a good soldier.

"I could take pills."

"Do you have pills?"

"Yes."

"While we talk, could you just put the pills in another room? You don't have to throw them out, but I'm not comfortable with them so close." TJ was aware it was the second time in two days she had used this technique.

"OK, just a minute." A moment passed.

"They're in the bathroom now," the woman said.

"Good." TJ, amazed the techniques worked, felt a sense of relief. "Do you have a plan for carrying out your suicide?"

"It's funny. You're going to think this is weird and I'm really fucked up."

"Go ahead."

"I was going to wait until *Law and Order: Criminal Intent* was over. I like that show."

TJ had learned in training that people often set times for when they would commit suicide. Waiting until a show ended wasn't unusual. It meant clarity of the caller's plan.

"I don't think you're strange at all." TJ didn't. She felt the excitement of crisis and the sharpening of her senses. She had felt the same thing in Iraq when shit hit the fan.

"I've never had anyone listen like you," the caller said. "People tell you to get over it. Find someone new, or something like that. They don't understand that he was really the only man I ever had."

"That must hurt a lot." TJ reflected feeling again.

"Yeah…" This time she heard tears. The woman began to weep hard. The kind of crying that caught in the throat and choked. It went on.

TJ listened.

"Oh God…it hurts."

"I know it does," TJ said.

She cried like that for a while. TJ stayed on the phone. She felt focused, not frightened, and she felt present, like what she did mattered. It was what drew her to the work. She resisted telling the caller everything would be all right. She knew that could be a lie.

"Can you tell me your name?" TJ asked when the crying subsided.

"Jennifer."

Jennifer was TJ's given name.

"Jennifer, can you promise not to hurt yourself today?" she asked.

"I'm not sure." The caller hesitated. "I'm not sure I have the energy anymore. I almost feel when I get this depressed I don't have the strength to do it."

TJ felt a small sense of relief.

"I loved my fiancé so—" She started crying again. TJ twinged at the sound of the term "fiancé."

"Now that he's gone, I just don't know if I want to live."

It dawned on TJ that Jennifer's fiancé had died, not merely left her. She felt a wave of something go through her.

"He was everything I had, everything. I don't understand why he could be gone," Jennifer said.

"Uh, I know that hurts," TJ said. It wasn't merely a therapeutic technique.

Jennifer cried and cried. TJ felt flushed and panicked. The name, the situation; this one was too close, way too close. She did her best to push out the image of the chaplain and Strickland and just listen to Jennifer. It was very hard.

"I don't want to live. I just don't want to live," the caller said.

TJ could feel her heart pound. She began to sweat and her breathing escalated.

"Oh God…I just…Oh God!" The caller was escalating and TJ got flustered. She didn't know what to do as an Aquarius counselor, and she didn't know what to do with her own feelings.

"Please, don't harm yourself." It was all TJ could think of saying.

"Oh God…" TJ heard the wailing that came with out-of-control grief. TJ knew it well.

"Please, I—" The caller had hung up.

TJ placed the receiver on the desk without hanging it up. She just stared straight ahead. She could feel her body begin to tremble. She went almost numb; her body felt the emotional wave, but TJ couldn't process anything. She just stared straight ahead.

She had no idea how long she had zoned out, but the phone on the other desk rang and brought her back into the moment. It took TJ a moment to orient herself, but she found a way to answer.

"Aquarius, can I help you?" she heard herself ask.

"Yeah, I guess so," a male voice said. TJ noticed something odd about the connection.

"Tell me what's going on today," TJ said.

"Listen, you are in a unique position." TJ identified the sound of a voice-altering program to disguise the caller's voice. "There will be several well-publicized military suicides in the next few days. They aren't what they appear."

"Who is this—"

He hung up.

• CHAPTER NINETEEN

At the Taco, TJ dressed without talking to any of the other dancers. Maria asked if she was OK and got a nod in return.

Gloria prattled on about an English test and something about having to read *Walton's Pond* and how boring it was, but this time TJ didn't correct her. Instead, she got dressed.

TJ set out costumes a week or so in advance and threw them in her knapsack. It was part of her always-be-prepared military training. She hadn't planned it, but tonight's costume was a soldier send-up. Her sand-colored cutoff camos showed the bottoms of her rock-hard ass cheeks, and a plain white crew T-shirt completed her ensemble. The shirt, cut off to show her six-pack abs, covered more than a bikini top, but that was by design. As she got dressed, the camo outfit registered with her but she fought back the thought of it or assigning any meaning to it all. She barely glanced at the scar on her bicep when she put on the shirt.

The outfit was on the conservative side for the Taco, in that it showed, at least initially, less skin. TJ knew that when she danced she'd begin to perspire, and by the second AC/DC song in the set, her sweat would allow her nipples to show through. No one would complain.

Something was bad inside of her, and she couldn't get in touch with it. The calls, therapy, and memories tormented her, and all at once. Too much ran through her. On stage, she danced with fury, sublimating her rage with as much energy as possible. She spun around the pole with anger, dropped down in a full split and sneered at the crowd. The anger, tangible and obvious, seemed to send a chill through the patrons paying attention, and somehow, even with their absence of insight, she could see they felt the danger inside her. No doubt it aroused them, but with an unapproachable sexuality that no one in the room had the guts to respond to. Tonight, even Roy would stay away.

In the second-to-last song in her set, her T-shirt was soaked through. She hadn't removed her top despite the rule that it was supposed to come off by the middle of the third song. She was oblivious as she danced out, or at least tried to get out what she felt. The men were transfixed by her power juxtaposed with her pure animal sexuality. She never took off the shorts, yet revealed way more than if she had gotten completely naked.

To "You Shook Me All Night Long," she worked clap push-ups into her routine, then one-armed reps. A hush filled the Taco and the playful air left the place. TJ bounced up, spun around, and launched two successive spinning hook kicks and landed in a split just as AC/DC's anthem came to an abrupt end. She was in a full-fledged fight, and not with an imaginary opponent. She was in a knock-down, drag-out brawl with her very existence and her inability to make sense of a life that just seemed wracked with pain.

She walked off the stage without looking, without smiling, and without caring what the reaction was to her. Her chest heaved; the perspiration matted the T-shirt to her skin, revealing the shape of her breasts and the flat of her abs. The sweat also hid the tears in her eyes.

"Holy fuckin' shit," Gloria said as TJ walked past her into the green room. "What the fuck was that?"

TJ walked by, head down, without acknowledging.

"TJ, are you—" She didn't get to finish. "Back in the USSR" cued her to the stage and TJ's body language told her to back off. TJ hadn't circled the room for her dollar dances.

Maria poked her head in and looked TJ up and down but said nothing. She had made a living reading people and knew when to back off. TJ threw on the oversized Notre Dame sweatshirt and baggy black karate pants and went out to the parking lot. The humid air didn't refresh her, and she walked to the back of the paved area where the woods began behind the dumpsters. She found a tree stump and sat down. Her breathing remained elevated and her body refused to cool down.

The tears came all at once, violently. She bent over and vomited between her legs, and the combination of puke and grief choked her. She began to shake, and then that feeling, the one that brought her back to when she heard that Trent had blown his head off, washed over her. She vomited again, her stomach contracting and her chest pounding.

On her knees now, she grunted through the pain and nausea. She shook and dropped to her hands. The pain was physical and she felt like it could kill her. She flipped over to her side, not feeling the gravel and dirt from the edge of the pavement.

It hurt more than she thought anything could, and she continued to cry. There was no thought or even consciousness that came with this physical reaction. There wasn't memory of Trent or that day on the UAH or even today's calls at Aquarius. This was a purely physical reaction to what went on inside her, raw emotion not tethered to any specific thought but rather a cathartic reaction to her existence. It was like an exorcism, but one in which the demon did not leave her. Instead, it just shook her to her soul, violently assaulting her physically, emotionally, and spiritually.

TJ vomited again, and it strained her abdominal muscles. She coughed more vomit out and her eyeballs tensed with the pain. She felt cold all over despite being covered in sweat. She had never experienced anything close to this; not in combat, not upon hearing about her father's or fiancé's suicides, not in therapy, and not while consoling others.

The retching stopped and the crying slowed, not because she felt less, but rather because her body was depleted of the energy to continue. She lay on her side in the dirt and gravel of the parking lot and curled her knees to her chest in the fetal position.

A voice snapped her out of her world of pain and back into the moment.

"TJ, my God, TJ." The voice filled with panic, then hesitated. "TJ, are you all right?"

TJ looked up to see David Strickland.

• CHAPTER TWENTY

At first TJ wasn't sure if what she saw was real.

"David?"

"My God, are you OK?" Strickland had dropped to his knees in concern over TJ. She sat up with her knees bent in front of her. She wiped at her tears with her forearms as casually as she could.

"What the hell are you doing here?" TJ asked.

"I've been looking for you. It's been a while now." Strickland had on army-issue boots and he had army-issue gloves stuffed into the back pocket of his loose-fitting jeans.

"So that *was* you last week. What was that all about, showing up, not saying anything, and disappearing?"

Strickland looked at her without a trace of apology in his face. He hesitated before he spoke.

"You're working as a *stripper*, TJ." TJ pursed her lips and rolled her eyes.

"Yeah, suddenly you morally object to stripping? I seem to remember you and Trent having a different view of the profession in OCS."

"Yeah, it's a little different when it's a woman you care about whoring it up in front of a bunch of pigs." Strickland felt his anger surge.

"You think I give a shit? I take home between three and four hundred a night and twice that on a Friday or Saturday. That's cash. You tell me what other job I'm going to get that will give me that." TJ's anger matched Strickland's.

"Showing your tits?"

"Look, you got a job? I'm guessing if you've got the time to travel across the country to look up old friends, you don't."

"I haven't even started looking."

Strickland stood up. TJ followed. She ignored the gravel and dirt that clung to her pants, resisting the urge to dust them off.

"Well, let me tell you what it's like. People read that you were in Iraq and they give a cornball 'Thanks for serving our country.' Then they look at you and wonder how many people you killed or tortured. They don't want you anywhere near their workplace."

Strickland folded his arms and exhaled.

"I don't remember you being this filled with self-pity," he said.

"Fuck you. You asked why I dance."

"So you show your tits to horny dudes for a living. Doesn't that get inside you? Don't you think it's eventually going to fuck with your mind?"

"It doesn't, plain and simple. I do it two or three days a week, make the money I need to live, and get the hell out of here."

"What about the men?"

"They're the ones being exploited. If they get their rocks off watching me or tucking a bill into my underwear, what the hell do I care? I don't do it because I didn't get enough hugs from my daddy or to support a crack habit. I do it to make money. And I do. I make a lot of it."

"I don't believe you."

"And I'm supposed to give a fuck about what you think?"

"You were the one curled up in a ball crying just now. Don't tell me this shit doesn't affect you."

"Fuck you. You know damn well that's not why I was like that."

TJ glared at him with rage. Strickland locked eyes with her and said nothing. They stayed like that for a long time.

"You never answered the question," TJ said.

"What question?"

"What the hell are you doing here?" TJ's hands were on her hips.

Strickland looked at his boots, exhaled, and kicked at the gravel. He looked up and looked into TJ's eyes.

"I came because I need your help."

• CHAPTER TWENTY-ONE

TJ dusted herself off, wiped the mascara stains from her cheeks, and looked at Strickland.

"My help?" she asked. His statement brought her back to normal consciousness.

"Yeah," Strickland said.

"Help with what?"

"I don't know how to say this. I'm afraid to hurt you..."

"What the hell are you talking about, David?"

"Trent's death." Strickland had his hands in his pockets and he looked at his boots. He couldn't make eye contact with TJ.

"What about Trent's death?"

"I'm not sure he killed himself." The statement hung there. Though afraid of her reaction, Strickland looked at TJ. She glared at him, no other expression on her face.

"Maybe suicide made it easy on some people," Strickland said.

"What?"

"I'm not even sure, TJ. Look, hear me out. It never sat right with me and I know it didn't sit right with you. Not Trent, not him. Suicide just didn't seem like something he'd do, you know?" Strickland did his best to communicate, but he knew he fell short.

"You're telling me this shit? Of course, it never sat right with me. But if he didn't do it then, then…what? What happened to him?"

Strickland didn't know how to answer. He didn't know what to tell her and what she could handle. He didn't want to mess with her head, but he wanted to tell her enough so she'd believe him.

"David, you just don't drop into my life after all this time, track me down, and start speaking in conspiracy theory. What the hell are you talking about?" He could feel the heat of her rage and he knew he had to tell her.

"Trent and me had gotten in to some shit. It wasn't real bad but it wasn't something we were supposed to do. We made some money before it went bad. There was so much money and it didn't seem right that it was going into everyone else's hands—private security, engineering firms, logistic outfits, rebuilding corporations—there's been millions, no, *billions* in cash and none of it went to the guys risking their lives. It wasn't right."

TJ just stared at him.

"We found a way to get some, not much, for us," Strickland said.

"Who was 'us'?"

"About a dozen guys in our outfit were in on it. We made a deal, we provided some necessary info, and we worked with certain Iraqi contractors doing some work that would've gone to someone else—someone nonmilitary. We just redirected it and gave them what they needed and they gave us the cash instead of someone else. Trent was in at the beginning but then got out. That's why he was a problem."

"What was the cash for, David?" TJ's mind raced.

Strickland kept silent. He went back to looking at his boots.

"David, what were you doing for the money?"

"It didn't hurt anyone."

"David!"

"We protected people who needed protecting and they gave us money."

"Who?"

"I can't—"

"Oh, you better, you son of a bitch. You come all this way and—don't you fuck with me."

Strickland took a deep breath and thought. His mind raced. He had no idea what to tell her and what to keep to himself. TJ didn't make it easy.

"David!"

"The CIA."

• CHAPTER TWENTY-TWO

Jonathan Jordan loved Venice, Florida.

It afforded him the luxuries of the Caribbean without having to deal with, well, Caribbeans. Here, everyone spoke English and crime stayed within acceptable limits.

Not that he had to worry about safety. He had a twenty-four-hour security force around him. Barely visible, they wore civilian clothes and blended nicely with the vacationers and super-rich retire-early types that lived out their Hemingway fantasies. You couldn't tell their Special Forces backgrounds by looking at them. The good ones never showed their capabilities. Jordan wanted to look like everyone else in Venice, and he took great pains to live a life that appeared exceedingly normal, at least for down here.

His cover story of retiring from the technology business before the bubble burst seemed entirely plausible. In his early sixties, but fit and tan with perfectly capped teeth, Jordan looked the part of someone who had landed on the right Monopoly square. If you believed a few lucky souls could get out of the market before it went to shit, you could believe that Jonathan Jordan could.

Jordan nodded to Daniel, his security man on the front lawn, who was dressed as a landscaper. Jordan knew all the men personally; they all had worked directly for him in Afghanistan. He insisted on that; he didn't trust many people. Why would he? He had screwed enough people and double-crossed even close allies to get where he stood today. That kind of history left a man feeling paranoid.

Daniel's nod assured him that everything remained secure. Jordan headed out to the screened-off pool area he had come to call "the lanai," a term he hadn't heard until coming to Florida. He dialed the number of his connection still in the country.

"Yes, Coop. How's the weather?" General Atwater asked. Jordan's caller ID negated the need for formal hellos.

"It's like a damned Jimmy Buffet song," Jordan said. "Look, I've got to ask you something."

"Shoot."

"I hate to sound like Tony Soprano, but 'this thing of ours,' it remains safe?"

"Man, you're a worrier. We've got a half dozen redundancies and safeguards in place. Every one involved remains enthusiastically on board and those who aren't have no idea—and no way of finding out what's going on." Atwater spoke in the singsong manner people used when they were repeating information.

"And the neutralizations? I'm afraid they will haunt us." Jordan used the term *neutralization* without hesitation, probably because he had used it so many times.

"Jonathan, do you read the papers? Suicide has reached epidemic proportions in the armed services. We're doing everything we can, but war is tough on these men," Atwater said with obvious sarcasm.

"I worry about Strickland."

"Why? With the money he makes, he, as much as anyone, should be committed. Besides, we checked him out thoroughly. We worked side by side with him for four years. We don't have to worry about David Strickland," Atwater said with confidence.

"He's with Dunn now. They were friends—he was friends with Trent's fiancée."

"My God, how many times do we have to go over this?" Atwater asked, not angry but with a reassuring tone that encouraged Jordan not to worry. "Is there anything in particular that is making you anxious?"

"Just an instinct," Jordan said.

"You mean paranoia." Atwater laughed.

Jordan exhaled. His insecurities remained the price he paid. He knew it would come and go. After all, his tendency toward suspicion and security had always served him well.

• CHAPTER
TWENTY-THREE

"You OK?" Maria asked. TJ had just walked in from the parking lot. It was clear she had been crying and her clothes were a mess.

TJ, a thousand miles away, nodded. She was on next, but despite having just five minutes she hadn't dressed yet.

"You gonna get ready? Dead stage time ain't good for business, you know." Maria raised her eyebrows as she looked at TJ.

TJ went through the motions of getting ready. She couldn't stand to wear the soldier outfit again so she got out of it. She slipped on a thong and got into a pair of royal blue boy shorts. A cutoff Giants T-shirt that made it just over her breasts filled out the second set costume. She didn't have the energy to get creative.

Trent, Strickland, the CIA, none of it made any sense. It also didn't change a damn thing. Trent stayed dead, she stayed fucked up from the war, and life still sucked. She didn't love her existence, but it had gotten predictable and manageable until Strickland had showed up, dropped this bomb on her, and then split. They were supposed to get together after her shift.

She hit the stage and spun around on the pole to Billy Idol's "White Wedding." The lyrics were stupid, but the bass line drove her and she worked out in front of the desperate men like they didn't exist. Oddly enough, the empty stare in her eyes combined with the ferocity of her work turned many of them on. TJ became an object, a moving and grinding one, that fueled their fantasies.

The men liked the set. TJ didn't care, but she could put it in automatic even while her mind raced. She left the stage; the Giants T-shirt had soaked through with her perspiration and she began to work the crowd. The air-conditioning hit her hot skin and made her nipples push through the damp fabric. It gave the crowd what they wanted.

"Hey, little girl…" Roy said from his usual spot at the end of the bar. Harmless and ignorant as he was, TJ didn't mind his lack of political correctness.

TJ took his cheek kiss and swayed in front of him. She never got into this, but plenty of nights she tried harder to fake it. Tonight she couldn't pull it off.

"Something's wrong, isn't it?" Roy asked.

She shook her head, turned her back to him, and lightly brushed up against him. Oddly enough, Roy knew her on some level. The guy actually cared to the degree that he could tell when she didn't feel herself.

TJ felt the ten-dollar bill slide into the side of her thong way before its time. TJ knew Roy tipped her in multiples of ten, and she usually gave him his money's worth. Tonight, Roy had obviously cut it short, sensing she didn't feel it. It made her feel worse; it was proof that her feelings showed so transparently.

She kissed Roy gently on the cheek and moved on. She was a body to everyone else, and that made it easier to get lost in her duties; TJ went to that place where she moved, swayed, and ground, but in her head, she went someplace else, someplace far away.

Her shift ended and TJ regretted agreeing to meet with Strickland. It opened the scar and it brought back what she had worked hard to leave behind. Still, somehow she felt like she was obliged, and so she toweled off the sweat from her last set, threw on her sweats and Yankees cap, and took a deep breath. The night was too weird, what with her emotional breakdown combined with the visit from David. The whole thing about Trent's death being a CIA murder just was too difficult to process. She didn't live in the world of conspiracy theorists. She did her best to live in the here and now.

She brought the Suzuki to a stop in front of the all-night diner and found Strickland alone in a booth toward the back. The place smelled like a combination of grease, sausage, and stale coffee. It was empty except for a few solitary patrons who TJ figured maybe drove trucks or were night security guards waiting for their shifts to start.

"You look exhausted," Strickland said.

"Thanks," TJ answered, putting her motorcycle helmet on the padded booth bench next to her. She ran a hand through her sweaty hair. She ordered a coffee.

"Uh, this is hard to talk about, TJ, but I think it's important enough for you to know. I also want you to know that what I'm about to tell you may put you in danger."

TJ, tired and pissed off, didn't want to play games.

"Look, Dave, it's been a long day and an even longer night. Get to it and then let me get on with my life."

"The CIA thing, it's complicated. There was a fraction of guys within our outfit who were working for them undercover. The outfit leaders didn't even know."

Strickland looked at TJ, trying to read her reaction. She gave none. He went on.

"They were trying to turn what we were doing into a real business and determined that if our military actions were too effective, it wasn't going to serve their purposes."

"Their purposes?"

"They were in the pockets of Telewater, the security firm. If things ended and we moved on, then money would be lost—lots of money."

"Yeah, and?" TJ sipped the coffee to be doing something.

"Cash flowed like water over there to the security firms. It was crazy. Cargo containers filled with cash came over with no accounting. Sure, it was supposed to go to rebuilding efforts and engineers and that shit, but it was cash. There was no chance of it getting there." Strickland stopped to take a breath.

"What does that have to do with the CIA and Trent's suicide?"

"Trent, Mr. Gung Ho, had a change of heart. At first, he was on board, but then his conscience started to bother him and he decided he didn't want any part of it. He didn't make a big deal out of it but he made it clear he wanted out."

"Well, so why was he a threat to the rest of them?" TJ asked.

"They don't like uncertainties. They don't like things they can't control. The CIA, or at least some agents in it, were making connections with soldiers, paying them handsomely and getting the cash delivered where they wanted it. I mean, I saw a guy deliver four pizza boxes filled with cash."

"Slow down, Dave. You're saying: One. the CIA, or at least crooked agents in the CIA, found ways to steal money earmarked for Iraq and Afghanistan rebuilding efforts; two, they got help from members of your outfit to help deliver, channel—whatever—the money where they wanted and got paid handsomely for it; and three, Trent knew about it and wanted no part of it."

"Exactly."

"And then they had him killed, only they made it look like suicide. That way he'd get counted as one of the many PTSD casualties of the war and no one would ask questions," TJ said.

"Yes."

"And this is still going on?"

"Yes, that's why we keep hearing about more and more suicides from our old outfit."

"Because 'whoever' is getting nervous and they're eliminating everyone who might know something?" TJ asked.

She ran it through her head. "But that's got be a pretty big number—soldiers talk, and if there's as much money as you say there is, that would create a lot of gossip."

"That's right."

"Dave, there are a ton of people who could probably know *something*. Anyone in that outfit, anyone who was family or friends with any soldier in that outfit, could possibly know something," TJ said. She was figuring things out as she spoke.

Strickland just looked on.

"That would mean you could be in danger," TJ said.

Strickland mulled it over. He exhaled and struggled to find the right words.

"TJ, I'm still involved. I'm out of the army but I haven't left this operation. They think I'm safe, for now."

"So why'd you come here?"

"I can't live knowing what they did to Trent. I can't live with it anymore."

TJ tried to let it sink in. She tried to understand.

"Can I ask you a question?" TJ looked right at Strickland.

"Yeah."

"What happens if you get out? Tell them you're not interested anymore?"

TJ looked into his eyes to try to measure in any way what went on inside him. They sat in silence for a long moment.

"They'll kill you, won't they?" TJ asked.

Strickland nodded.

TJ thought about saying more but decided against it. She wasn't sure she trusted David enough.

Not now, not yet.

CHAPTER
TWENTY-FOUR

"Tell me about your father," Dr. LaMontagne said. She said it like she said most things, with dispassion. She presented a blank slate most of the time when she spoke. TJ assumed that was purposeful.

"We've talked about him," TJ said.

"Not to the extent that I think we should. I want to talk about him again."

"Why? I think I'm settled about him."

"Settled…"

"I mean, I don't think I'll ever be OK with the fact that he killed himself, but I believe I'm to the point where I can move on."

LaMontagne had her hands on the arms of her chair and her feet crossed at the ankles. She was smartly dressed in a tan business suit, a dark brown chemise, and a single strand of pearls. TJ admired the woman's concentration.

"Tell me about the anger," LaMontagne said.

"I'm not angry. I'm sad he's not here to talk to and see how I've grown up. I'm sad for my mom. I'm sad he never saw me graduate from Notre Dame."

LaMontagne maintained eye contact. She pursed her lips as she seemed to ponder TJ's words.

"The fact that he chose to leave this world and chose not to be here for those events in your life…that doesn't anger you?"

TJ thought. Her father's suicide had impacted her like nothing else in her life, at least until Trent's death. She tried to get in touch with how she felt but she couldn't identify any specific feeling. She struggled to retrieve her emotional memory connected to him.

"Dr. LaMontagne, I try really hard to be straight. I try really hard not to deny things…I just don't recall any anger," TJ said.

LaMontagne nodded with a half smile.

"TJ, you do, indeed, work very hard, and like most things in your life you demonstrate courage and tenacity. Sometimes anger lies below the surface."

TJ started to get frustrated, and it showed.

"Stay with me."

"OK…"

"You said your father killed himself your junior year at Notre Dame. Tell me about him and what you were like up until then." LaMontagne sat back.

"He worked in Special Forces. My mother and I didn't get to know a lot about what he did in the service. He was in Afghanistan at the start of the war but we weren't sure where or what he did. I believe he worked in intelligence to some degree, but we were never sure."

"Was he affectionate?" LaMontagne asked.

"Uh, I don't know. He was military. He loved my mother and me."

"That's not what I asked," LaMontagne said.

"He was OK with affection. I didn't get a lot of 'I love yous' or hugs, but I knew he loved me."

"And you chose to go into ROTC…"

"Yeah."

"Why?"

"It paid for college. It gave me expense money. I had lived with my father in the service my whole life, so it was familiar to me." TJ did not know where LaMontagne was going with this.

"So you followed in your dad's footsteps."

"I never really looked at it like that. I mean, I entered the military but it wasn't like I was obsessed with following in his shadow."

LaMontagne hesitated before leaning forward and resting her elbows on her knees.

"Do you think you were trying to move close to him?"

TJ sat and thought. This topic didn't seem to fit, but she didn't want to seem resistant to LaMontagne.

"The military is huge. I knew the chances of me getting closer to him were small."

"That's not what I meant," LaMontagne said and looked right at TJ.

"I wasn't, or at least I wasn't aware of, trying to move closer to him," TJ said.

LaMontagne sat back and ran her pearls through her hand.

"Let's change the subject just a bit," LaMontagne said. "Tell me what you were like in college before your dad killed himself."

TJ noticed that she used the expression "killed himself" and not "died." TJ knew LaMontagne did everything with purpose. "Killed yourself" felt more direct, more purposeful.

"I was more of the preppy Notre Dame type." TJ rolled her eyes with embarrassment. "I was in ROTC but I had my Izods and my penny loafers and my rich Republican boyfriend."

"What happened to him?"

"We broke up three months after my dad's thing. I was a mess. I don't blame him."

"Go on."

"Uh, I don't know. I was twenty. I cut my hair, bought a leather jacket, threw myself into tae kwon do, and started working out like a fiend. It was how I dealt with it."

LaMontagne leaned forward and rested her elbows on her knees again.

"Did you date?"

"No, not until Trent."

"Why not?"

"I didn't meet anyone I liked. I started getting sick of Notre Dame and all the 'rah-rah' bullshit."

"Your dad went there…"

TJ didn't respond. She furrowed her brow a little, thinking it was a cheap analysis.

"I was twenty. I was finding myself. Some people pierce their noses or their lips and dye their hair purple. I got to be a tough guy, I guess."

LaMontagne bit her lip but remained silent. The silence went on for a while.

TJ broke it.

"So, you're saying I got so angry I changed who I was, I revolted against being the girl my daddy loved, and that I got hard and tough. That I rejected what my dad loved."

TJ didn't realize it, but her voice had gotten louder.

LaMontagne didn't say anything.

"He killed himself. I was twenty and of course it impacted me. I started to rebel a bit, but I was a junior in college, at an age when people start to think differently no matter what…"

TJ didn't complete the thought.

"And now?"

TJ squinted, not understanding.

"What in your current behavior, what eight, nine years later, reflects that same rebelliousness?"

TJ sat back hard and exhaled, annoyed that she didn't get what this was all about.

"I'm just getting by after the army, after the stress of my fiancé's suicide. There's no rebelliousness."

"You're a stripper and you are a loner. You tell me what you're rebelling against," LaMontagne said. Her volume increased, but it was for emphasis, not a reflection of anger.

TJ got quiet. She shook her head slightly and looked at her boots. She stayed quiet for what seemed like forever. LaMontagne didn't break the silence.

TJ exhaled hard. Tears ran down her face and she ignored them. She was slouched in the chair, pursing her lips, when LaMontagne finally spoke.

"It's not an accident what you've chosen to do."

"We've been over this. I dance because I make good money—cash—quickly and easily. I volunteer at the hotline to give me something to do and to give back to the community. I spend a lot of time by myself because I'm new in town and I'm not the 'single scene' type. Jesus fucking Christ, is all that so hard to understand?"

TJ slammed her arms down on the arms of her chair. She couldn't ignore the tears now, and she bent over and held her head in her hands while she cried almost to the point of convulsing.

"Fuck! I hate myself!" TJ screamed and pounded her clenched fists into her thighs before burying her face into her hands again.

LaMontagne let her go. TJ continued to cry.

"TJ?" LaMontagne asked. She spoke softly to get her attention.

TJ looked up without saying anything.

"You work hard here in therapy. You try to face everything head-on, but like we've gone over before, not everything is what you think it is. We're uncovering things that are important in your life that maybe you didn't think were."

TJ wiped her eyes with the back of her hand.

"Like what?"

"I think you've convinced yourself that your father wasn't as important in your life as he truly was. I think, in many ways, he's been a guide for you," LaMontagne said, and then hesitated. "I think you vacillate between emulating him and rebelling against him. You want him and you want to forget him at the same time."

TJ sat back and tried to let it sink in. Why did the doctor always have to be right?

• CHAPTER
TWENTY-FIVE

"It's difficult to say what she knows," Strickland said. He was back in the extended stay hotel. With his feet up on the coffee table, he tuned the TV to *Sports Center* and muted the sound.

"I still don't like it. He must've told her; she was his goddamned fiancée," Jordan said, his intensity coming through the phone.

"Just give me some time. We shouldn't underestimate her. She's, I don't know...different."

"Different?"

"When she gets something in her head, she's determined. If we do anything, we'll have to make absolutely sure it's complete. There's no chance for mistakes."

"That's how things should be in every situation, Strickland. You should know that by now."

Strickland didn't like his tone, nor did he care for lectures. He didn't deserve that type of treatment, even with the money he was paid. He had come to learn that just like the cliché said, money didn't buy everything. After all, he had more money than he had ever dreamed of having and he still wasn't enjoying himself. Nights in sterile hotels, staring out the windows of rental cars all day and double-crossing old friends—this wasn't his idea of the high life. He knew he deserved the wealth and he stopped short of sanctimony, but he wanted some pleasure out of life.

Trent and he had been best friends. He had liked TJ from the start even if he saw less of Trent because of her. She was cool for a woman and didn't get in the way like some girlfriends could. She even hung with the guys on occasion and held her own. Not in that needy, clinging way when women tried too hard to be part of something; no, her casual way made having her around comfortable.

Trent, on the other hand, had become a pain in the ass. He had gone along with things at the beginning but then felt guilty and started questioning everything like a fucking philosopher. If he didn't want a part of things, that would've been fine, but he wouldn't make up his mind one way or another. He'd take the cash one day but the next day want to rehash his decision and get into a long talk about whether it was the right thing.

Strickland didn't complicate things like that. He figured the money existed and someone was going to take it. Whoever took it didn't have a right to it—there was no way it was going to get into the right hands, anyway. The right hands? Geez, there were no right hands in this hell. The whole thing was bullshit and everyone knew it. If they were the ones willing to put their lives on the line, all bets were off. They deserved to be taken care of more than anyone. It was a different place with different rules, and getting something for living this bullshit seemed to be the only thing that made sense.

He hadn't counted on the complications. He hadn't counted on having Jordan as a partner for life. He hadn't counted on seeing so many old friends die.

And he hadn't counted on TJ.

Strickland got another beer from the half-size refrigerator. The TV remained on in the background as he thought. TJ would be heading to the hotline in the next hour or so. He should keep an eye on her. That's what Jordan would want and that's what the protocol was. Strickland hated the idea of waiting in a car with binoculars for hours. That was the bad part.

The good part? He hated to admit it, but he felt better when TJ was close by. He didn't understand it at first, and then he began to realize that he felt some guilt. Not about the money, not about the dishonesty or his own greed. No, he didn't care.

He didn't feel right about TJ.

• CHAPTER TWENTY-SIX

TJ struggled to sleep. Hot, damp, and restless with everything running through her head, she stared at the ceiling. The radio sitting on the milk crate that functioned as a nightstand cackled with sports talk. The Yankees continued to have middle relief issues and a certain quarterback pondered coming out of retirement, again.

Before sleep came, she thought about therapy. Half the time she saw it as utter bullshit and the other half she believed it was the only thing that kept her sane. She did what she did—stripped, volunteered, worked out, went to therapy—because at this moment in time they seemed to be the right things to do. She had made a commitment to herself to do just that—do whatever occurred to her that felt right, and if it turned out to be a mistake, so what?

At times, it felt robotic, though. Dancing half naked in front of mindless men brought more than enough money to live on. She avoided the mind games and counted the cash. She couldn't do that in an IT job, a retail store, or in some office. She could work two nights a week and have cash at the end of the night.

The volunteer job at Aquarius leveled it off. It got her through the powerlessness of missing Trent and it made up for the superficial nature of exploiting stripping. Sure, she knew she rationalized, but so did everyone else.

Then, Strickland showed up, bringing back the past and the news of some master plot that Trent got involved in. It didn't fit, and Strickland's sudden appearance didn't either. But did it not add up because she didn't want it to, or was her bullshit radar on target? And if Strickland was lying, what was his motivation?

When sleep came, she dreamt.

She makes love to Trent. Her legs wrapping around his body as she rides him. They are on a chair in his apartment. She can feel him inside her and she grinds into him with all the energy she has. Trent's tongue lightly dances over her nipples, and she leverages her thrusts with her hands around his shoulders and head.

She begins to feel the tingling that leads to her climax. It intensifies, and she rides the wave of it. When she comes, it spreads through her with an explosive release and it continues, cascading and multiplying. She feels his sweat mingle with her own and she hears his breathing quicken. He begins to quicken his pace; he lets out a half moan, half growl, and she feels him first tighten and then spasm in his own orgasm.

His contractions bring her to climax again. This time faster and shorter than the others, but in a strange way, more intense. It takes a long time for them to separate simply because of a combination of it feeling far too good and because the two of them are too tired to move.

She awkwardly hikes herself off him and looks down at their wet bodies. Crimson covers the two of them and TJ wipes at her abdomen to get a closer look at the liquid. The two of them are covered in blood.

TJ screams and looks at Trent. Half of his head is blown off, and the wound steadily pours blood. He is dead from his own bullet.

TJ realizes she just made love to a corpse.

She screamed as she awakened. She was confused, still unsure of what was real and what was not. Sweating, panting, and now crying, TJ tasted vomit in the back of her throat and hurried to the toilet. She didn't make it, and though she tried to hold back, she vomited down the front of herself and onto the floor of the studio kitchenette.

"Fuck!" she screamed and collapsed to the floor.

She just lay there and wept.

• CHAPTER
TWENTY-SEVEN

"I'm not even sure this is something you talk about in therapy," TJ said.

"You can use the time in whatever way you want. I'll let you know my opinion on whether I believe we're being productive," LaMontagne said. She, as always, was collected and measured without being cold.

"I've been getting strange messages on the hotline."

"Hotlines frequently get obscene calls, prank calls, or even people making up stories for their own amusement."

"No, I've gotten used to those. I've gotten several calls telling me that the military suicides everyone is hearing about aren't really suicides. They are murders being made to *look* like suicides."

LaMontagne leaned forward, interested.

"Both times I've gotten the calls, soon after I got a military person calling in. In both cases, they were suicidal but didn't want to be talked out of it. They just wanted someone to know." TJ heard her voice quiver just slightly.

"Suicidal people often do that. They want to kill themselves but they want someone to know. It's almost hygienic. They want to take care of the mess they are leaving behind as much as possible," LaMontagne said, then leaned back and raised her hand to rub her chin.

"But to get those calls right after the other calls is a pretty weird coincidence. The other thing I didn't mention—the caller's voice is altered through one of those voice machines," TJ said, looking at LaMontagne.

"TJ, the high rate of military suicide since Iraq and Afghanistan is well documented. And weird phone calls are a fact of life on a hotline. Perhaps it's their juxtaposition that is making them seem more concerning than they really are." LaMontagne raised her eyebrows as her way of forming a question.

"There's something else…" TJ hesitated.

LaMontagne merely tilted her head.

"Trent's best friend, David, has found me. He said he needed to talk to me. He said there was some sort of corruption going on in Iraq involving the reconstruction money and that he and Trent and their outfit had found a way to get some of the money." TJ felt like she was betraying her fiancé's memory.

LaMontagne crossed her legs and smoothed her suit pants.

"That doesn't sound like the Trent you've talked about. Hearing that must've been difficult for you," said LaMontagne.

"The thing is, I'm not sure I even believe it. I guess after a while he wanted to not be a part of it. I know I don't want to. I just think I would've known something if it were true," TJ said.

"The two of you weren't stationed together, right?" LaMontagne asked.

"Yeah."

"TJ, it was war. People do what they need to survive, physically and emotionally."

"It wasn't something the man I knew would get involved in."

"Did you know this man under the stress of war? The stress of having his life threatened daily? The stress of killing others? Don't you think that type of stress level takes its toll?"

TJ rarely thought about it. She didn't want to admit it was possible. Tears ran down her face. She didn't wipe them away.

"The whole thing was fucked up. It was bullshit, fucking bullshit—"

LaMontagne didn't say anything.

"He was a good man. I loved him more than anything. He went and fucking killed himself like a fucking coward!" TJ wiped the tears from her face with anger. She felt sick to her stomach. She felt anger so intense she didn't know what to do with it.

LaMontagne didn't say anything but TJ felt her absorb everything she had said.

"Why, why the fuck would he kill himself? That wasn't him."

Even though she'd come in wanting the doctor's opinion on whether David was right or was full of shit, somehow it didn't matter anymore. She hadn't coped with Trent's death, period. With so many questions and no definitive answers, Strickland's conspiracy theories just added on to the pile of grief and loss.

"Circumstances change people. Drastic, dramatic circumstances change people in a drastic and dramatic fashion. It doesn't mean the man you knew was a lie," LaMontagne said.

"Fuck!" TJ stood up and walked to the window. She kicked over an end table, shattering the glass, and walked back to the window. "Oh my God…" she wailed.

LaMontagne left her chair and walked to TJ, stepping over the shattered glass.

"TJ…" LaMontagne said and extended her arms.

TJ moved to LaMontagne and the therapist held her. It felt as natural as anything. TJ wept violently into LaMontagne's breast and cried so hard that she shook and then gagged.

LaMontagne lightly massaged her back without saying anything. TJ didn't think; she let herself be held.

She needed to.

CHAPTER
TWENTY-EIGHT

Strickland waited. He knew TJ's shift on the hotline ended at eleven.

Now it was quarter after and she hadn't come out yet. He wasn't sure what that meant, but it made him uneasy. He already felt strange about going to talk to her again. They hadn't spoken since the night he had found her crying, when he told her about all the conspiracy shit. When they left that night he couldn't get a good read what she made of all it.

It was almost eleven thirty when she finally came out of the storefront. Strickland called to her before she climbed on the Suzuki. She turned, squinted in the streetlight's glare, and adopted a defensive stance. Strickland recognized the almost imperceptible posture change and smiled to himself, wondering if the woman ever let her guard down. Of course, he thought, she danced topless but, then again, Dunn found ways to be on guard then too.

"It's me, Strickland," he called. He noticed her relax just a little as he approached.

"David, I'm beat. Can this wait?"

"I don't get it. After everything I told you the other night, aren't you interested?"

TJ looked at him impassively.

"So, what the hell am I supposed to do with the information you gave me? Trent's still dead, and if somehow I know too much about some bullshit I might get dead too. Listen, David, I sometimes think being dead doesn't sound all that bad."

Strickland hadn't expected this type of response.

TJ raised her eyebrows, cocked her head, and made a face at him that said *Say something or I'm leaving*.

"It doesn't bother you that they'll get away with it and keep doing the same thing to others like us?"

"Oh, stop the bullshit. All I know is that you're telling me that the CIA is involved and they may want us dead. What does that even mean? You might as well say that the boogie man is out to get us, David," TJ said. She was getting louder.

Strickland thought hard about his response. He felt he was losing her.

"I think I know who they will send."

TJ remained silent and just looked at him.

"If it's who I'm thinking, there won't be a warning. There won't be a sign."

She just stared at him. Their eyes locked—his questioning, hers defiant—but the two of them remained silent. TJ let out a long exhale, then shook her head, put on her helmet, and started her bike. She didn't look at Strickland as the engine revved, and she didn't look in her mirror as she pulled away.

She drove fast through Albany, heading back up Central in the direction of the Taco. It was the middle of the week and the traffic was light. She cruised through the lights, pacing the bike so she wouldn't have to stop. Flashing red lights a couple of blocks ahead got her attention.

She counted three or four patrol cars and a fire engine, and an ambulance was pulling up. TJ thought that the fire engine probably meant paramedics. Her curiosity got the better of her and she headed to the excitement.

A man and a woman raced out of the ambulance and took over for the two cops working on what looked like a woman bleeding from the head. She was unconscious and motionless; it didn't look good.

TJ glanced around and saw no one else. TJ's experience kicked in and she knew the woman looked bad, maybe dead. She surveyed the area to get an idea about what had gone down.

She saw a cream-colored two-door Lexus with the front driver's side door open, parked at a funny angle fifteen feet or so from the scene. She glanced back at the woman being lifted into the back of the ambulance and noticed a bright pearl necklace catch the streetlight.

TJ froze when the realization came over her.

The Lexus, the necklace, the sharp tailored suit. The woman being loaded into the back of the ambulance was Dr. LaMontagne.

CHAPTER
TWENTY-NINE

TJ tried to help the paramedics and resisted when they told her to mind her own business. They told her they had already called next of kin and that everything that could be done was being done. Efficiently, they lifted the stretcher and it clanked into the back of the ambulance.

Several patrolmen and what had to be detectives in plain clothes gathered around the Lexus. Already a burly guy with a red mustache and wired-rimmed glasses was dusting for prints. Paint got sprayed around the bloodstain on the pavement that had spread out to the size of a manhole cover.

TJ had never thought about LaMontagne's personal life, at least not in any detail. She didn't know about a husband, kids, parents, or any of the things that made her human. All at once, it made her feel selfish and self-absorbed. Here this woman knew all about her, but she knew nothing in return. Professional relationship or not, it just didn't seem right.

She thought about following the ambulance to the hospital but changed her mind. LaMontagne would be rushed into surgery or something and TJ would be left to wait. There would be nobody to console or keep company. At least, she figured there would be nobody who would want to be kept company by one of Dr. LaMontagne's nutty patients.

TJ walked toward the bike, hypnotized by the flashing red lights and the cops' activity.

"You want to hear what I say now?" It was Strickland. He came up from behind her. His voice startled TJ. She took a deep breath before responding.

"David, not now, OK?" she asked.

"This is part of it, you know."

TJ just looked at him. Too much ran through her head. She didn't need riddles.

"I'm guessing this shrink knew your secrets. Then she gets killed? Pulled out of her Lexus at an intersection and beaten. You think that's a random act?"

TJ didn't move. She just looked at Strickland.

"I'm telling you, this ain't no joke. If you're not going to listen to me, at least keep your head up."

"You're saying she got hurt because of me?" TJ asked, almost to herself.

"I'm saying it's because of all this shit we're involved in, whether we like it or not."

TJ looked in the direction the ambulance had gone. The image of LaMontagne holding her as she cried in the last session washed over her. The tears ran down her cheeks.

Too much; it was all too much.

"We've got to make a plan," Strickland said. He put his arm around her shoulder.

TJ wept hard and tried to hold her head in her hands. Strickland reached out for her and held her. She buried her face in his chest and let loose. She cried for a long time.

When she calmed down enough to get a handle on things, she pulled away from Strickland. Embarrassed, she didn't make eye contact as she walked toward her bike.

"Meet me tomorrow at Denny's. I'll be there at eight," Strickland said. He wasn't sure she heard him. She started the bike and pulled away.

• CHAPTER THIRTY

Jordan was nervous. A cautious man, he didn't like taking chances. The more people who knew his business, the more he felt exposed. He trusted very few; actually, he trusted no one, but had to use a select few to get what he wanted accomplished.

He liked redundancy when it came to safety. He liked to know that nothing was left to chance. It made him a great colonel and it made him a leader. In his present position, it made him a multimillionaire.

He had almost unlimited resources but still he didn't have everything he wanted. He didn't have the ability to control all the variables. So far, his way of making up for the lack of control was simply to eliminate anything that hinted at chaos.

Now he worried about something he hadn't given much thought to before.

Strickland.

Jordan saw the former soldier as both loyal and greedy, a good combination, without a lot of ethics to get in the way. It made him perfect for what they were doing. But now he couldn't be sure.

Just as Strickland's assignment was to gather intelligence on Dunn, Forbus's job was to let Jordan know about Strickland. Jordan had set this up without suspecting anything in particular; it was just part of his usual redundancy to make sure the situation was safe.

Now he had concerns.

"They've met to talk several times. I've seen them hug. I've seen him hold her when she's broken down," Forbus reported.

Perhaps that had been Strickland's plan all along, to get her to trust him, but Jordan didn't feel sure about that. Strickland didn't seem that slick. He was more of a straight-ahead soldier and not very clever. Creating a romantic ruse or even a warm, befriending cover seemed beyond what he was capable of. No, Jordan was worried that Strickland was getting feelings, or had feelings, for the target, and it was interfering with his assignment.

Dunn was still alive, and if she knew anything, she had the potential to blow the operation sky-high. She remained unpredictable and by that very nature, dangerous. The suicide hotline, the therapy—for Christ's sake, the exotic dancing—who knew what she was capable of.

He didn't like it. She wasn't easy to control, and that was not acceptable.

Forbus didn't suffer from feelings. Forbus was a rare breed, a machine, a soldier who could kill without regard and then eat a ham sandwich. "T-Rod" had done just that, whenever Jordan asked. Not every assignment was appropriate for Forbus because of those lacking social skills. Shit, how could you operate normally in society and still be robotic about killing?

Now Forbus was in Albany and following Strickland from a safe distance, biding time, and waiting for the word from Jordan. Jordan hesitated, not out of any moral concerns or loyalty to a soldier. That was the last thing on his mind. No, Jordan was careful about murder because it received attention. Attention that could screw everything up.

He would have Forbus wait and gather as much information as possible. When and if he needed someone killed, all it would take would be a word to Forbus.

• CHAPTER THIRTY-ONE

The UAH explodes, a ball of fire and smoke searing up from its center. TJ is underneath it, helpless. She witnesses burned bodies falling from the vehicle. First Milford, then Alvarez, and finally Marquason land on the side of the burning vehicle and turn to ash in front of her.

Trent appears, his face blackened from smoke. He looks right at TJ and says, "I love you, marry me." Then he puts the pistol in his mouth and fires.

TJ awoke covered in sweat and disoriented. It took a long moment for her to realize where she was. The red numbers of her alarm clock read 4:15 a.m.

She cursed the dream. Though embarrassing, she admitted to herself that she preferred the sexual ones. Reliving the attack on the UAH horrified her. She thought for a moment that she would need to talk to LaMontagne about it, and then the night before came back to her in a rush.

A wave of panic went through her. Not just at the trauma of seeing another violent act to someone she cared about, but because she now had no idea what to do with the feelings. Those feelings were frightening, unpredictable, and she didn't like the idea of not having an outlet to do something with them.

Strickland had been on the scene. His timing had been disturbingly precise. He had to have followed TJ to be there like he was. She had said good night and had agreed to meet him. Why would he feel the need to follow her? Maybe it was as simple as two people heading in the same direction.

Maybe not.

She'd known Strickland for years in that hard-to-define way that girlfriends knew their college boyfriends' buddies. They had spent enough time together partying and traveling, but she didn't know much about him other than his love for Southern Comfort, the Dallas Cowboys, and girls with long blond hair. He was Trent's friend.

Trent got frustrated with him, but it seemed within the bounds of normal guy friendships—whatever that was. Sometimes Trent saw him as shallow, sometimes as a womanizer, but the two were loyal to each other. They liked to say they had each other's backs.

Now, with Trent gone, she realized she didn't know much about him. In short, she didn't know if she could trust him. And not just trust him, but trust Strickland with her life. Still, why would he make up this CIA shit? It was a long way to come and it had to have been hard to track her down, so why else would he have come?

The instant coffee tasted bad. TJ ignored the taste, focusing instead on getting it down her system to clear her head. She pulled on her nylon running shorts, cutoff T-shirt, and Nikes. A morning run on no sleep was going to be tough, but once she got into it, it would do wonders to even her nerves.

She walked down the wooden garage stairs and went out the side door. She ran down the dead end, rotating her shoulders to work out the kinks. She heard the crack of her joints and it reminded her of her years spent kickboxing. She could mark almost every belt promotion with a shoulder or joint injury.

Half a mile in, she started to pick up the pace. Her body warmed and she turned down Central, cruising down a long slope that made her stride easy. This was the best part of running. Alone, at a hypnotic rhythm where thoughts cycled rapidly. She noticed them, but then let them go on their way. She let the road take her where it wanted and she could see the orange sunrise backlighting downtown and the Alfred E. Smith, a mini art deco version of the Empire State Building.

She checked her watch. It was 6:45. She hit the button and found her heart rate was at 143. She kicked it up just a bit, hit the button two blocks later, and found she had increased to 152. She knew to stay there for only a few minutes or she would pay with lactic-acid-induced soreness for days. Still, the heart rate increase brought with it a short-term euphoria, an immediate gratification she couldn't pass up when she felt this kind of stress.

She cruised past Ontario and Quail without slowing and picked up the pace in the long block before Lake. She was almost to the corner when she realized she was in front of last night's accident scene. All at once, she left the running trance and was brought back fresh to the horror.

She slowed to a walk, crossed to the other side of the street, and let her eyes sweep across her field of vision. It was a technique she had learned as an MP, to keep an eye out for roadside guerillas.

She saw the large circular stain where LaMontagne had lain unconscious. She saw splats of blood where she imagined the first confrontation and struggle took place. She saw rust-colored stains sprayed over an area ten feet by ten feet. Breathing hard from the run and from the emotional memory, she walked slowly with her hands on her hips.

She didn't know where to put this emotionally. She didn't know where it fit. LaMontagne wasn't a loved one or a comrade. There was no doubt she was an important part of her life, maybe the single most important person since TJ found herself here in Albany.

TJ wanted to get going. She hadn't gone there on purpose and blamed ending up there on the sleepy start to the run. She'd lost the runner's high and now wanted simply to lose herself in more exercise.

She turned on her heel, glanced at her watch, and headed back toward where she came from. She walked with her head down, trying to put this away, and tried to focus on getting back into the running meditation. She concentrated on her breathing, checked her watch and her rate, and got ready to run. She still had her head down when she got to the curb at the Lake and Central intersection. That's when she saw it. She froze.

It was wedged into the curb, half covered by a littered Burger King wrapper, an empty Gatorade bottle and street dirt. Since she had entered the military, she'd always noticed anything that was military issue. It always signaled to her that she was around the familiar.

It was a left-handed glove.

And it had dried blood on it.

• CHAPTER THIRTY-TWO

"It's not a coincidence that your shrink got beat up," Strickland said. He had coffee and an egg sandwich on a hard roll. The Denny's was about half full, with salesmen getting ready for the day, seniors killing time, and the other random patrons that filled up restaurants like Denny's.

"So, what is it, then?" TJ asked. She had on her Notre Dame hoodie over her running shirt. She still wore her running shorts and shoes.

"They figured she knew whatever you knew. She was dangerous."

"And I suppose you're about to tell me I'm next." TJ noticed a scratch on the back of Strickland's left hand. She made a point of not staring at it.

"Go ahead and be flip about it, but you know that makes sense."

"This has something to do with the CIA?"

"Yeah, it does."

TJ just looked at him without saying anything. Strickland sipped his coffee and took a bite of his sandwich.

"If I tell you any more, then it makes you that much more vulnerable," Strickland said.

"You know I don't buy that. Shit, look what happened to LaMontagne. She *didn't* know anything."

"They assumed she did. They assume you do."

"Do you know this for a fact? I mean, so far all I know is you and Trent were stealing money and then Trent killed himself."

"You say it like we were—"

"Thieves?"

"You know what I mean."

TJ sipped her black coffee, put it down, and shook her head.

"David, stealing is stealing."

"Look, you can be as righteous as you want. Everyone around us was swimming in cash. They were getting rich off the war without putting their lives on the line. I don't see it as stealing."

"Whatever."

Strickland sipped his coffee. He hated arguing with TJ. She was relentless. She didn't give an inch.

"That shit doesn't matter now anyway. I want to tell you a little about what I know about the CIA."

TJ rolled her eyes and moved a spoon through her coffee.

"Is this the part where I'm supposed to get all spooked and start to shiver?"

Strickland tried his best to ignore her.

"The money came easy. No one even missed it. A plane would come in with boxes of it and we would move it. We figured out after delivering it that it was never counted. It was so crazy and there was so much of it that we would just deliver it."

"Who got it?"

"Contractors, engineering firms, those fucking private security firms, and there were others."

"Why were they getting it?"

"Supposedly for the rebuilding of Iraq. That place was so fucked up. There was no rebuilding going in. Everyone knew that. It was people sitting around waiting for money to show up."

"So you just didn't deliver some of the packages and kept them for yourself?"

"No, that was too obvious. We'd skim from each box of cash. There were higher-ups who were in on it. We were just, well, soldiers."

"Higher-ups? Who?"

"We didn't know. We dealt with a noncommissioned guy who dealt with another noncommissioned guy who dealt with a lieutenant. They did it that way on purpose, so no one was quite sure of exactly what was going on."

"I find it hard to picture Trent involved in this."

"Trent had been through some shit, TJ. He had seen men die, men really fucked up. That always gets to a person in the end. Even Trent."

TJ looked out the window, just to avoid looking at Strickland. She swallowed hard, determined not to show what was welling up inside her.

"It doesn't change anything about him," Strickland said.

"Fuck you, it doesn't!" TJ said. She slammed her coffee cup down. The crowd in Denny's got quiet. Two waitresses looked at each other without saying anything.

TJ left the booth and walked hard and fast to the parking lot. Strickland followed close behind her. She did her best to ignore him.

"TJ, wait!" Strickland yelled.

She kept walking toward the Suzuki. She pulled on her helmet and mounted the bike in one motion. Strickland straddled the front tire.

"Get out of the way," TJ said.

"You have to listen to *one* more thing. That's it."

TJ started the engine over Strickland's shouting.

"Come on!" Strickland tried to yell over the engine.

She revved the bike again. Strickland didn't move.

In frustration, she shut down the engine and whipped her helmet off. She held it in one arm and put the other on her hip.

"Look, I'm sorry. I'm really sorry," Strickland said.

"Fine." TJ went to put the helmet on again.

"Wait, there's something you've got to know."

TJ exhaled hard. She stared at him.

Strickland began to talk fast, as though he knew he didn't have much time.

"There was a guy. He started to show up after a while. He would be behind us or he'd just show up out of the blue. At first he stayed back, but then Trent told me the guy confronted him."

"C'mon, David, get to the point."

"Trent told me the guy confronted him. Wanted to know about the cash, how much, who was getting it. He told Trent he was getting into something he shouldn't. That the agency knew and didn't like it."

"And…" TJ had heard enough.

"And the next day Trent was dead."

CHAPTER THIRTY-THREE

TJ never thought she'd see the day when she actually looked forward to going to the Taco. She didn't despise the place, but it was little more to her than a means to make some cash. Today, she looked forward to doing anything besides thinking about this mess.

Being angry at Trent was never something she was comfortable with. Despite the work she did with LaMontagne, every time she allowed herself to feel the rage it inevitably turned to guilt. He was gone, she loved him, and it hurt.

It hurt a lot. That was the emotion that seemed the most genuine.

She called Albany Med and found out that Dr. LaMontagne was in critical condition. That made her stomach churn with guilt and fear. Guilt over LaMontagne getting assaulted because of her, and fear because if LaMontagne died, she had no idea where she'd go with her feelings. She felt embarrassed for feeling that way, which only increased her anxiety.

At the Taco, Gloria was talking to Tequila Sheila when TJ came into the green room.

"You see, Thorlo wrote this book, it's like, you know, famous. It's called *On Golden Pond*. He just hung out there by himself and like, *thought*," Gloria explained.

"That's what I do on Sundays when I'm hung over," Sheila said.

Gloria rolled her eyes as she turned from Sheila and caught TJ coming in.

"Hey, Tommie Gunn. What's up, girlfriend?" Sheila asked.

"Same old. You diggin' *Walden Pond* now, huh?"

Gloria furrowed her brow for an instant while it registered. TJ was already kicking off her Nikes and getting ready.

"I like it. It's deep," Gloria said.

"Yeah. Some of it gets a little dry. It took me a while to get into Thoreau's 'The Bear.'"

"I hear ya. Thoreau talks some deep shit, though."

TJ went behind the curtain to pull on her thong. After the military, she didn't really need the privacy but she figured the other girls would freak out if she just got naked in front of them. When she was in a hurry she'd get naked in front of anyone and not worry about it, but since this was chat time, it seemed inappropriate. It was a strange irony, but there remained some modesty in the strippers' dressing room.

"Hey, girls." TJ recognized Maria's call to attention. TJ smiled to herself as she realized that Maria was the equivalent of the ranking officer in this outfit.

"We got a new girl here tonight. Everyone say hello to Jennifer. She goes by Jenny," Maria announced.

The girls exchanged what ups before Tequila Sheila blurted out, "Damn, another long-legged blond. I ain't gonna make shit for money!"

The girls all laughed and Jenny took it in stride. She gave everyone a half smile and started to unpack.

TJ noticed the new girl had long blond hair and a beautiful Scandinavian complexion. She was fit too, with strong arms and shoulders. She could see the hint of a six-pack. Jenny's abs were maybe a little tighter than her own.

Sheila went on stage to Toby Keith's "How Do You Like Me Now" wearing her six-inch Lucite platforms. She was three strides across the platform when she slipped and fell on her backside. The green room erupted in laughter.

"That girl gotta go easy on the Cuervo," Maria said to herself, shaking her head and moving out toward the bar. The rest of the girls looked around the curtain and watched Sheila right herself and continue on like nothing had happened.

"Un-fucking-believable," Gloria said.

"Is she like that every shift?" Jenny asked.

"Pretty much," TJ said.

Jenny shook her head, lifted her eyebrows, and smiled.

"Comes with the territory," she said to no one in particular.

"Uh-huh." Gloria gave Jenny an exaggerated validation.

"How's the crowd when it comes to working the floor?" Jenny asked TJ.

"This is my first gig so I don't really have much to compare it to, but they're all right. Stupid, horny, and grabby, but nothing worse than that," TJ said.

"This your first time too? Oh, thank God. I thought I would be the only one," Jenny said.

"The hardest part is your first dance. After that, it gets easier if you got the right head for it. That is, if you're not too sensitive and want to make serious money," TJ said.

"That's it right there," Gloria said.

"Welcome aboard," TJ said. "We all kind of stick together, so we'll have your back."

Jenny smiled at TJ and Gloria.

"I thought this was going to be a nightmare. You guys are cool," Jenny said.

TJ shrugged and smiled.

"You gotta have each other's backs in this world."

• CHAPTER THIRTY-FOUR

Billy was sucking his teeth and reading the newspaper when TJ came into Aquarius for her shift. His glasses sat impossibly on the very tip of his Roman nose.

"Says here, the new hybrid cars are gonna clog up all the land-fills with toxic batteries." Billy often read TJ the news in lieu of a more traditional greeting.

"Hey, Billy. How's it been, quiet?" TJ replied, deliberately not engaging with him about the hybrid story.

"Says the batteries might be worse for the environment than the fuel emissions." His defiant tone sounded to TJ like he was in for an argument with her, though she had never brought up how she felt on the issue.

TJ instead went to the log, knowing eventually Billy would answer her question.

"Hannity had on this liberal pain in the ass last night. He lit into her good. She had all her facts wrong."

TJ started to scan down the log of the list of calls from the day and last night when the phone rang.

TJ got it. "Aquarius, how can I help you?" Billy didn't even try to answer. Instead, he sucked his teeth and flipped to the financial section.

"Hi, it's Marsha." The middle-aged voice was tired and slow. Marsha was a frequent caller.

"Hi, Marsha. How are you?" TJ asked. Marsha called two or three times a day to check in. Because she had a mental health diagnosis, she knew the system better than most veteran social workers. She used the suicide hotline as her main social outlet.

"I'm cooking dinner. Making meatloaf."

"Sounds good." TJ mustered as much enthusiasm as she could.

"My corns really have gotten bad. My doctor says I need to go to a podiatrist."

"Yeah?" TJ used her minimal encourager.

"The one between my pinky toe and the next toe—what's that toe called? Is it the fourth toe or is it the second toe? Is there a medical name for each toe? I bet there is. Anyway, I tried to cut it off with an X-ACTO knife once and it got infected."

"Oh…" TJ encouraged.

"Yeah, they said not to do it again but I don't like having to wait to go to the podiatrist and really all he really does is take an X-ACTO knife to it like I did."

TJ read down the log. Marsha was on her fourth call today. Three other frequent callers had checked in the last twenty-four hours and someone had called in looking for an AA meeting.

"I think being a podiatrist would be easy. I wouldn't have cut myself with the X-ACTO if I had the same angle as the foot guy. He just can get at it. Especially the ones between the toes."

"Uh-huh," TJ encouraged.

There had also been a call from a teenage girl whose boyfriend had cheated on her and she had taken a bottle of vitamins. She had thrown up quite a bit.

"People don't think corns are a big deal…"

TJ read further down the call list and stopped at a call from two nights ago.

Female caller asked specifically for TJ. Wanted to talk to her only. Asked when her next shift was and hung up when informed that giving out shifts was against policy.

"But they are a big deal when they're *your* corns," Marsha said.

Right after that log entry TJ saw a note that read:

Caller states that he is just back from Afghanistan. He claims to have been harassed by the CIA and they now are following him and they want him dead. He even said they've encouraged him to "do it himself" because it would be far less painful. Caller states that he doesn't want to kill himself, but that it would be easier than living the way he is now.

"...and after he said that I wondered if he did it to hurt my feelings on purpose," Marsha said. TJ had missed the first part.

"Uh, Marsha, it's more important what you think." It was what she was supposed to say, but it was also a convenient reply considering she had no idea what Marsha had moved on to.

Encouraged to 'do it himself'...far less painful. TJ got a chill.

"I better check on the meatloaf. I'll call you later." Marsha signed off.

Immediately, TJ turned to Billy.

"Billy, did you take the call from this person asking for me?"

Billy was almost done with an article on Walmart and refused to be rushed. He just sucked his teeth by way of response.

"Billy, what the fuck?" TJ asked, and instantly regretted it.

Billy's eyebrows went up and he put the paper down.

"Excuse me? I'm sorry I didn't respond to your every beck and call." He snorted an exhale by way of punctuation.

"This call asking for me—did you take it?" TJ didn't want to hurt his feelings but her desperation overrode her concern.

"I take a lot of calls."

"*This* one." TJ held up the log and pointed to it.

Billy squinted through his reading glasses like he felt no sense of urgency.

"Yeah, so?"

"What did she want?"

"Did you read it? That's what she wanted," Billy said and went back to his business section.

"You know what I mean. Was there anything else?"

The phone rang, interrupting the argument. Billy picked it up and gave the greeting.

"She is here." Billy raised his eyebrows and pursed his lips at TJ. TJ motioned to him to give her the phone. It was against policy.

"May *I* help you?" Billy asked.

"Billy!" TJ felt like she was going to lose it.

"It's against our policy to identify who is working. I—"

TJ picked up her phone and pushed down Billy's line.

"This is TJ," she said. Her tone was flat.

Billy slammed down his phone, shot TJ a look to kill, whipped his chair around, and went for coffee.

"Are you alone on the line?" The altered voice was unidentifiable. The best TJ could tell was that it was a woman.

"I am."

"I'll say this once. Listen closely."

"Who the hell is this?"

"Stay away from the suicide issue. Leave it alone. Ignore Strickland. Ignore the other phone calls. Leave it alone."

"Who the hell is this!"

The voice ignored her plea.

"Listen to my message."

"Why the hell should I?" TJ almost growled.

"If you don't, I will kill you."

The caller hung up.

CHAPTER THIRTY-FIVE

Strickland had grown tired of sitting in his car watching the Aquarius storefront for hours at a stretch. He had grown tired of a lot of this bullshit.

The yelling inside the hotline caught his attention. It sounded like TJ.

He watched the window closely. The old guy stormed away from his desk. TJ stood, talking on the phone. She had her hand balled up in a fist and she shouted into the phone.

Strickland shifted in his seat and did his best to listen closely but the phone call ended. TJ held the receiver at her side for a moment before hanging it up. The old guy returned. He immediately went back to his newspaper.

TJ went out the front door, turned right, and headed toward Central. When she went right, Strickland put the car in gear and slowly followed her. He wanted to keep her in sight but he feared being spotted. Strickland became aware of his sidearm tucked in his jeans under his oversized striped golf shirt.

By the time he made the turn he saw she was already to Dove and was running. She turned right on Dove. He accelerated but didn't rev the engine, hoping he wouldn't lose her. When he got to Dove she was nowhere in sight. He noticed that State was a one-way street.

He slowed when he cruised past State, but the tree-lined street was dark and there were only a handful of pedestrians. To make matters worse, the SUV behind Strickland laid on the horn.

He didn't want the attention. He cursed, waved a hand, and kept driving down Dove, knowing he'd lost her.

* * *

TJ sprinted up the State Street hill. She tried to amp up her heart rate when she felt stress, and hill sprints did it faster than anything else. She went anaerobic, felt the sledgehammer pounding in her chest as she reached the crest of the hill. She kept going, and from the times she'd trained with a heart rate monitor, she knew she was hitting close to two hundred beats per minute.

She cruised to a stop, doubled over with her hands on her knees, and heaved.

What the fuck was happening? She had done her best to do what LaMontagne had ground into her: Stay in the moment. Don't chase what might happen tomorrow or what happened a year ago. Stay in the now.

That seemed impossible.

Too much was going on at once, and with the trauma of Trent's loss, she couldn't evaluate her situation in the same way she had evaluated problems her whole life. In the past, she could look at all sides of an issue, weigh plusses and minuses, risks and rewards, and make informed decisions.

Now, she had things in front of her that not only defied evaluation, they also pushed her up against emotions that she was unsure about. She was out of control and she hated that feeling more than anything. She lived a life maximizing control, assessing and taking action carefully, based on evidence.

She had ghosts in front of her and didn't know what to do.

Her hear rate came down and her breathing began to slow. She felt the all-over tension of uncertainty. She took a deep breath, trying to calm and center herself.

She thought about being short and inconsiderate to Billy. He was a bug but he didn't deserve to be mistreated. He was ignorant, but he was a friend at a time in her life when she didn't have any.

The Blue Ribbon Diner served the best cheesecake north of New York City and was on the same block as Aquarius. On the walk back, she stopped and got an extra large piece of the chocolate turtle, Billy's favorite. She dreaded facing him but knew she had to.

She crept in Aquarius's front door and Billy glanced at her for an instant and then went back to his paper, pretending that he didn't notice her entrance.

"Billy, I'm sorry for being a total asshole. You didn't deserve how I acted. I'm really, really sorry," she said. He didn't react. He kept reading the *Post*.

She waited and looked at him. It seemed like forever.

Her eyes welled up and she did her best to hold the tears back. It didn't work.

Through her tears she managed to say, "Billy, please. I don't have anyone and I couldn't stand to know you won't be my friend." She wiped tears with the back of her hand, her own hurt overriding her embarrassment.

"Billy...*please*."

He looked up and saw that she was crying. His eyes moved to the cheesecake and back up to TJ. He half smiled.

"You had me with the cheesecake," he deadpanned.

TJ hugged him awkwardly around the shoulders and kissed his cheek.

• CHAPTER THIRTY-SIX

Jordan got the call in the middle of the night. He was used to that. It came with the territory of making money overseas. But while getting late-night calls might have been something he was used to, being told that his whole operation and his main source of income were being threatened was not.

"We're not shutting things down!" he screamed into the phone. It took a lot for him to lose his cool.

"Things are getting different over here lately. There's a campaign on to reduce usage. The soldiers can't control themselves and it is affecting their performance," the contact said.

"C'mon, don't hand me that bullshit. The soldiers want it and everyone knows that. The administration is running their usual PR routine," Jordan said.

"This is different."

"Don't let it be." Jordan hung up

He listened to the ceiling fan hum. Despite its high speed, the tropical air was heavy. He didn't like what was happening. There was the ongoing problem with Dunn and now this. Demand remained the fundamental base of what he did. The need would still be there, but if interference with distribution made sales harder, it would cut into his profit margin. Bad press and people talking too much would have the same result.

Jordan didn't like his control threatened. On the occasions when it happened, he strategically stepped up activity.

He called Forbus. Despite the hour, Forbus answered on the second ring. Forbus always did.

"Step things up. Don't get careless, but take care of things, sooner rather than later."

That was all Jordan said.

It was enough.

• CHAPTER
THIRTY-SEVEN

TJ didn't have to work at the Taco until just before midnight and she didn't have a hotline shift today. That meant a whole day to herself to do whatever she wanted. For TJ, that wasn't a good thing. Free time let her mind wander and she didn't like that, not at all.

She didn't need an alarm clock. Either she didn't sleep well enough to make it through the sun's reflection against the shades or she simply got out of bed after a night of little or no sleep at all. After what had happened with Billy, this was one of those nights.

Without the outlet therapy provided, TJ felt more frightened than usual. The fear stayed with her all the time and simmered constantly just below the surface. She had grown accustomed to it and most often, she simply acted as if it didn't exist. That strategy worked when she busied herself, exercised, or talked to others on the hotline. The fear was magnified both early in the morning and late at night, when she was alone.

The pot whistled, and TJ watched the freeze-dried crystals turn into bitter coffee. She had gotten used to instant in the service and liked the convenience of it. Her whole life remained in many ways much like her service existence. It was built around transiency and the ability to pick up and move when she wanted to. Careful not to put down roots or commitments, she kept her life in this purposeful in-between period, like she would actually begin to live again only whenever this was over. However, "this" had been going on for a while and there was no end in sight. It frightened TJ to think that "this" could go on forever.

She killed time at the kitchen table drinking a second and third cup of instant coffee and reading an article in the back of *Time* magazine. The op-ed piece questioned whether America could ever win in Afghanistan. TJ shook her head at the absurdity of it.

At quarter to nine, she got dressed and decided to head to Albany Med to say a quick hello to Dr. LaMontagne. TJ didn't know the rules or protocol regarding visiting a therapist but it felt like the right thing to do. This whole therapy thing didn't come with directions, like everything in the military did. Though she hated to admit it, sometimes the structure of the military made life easier. It took away the uncertainty. In its place, it gave you rote repetition and stupidity, but it took away uncertainty.

TJ parked the bike on the first floor of the connected parking garage right by the hospital entrance, taking advantage of the unused bike space. She asked at the front desk where she could find Dr. LaMontagne. The librarian type with the big Adam's apple and old-school reading glasses who was manning the front desk hit the keys in rapid succession without ever glancing down. Without looking at TJ and with an absence of warmth he said, "She's in ICU. She can't have visitors."

"She's in ICU?" TJ asked to say something.

Adam's apple nodded.

"Does that mean she's in bad shape?" TJ realized it wasn't the most cogent question.

"HIPPA regulations limit the information I can share with you." He said it like it was the Pledge of Allegiance and he said it a thousand times a day.

"If she's in ICU it can't be good, right?"

"I'm not allowed to say—"

TJ turned away before he could finish. She felt panic and a wave of raw emotion come over her that she wasn't ready for. Logically, she knew LaMontagne could be in trouble but emotionally she hadn't expected it. She hadn't realized the emotions were going to hit her like this.

She started to run in the lobby, and when she hit the light of the street, she went into a full sprint. She had the traffic light to cross the street and ran as hard as she could to her bike. Her face, now wet with tears, throbbed, and TJ did her best to not double over. She welcomed her motorcycle helmet's coverage, straddled the bike, and threw it into gear.

She took the right out of the parking lot and headed toward the highway. TJ grew impatient with the city traffic, and when she hit I-90, she drove the bike faster than she ever had before. Her heart pounded and concentrating got harder through her tears. After fifteen minutes of getting it out at high speed, she started to slow the bike down. Speed wasn't her thing, and even through her intense emotion, she knew this wasn't a great idea. She entered the rest area beyond Exit 11 and tried to think. Getting killed on a motorcycle wasn't how she wanted to spend this day, despite how she felt inside.

Methodically, she ran through her options, brainstorming what would be her best choices. Exercise was always her best stress management. A hard workout of throwing punches, kicks, and getting her heart rate up was a better answer. She put the bike in gear and headed home to get her gym bag.

When she got to the Crawford Y, she headed straight up the stairs toward the boxing gym. As she climbed, she could hear the rat-a-tat of the speed bag but not much else. She came around the corner and noticed there was only one guy in the gym, Duffy the left-handed heavyweight from her first visit. The rest buzzer sounded and he wiped his soaked forehead with the back of his wrapped hand.

"Hey, what's goin' on?" he asked, smiling at TJ and picking up a jump rope. "It's TJ, right?"

"Yeah, how you doing?" TJ asked. It felt good being remembered.

"Smitty's out of town at an amateur show. Most of the fighters are with him. We pretty much got the gym to—"

A loud bark came from the coach's office, followed by a very large basset hound. The hound waddled out of the office and stared at TJ.

"What the hell…"

"Al, be nice," Duffy said. "TJ, allow me to introduce Al, my roommate."

The dog kind of hummed, then yawned and stretched. He then flopped onto his side and began to snore.

"See, you wore him out. He'll be quiet the rest of the afternoon."

TJ couldn't restrain a smile. She loosened up by going half speed on the duct-taped heavy bag until she felt the first drops of sweat appear down her back. She wore a plain white T-shirt with sleeves cut off and heather gray shorts to go along with her running shoes.

Duffy was skipping rope. For a big guy he was surprisingly agile. TJ knew from experience that heavyweights could hit like mules, but most had a hard time getting out of the way of a punch. This guy could move. The buzzer for the end of the round sounded.

"Hey, would you want to do any work in the ring?" Duffy asked.

TJ wasn't sure what he meant so she didn't answer.

"I mean some sparring. You know, controlled. Obviously, I have a few pounds on you."

"Sure," TJ said.

It wasn't uncommon for fighters of different weights to spar together with the unwritten rule that the heavier fighter was to take something off his punches. Advanced fighters could get a lot out of such work. The bigger issue was how women were respected in gyms. The fact was, usually, they weren't. Men tended to dismiss their presence entirely. TJ hated being patronized.

"Headgear and gloves are in the cabinet," Duffy said, motioning with his head. "I don't think Smitty has any female foul protectors but I'm good at not hitting low."

He said it without a hint of awkwardness. TJ hadn't sparred in a long time, and the excitement and anxiety mixed with the rest of her pent-up emotions made her feel electric. Using the gym's gear was gross; she would've brought hers if she had known sparring was a possibility, but she could deal with it. She put on the headgear and years of sweat and BO from who knew how many fighters combined with the smell of old leather to fill her nose. It was the scent of fighting.

"You need help getting the headgear on?" Duffy asked. He already had his gear on and TJ was fidgeting with hers.

He came close to her and leaned down so he could see where the strap went together under her chin. He was soaked with sweat and TJ couldn't help but notice the veins in his arms and his biceps as he tightened the headgear. His shirt stuck to his chest, and she could see the chiseled pectoral muscles. Despite the sweat, he smelled good, not of cologne but in a more masculine way.

"Good?" he asked. She nodded and he gave her a quick slap around the top of the headgear and smiled. TJ, about to get into the ring, felt her heart race. When she climbed through the ropes with Duffy, she wasn't sure what she was getting into.

"Let's start slow, kind of feel each other out," he said. TJ nodded. Duffy threw a jab toward her face at about half speed and she blocked it. She countered, parrying off his punch, and it was clear the speed surprised him. He blocked part of it but a part of her glove got a little bit of cheek.

"Whew, you got some speed," he said.

He threw a double jab, this time taking the speed and power up a notch. His intensity increase told her he respected her skills and the uptick in power was his way of letting her know he knew she could handle it.

She stepped inside his next jab and threw a three-punch uppercut to his body. His abs were firm and she knew the punches didn't take anything out of him. Still, getting inside him and scoring was a victory in and of itself. He spun to his left and tapped her with two jabs. He shot them to her face and she could tell he opened his hand to lessen the impact. She deflected most of the jabs, taking just a little leather on her cheek.

"Nice movement," TJ said.

She moved toward him, hitched her left shoulder to feint a jab, and drove a straight right down the middle of his guard. He went for the feint. The right landed harder than TJ expected. She felt his nose against her knuckles through the padding of the glove.

"Oooh, sorry. I didn't mean to—"

"Nice shot, you caught me," Duffy said, offering his glove to tap, the universal, nonverbal boxing language of affirmation. Immediately, TJ felt embarrassed and silly for apologizing. The last thing she wanted was to come out sounding girly.

"I need to work on the ropes," Duffy said. "Can you pressure me a bit?"

It wasn't unusual for a fighter to work on strategy during sparring. Working on the ropes required advanced skills.

"Just throw at me," he said.

TJ let go with combinations focusing on speed. She'd jab right, jab, jab, right, and finish off with a hook. Then she alternated going upstairs and to the body. Her rat-at-tat-tats to the body came lightning quick, and when she ended it with a left to the head it caught him flush on the jawline.

She heard him grunt, and it let her know that her hook had something on it. He tightened his guard and lowered his crouch. TJ was breathing hard, really hard, from the work, but she was loving every second of it. She mustered all she could and let go with another combination.

Duffy took three punches on his gloves. Her next right came down the middle but he was ready for her. He stepped into the punch, hooked his upper arm around it, and trapped it. Then, he turned TJ so that she was the one against the ropes.

The move caught her by surprise and almost took her breath away. Her face was planted on his chest and she needed to breathe deeply to get her wind. Her arms, needing to balance the rest of her, wrapped around his waist, forcing her even closer to him. Duffy leaned his weight into her and her back went into the ropes. The ropes stretched and bent with the force of the two bodies.

It was some advanced movement and it was clear this guy knew what he was doing. TJ felt his weight, his hard upper body pressed against hers, and she knew he had her tied up. It was both offensive and defensive at the same time.

She was breathing hard and she took the clinch to rest, as fighters often did. She let Duffy support her as she leaned back into him. He was warm—almost hot—from the work, and so was she. Her breathing didn't come back as fast as she wanted it to, and she realized she was not only winded but wet from the exertion.

After what seemed like a long moment, she worked out of the clinch and they danced to the center of the ring. She threw a double jab without much steam, and he caught both of them. The buzzer sounded and TJ was grateful for the rest.

Both of them were winded from the exertion.

"Hey, you really got something," Duffy said.

"So do you," TJ said with a heavy exhale.

They went at it again for two more rounds and found that rhythm that fighters who worked together for a long time enjoyed. They could challenge each other, they could make the other work, and they could also slow things down to a comfortable pace just for the good of the movement.

TJ hadn't had anything like this in a long time.

· CHAPTER
THIRTY-EIGHT

Finding where she lived took longer than expected.

The strip club didn't keep records. She had no credit cards and an e-mail address was nowhere to be found. Following her gave an idea of the general area but not the specific location. Narrowing it down took a couple of days.

She had to live in a rental property, and the neighborhood didn't seem to have any. The semi-industrial section was littered with light manufacturing bordered by run-down single-family houses. The neighborhood had once belonged to the blue-collar laborers who had worked there, but now it was all welfare recipients and old people who didn't have the strength to move.

Spotting what looked to be an apartment on top of the old garage was just luck. It was in the backyard of a piece of land filled with fast-food wrappers and beer cans old enough that the color of their labels had changed and faded. The motorcycle tracks partially hidden behind a weathered bush served as confirmation.

Getting in was no easy trick. The windows were locked and the door leading up to the apartment was dead bolted. Breaking glass would give too much away. There'd be no reason to rob a dirty, sparse apartment, especially one that was so well protected. It had to go unnoticed. Fortunately, taking time with the locksmith's tools wasn't an issue. In this neighborhood, no one looked up, and back here, no one cared at all. The only problem would be if she came home.

The neatness and economy of her personal property spoke of her military background. A duffel bag filled with lace thongs, patent leather bustiers, and sequined boy shorts was the only thing that would make anyone question the occupant's background.

There was an art to searching a place. One had to be thorough and meticulous but efficient. Making sure to check under dresser drawers and tapping for hollow areas was important. Of course, the freezer, oven, and all the cans in the cupboard were searched. There was barely anything here that gave any evidence of what she knew or what her intentions were.

The apartment didn't reveal any new information. There was one thing left to do.

The package, neatly wrapped in brown paper and tied with twine, was left anonymously on her counter. A standard military cardboard box used for shipping would send a subtle message when she opened it.

It was an old box being repurposed.

• CHAPTER THIRTY-NINE

"I'm getting a beer. You feel like coming?" Duffy asked. It was nonchalant and seemed to come without an agenda.

TJ hesitated just a second and wished she hadn't. It set some awkwardness that didn't have to be there.

"Sure," she said.

"You're not from around here?" It was a question.

She shook her head.

"There's a place I go to around the corner." He was pulling off his sweat-soaked T-shirt. TJ noticed the hint of washboard abs and the prominence of veins in his wiry upper body. She did more than just notice. She actually kind of felt something.

He pulled on an old, ripped, gray sweatshirt with the arms cut off and the neck collar cut.

"You wanna ride with me or follow?"

"I'll ride with you if it isn't far," TJ said, this time without hesitation.

TJ walked with him through the Y out to the parking lot, feigning nonchalance. All at once, she became hyperaware and her senses sharpened while trying to pretend that going out for a beer with a gym mate, who just happened to be male, was no big deal.

The fat hound trotting alongside made things a tad weird. They reached his car, a burnt orange Cadillac from the seventies. The car seemed like it was a block long, and TJ found herself smiling.

"What year is this thing?" TJ asked.

"Seventy-six."

The dog jumped in the backseat, stuck his nose between the seats just above the elbow rest, and looked at TJ. She thought she heard a low growl.

"Is he mad at me about something?"

"Al, sit back." He nudged the dog into a sitting position on the backseat, which was the size of a sofa sectional. The hound growled once more then lay down and started to snore. "You're in his spot. He generally rides shotgun."

TJ noted that if the hound usually rode in the front, then it sounded like Duffy didn't have a girlfriend. She felt embarrassment for thinking like a girl in the seventh grade. They drove about a mile and a half and pulled in front of an old building in between a cookie factory and series of warehouses. TJ couldn't believe her anxiety.

The three of them walked in the front door just under a red neon sign that said "AJ's" except the small "s" was burned out. She was immediately hit by the smells of old beer, smoke, and old customers—the smell of a classic dive bar.

Four guys were sitting directly in front of the taps. Duffy walked around them to the far left and took what seemed to be "his" seat. An opened bottle of Schlitz was waiting for him. TJ sat next to him and the dog lay down at her feet.

"Hey, Duff," the bartender said. He didn't smile, and he had a look of weariness. The four guys offered no greeting. In fact, they seemed to be in a heated argument. TJ thought she heard something about David Carradine and his death, except one guy kept saying that he asphyxiated himself in his car.

"Schlitz?" TJ asked.

"Don't start," Duffy said.

She ordered a Coors Light.

"You've got nerve," Duffy said. TJ feigned anger and then smiled. He smiled out of one side of his mouth and offered his bottle for a toast. "Nice work today."

TJ clinked the neck of her bottle with his.

"What do you do?" he asked.

Off guard, she hesitated. It was a normal question, but she wasn't ready for it. She could see his expression change.

"You don't have to—"

"I was in the army. Not really doing anything yet." She felt like she recovered well.

"Oh, sorry."

"No, don't be. I just still feel funny talking about it."

"Did you see action?"

"Yeah, I was an MP."

He nodded and seemed to think about it. She was impressed that he didn't immediately say something about her being a women or show surprise.

"So what do you do now?"

"Mostly, I volunteer on a suicide hotline." It felt good not to lie.

"Hmmm, I work as a counselor at JUS, Jewish Unified Services. Mostly ghetto-type stuff: addiction, spousal abuse, welfare issues…"

"Really? You like it?"

He half-laughed.

"Do I like it? Well, I like it when I genuinely get to help someone who really wants to change. I hate paperwork and the administrative bullshit, I hate manipulative clients, and I hate my boss.

Percentage-wise that means I like my job about three percent of the time."

TJ laughed and instinctually bumped his shoulder with hers. He was hard and steady and he didn't pull away. He laughed back with her. She felt something. It felt nice, and it felt scary. She finished her beer with a bigger gulp than she was used to.

She wondered if she was completely out of touch with reality. They were quiet for an instant, but the chatter from the guys to their right filled the space. They were going on about *Hogan's Heroes*, Bob Crane, and "auto-a-pixelation."

She felt Duffy's hand on her shoulder and the weight of him leaning on her. It startled her. Then she heard him whisper in her ear. "Check it out."

He pointed to the swinging half doors to the kitchen area. Al the dog was up on two legs, reaching for a slice of American cheese.

"Ready, three, two, one…"

"Goddamn it! Al! Shoo! Shoo! You bastard!" the bartender screamed. The dog dropped to all fours, waddled out of the kitchen, and returned to his position at TJ's feet.

"Goddamn it, Duffy. I keep tellin' you to keep that bastard hound out of here!"

Duffy was laughing so hard he couldn't speak. TJ cracked up at the absurdity of it all. She laughed really hard and looked up into Duffy's eyes. They both laughed for a long time.

It felt good.

• CHAPTER FORTY

"Some of the product was compromised," Atwater said. His voice was tight.

"In what way?" Jordan could feel his senses sharpen.

"The Afghanis are making a show of cracking down."

"They do that twice a year. You've made the payments, haven't you?" Jordan let a little intensity creep into his voice.

"Of course, but I'm concerned with some of the personnel changes. They seem to be going in a different direction."

"How so?"

"I can't put my finger on it. It's more instinct." Atwater didn't like to sound uncertain.

"So what happened to the product?"

"One of ours was caught and arrested in possession during a drop-off," Atwater said. "He had three hundred pounds."

"Christ." Jordan's voice tightened further. "Have you paid them off to make it go away?"

"Of course. That's the problem. The usuals weren't there. There are some new people, and they are at least making a big show about stopping this."

Jordan went silent. It had happened before. New Afghanis came in and he changed the game a little for a time. He showed them the money and business boomed.

"Hold tight. Let it get quiet. Things will go back to the status quo. They always have," Jordan said.

"Yeah, you're right." Neither man sounded completely confident. There was too much at stake.

"Jonathan, what do you want me to do with the soldier?"

"Who is he?"

"He's relatively new. Pretty stupid kid. I blame myself, but it is getting tougher to recruit." He waited while Jordan thought.

"Go with procedure," Jordan said.

• CHAPTER FORTY-ONE

Forbus watched Dunn leave the bar with the boxer. They were laughing, and Forbus noticed Dunn lean into him and laugh after he said something. Hmm, Forbus wondered, could the little head case be hooking up?

Forbus followed at a safe distance and watched them return to the YMCA parking lot. TJ seemed hesitant to get out of the old Caddy, but she did. Forbus didn't see her give the guy a kiss or anything. Forbus, hard-nosed and all business, could still read the body language.

Forbus didn't know if this affected the plan, but figured it was too small to let Jordan know about it. The goal was to take care of business and eliminate drama, not create it.

Forbus let the motorcycle get a comfortable distance before the trail began. Odds were good that TJ would be heading home, and if her dance schedule had been studied correctly, tonight was a work night. It was a couple of hours before she would get ready, so when Dunn entered the general area of her apartment's neighborhood, Forbus let her go. Later, they would meet, one way or the other.

• CHAPTER FORTY-TWO

TJ was embarrassed even though she was by herself. But as she drove the Suzuki toward the Taco she couldn't stop thinking about Duffy and how she felt. It was too intense to dismiss, and the feelings confused her. She didn't know where they belonged, and she didn't want the complication of being attracted to someone right now. Still, it was nice to feel something romantic that involved a man and some attraction. That girly high school feeling conflicted with her usual dark outlook on life. She tried her best not to filter it through Trent and that complicated mess.

The lot at the Taco was only half-full. It was early. TJ was glad she had someplace to go and something to do so she wouldn't have to think, or for that matter feel, much. She began to dress in the green room. Sheila was on stage; it was early in the evening and she wasn't drunk yet. Gloria, Dee, and Jenny were also getting ready for their first shifts of the night.

"I can't believe I'm going to say this, but I'm actually glad to be here tonight. I'm so sick of studying," Gloria said. "Fuckin' midterms."

"Girl, why you wastin' your time? You know what social workers make—like nothin' compared to this," Dee said.

"I'm just doing this until I can get a good job, and college is a way to make that happen."

"You trippin'. Every girl think she's doin' this as a hobby and shit."

Gloria turned away and exhaled. TJ decided to give her an out.

"Which midterms are coming up?" TJ asked.

"I got an essay test on counseling theory. He wants something on comparing Jung and Rogers."

"Existentialism versus humanism. I had that same type of test once. Here's a shortcut for you: Existentialists believe life has no meaning and that each individual has to create something to live for. Humanists believe that just living is enough of a meaning and the individual's goal is to be consistent with their internal meaning," TJ said. She raised her eyebrows to see if Gloria got it.

"That's some crazy bullshit," Dee said.

"In other words, the existentialists believe that there's really not much to live for unless we create something. Humanists believe that life is worth living on its own and we have to find our own meaning," TJ said.

Gloria looked blankly at TJ.

"If you were an existentialist you would believe that going to school, getting a career, and bettering yourself gives your life meaning. If you were a humanist you'd believe that this life of yours is worth living and enjoying and you need to be true to yourself by going for everything you can," TJ said.

Gloria smiled.

"So they're both kind of the same but the humanists are a little happier about life," Gloria said.

"Exactly," TJ said and put her fist out for a bump from Gloria.

"Fuckin' white people are a trip," Dee said, putting a hand in the air and turning her head away.

The power chord intro to "Hit Me With Your Best Shot" came on, and that meant Sheila was on the floor for tips and Dee was on stage. The awkward DJ transition from Pat Benatar to Michael Jackson's "Beat It" didn't seem to bother the customers and was so second nature to the dancers that they never noticed.

Jenny was wearing a pale green velour tracksuit. It was real athletic gear, not a sexy fashion twist on the warm-up. She slid off the velour suit to reveal shiny metallic boy shorts and a matching skintight halter. She took a pair of Lucite-heeled shoes out of her gym bag and kicked of her Nikes.

"Girl, I love your arms. What kind of working out do you do?" Gloria asked.

"I like the kickboxing classes. Feels good to hit something, you know?" Jenny said.

TJ smiled.

"Your thighs are rock hard too. Is that kickboxing?" Gloria asked. "I gotta get into that."

"You'd love it," TJ chimed in. "Especially after a few Taco shifts. Then it feels even better to hit something."

The Beatles' "Revolution" cued Gloria to the stage, leaving TJ and Jenny alone.

"I think it's sweet the way you help her with the college stuff," Jenny said.

"I guess it just feels good to see someone trying to better themselves," TJ said.

"No, it's not just that. I know you do it in a way that lets her keep her pride. That's pretty awesome."

TJ smiled.

"One of these nights you want to grab a drink or something? I mean, I really don't know anyone in Albany. I pretend that this stuff is no big deal, but sometimes, I don't know, it's hard."

It seemed to TJ that it took a lot for Jenny to offer that.

"Yeah, I'd like that."

The two women smiled at each other. TJ felt a little warmth spread through her. In one day, she seemed to have made some real connections. Two more than she'd had in the previous twelve months.

"Born in the USA" began, and TJ knew it was her time. She wore a red, white, and blue star-spangled bikini under a ripped-flag-decorated sweatshirt and cutoff sweatpants combination. She spun around the pole and danced away, dropping down into an almost violent front split. The move got the room's attention.

"Ain't That America" cued her to remove the sweats, and she even drew a little applause when the customers saw the bikini. The bottom thong was ridiculously brief, so much so that TJ had to give the razor extra attention in the shower that morning. Not every dancer could wear something like this. TJ's fit abs were required. Midway through the song, she removed her top.

A Bob Seeger song moved her toward the end of the set. She did an ultra-slow slide into a side split and actually felt a little pride at some of the looks the audience gave her. Not so much the leering, but the gap-mouthed look that told her that they, at least for a moment, were impressed by her fitness.

She came up from the move and bent down to retrieve her top before moving to the customers. She glanced toward the green room to see if Jenny was ready. Jenny smiled back at her and it made TJ feel good.

TJ gave her a nod and a wink and headed toward the tables.

• CHAPTER
FORTY-THREE

It was close to five in the morning when TJ got home. The Taco had stayed busy right till closing, and it was after four when Maria let everyone go. TJ had stopped at home briefly after the gym before her shift, but just long enough to shower and change.

She nearly collapsed after climbing the garage stairs, and all she could think of was her bed. The bumpy pullout even seemed gloriously luxurious after the day she'd had, and she simply kicked her shoes off and left her jeans in a pile on the floor. The street-light coming in from the dirty kitchen window was hitting her right in the eye and, as much as she didn't want to get up, she relented.

After she pulled the shade and turned back, she noticed the package on the counter. It was the size of a shoe box and wrapped in brown paper. TJ got chills. The package sat, with no explanation and no invitation, and TJ knew something wasn't right.

She stared at it for a long moment before touching it. Her military experience made her cautious. In Iraq, they could booby trap anything, and friends with missing digits and limbs were a constant reminder that anything that appeared to be unusual should be treated with caution.

Still, TJ felt just a little silly imagining all the espionage shit. After all, she was now a stripper in therapy and her military operations area had been MP—not exactly the espionage stuff. All of that, combined and multiplied by ten, didn't exactly put her in James Bond's league.

TJ poked the box with her right index finger and was surprised to feel no resistance. The box was empty, or nearly so. She knew all about plastic explosives and how light they could be, but they weighed *something*. She pushed it again, this time with more force, and again—nothing.

She got a an old steak knife out of the drawer and cut the knotted twine that joined neatly from the four sides of the box. It was amazingly uniform in that way that told her whoever had prepared this was undoubtedly in the service or at least suffering from a mild form of OCD. She ran the underside of the knife toward the middle of the box and snapped the twine.

TJ undid the brown paper deliberately, without hurry. Immediately, something on the cardboard stood out: the box carried the imprinted inscription "Property of the US Army" and it set something off inside of her. She took off the top of the box, holding her breath, and waited for something to happen. Nothing did.

Inside was a clear plastic sandwich bag. In it was what looked like four or five tablespoons of beige powder. TJ's mind flashed back to hazmat training and chemical warfare seminars and felt a sense of panic. If this was anthrax or Ebola, it was probably already too late. She was too close and had probably contaminated herself with a granule or two left on the outside of the baggie or cardboard.

She felt a little better when she recalled that beige was never one of the colors that were supposed to bring concern. Anthrax and the other chemicals were generally white, or near white, as were most chemical weapons. It didn't matter, anyway; it wasn't like she could call the chemical weapons unit or a hazmat team.

She opened the sandwich bag, trying not to think. She tried to go to a neutral place since she knew she was defying reason and logic. It was after five in the morning, and she was exhausted and didn't need this in her life at the moment. She wasn't in the mood.

She brought her nose to the opening and gently sniffed. Gently sniffing anthrax, or anything else for that matter, was enough to kill her one hundred times over, but right now, she didn't have any better ideas. She didn't pick up a strong odor, but instead a faint, bitter, sour smell. She allowed herself a deeper inhalation and picked up a vinegary aroma, almost like ketchup that had turned. She sniffed again, this time lifting the baggie out of the box.

Underneath the bag was a plain white sheet of paper cut to the size of an index card. It had one sentence typed across it in Courier font: *This is heroin and this is what it's all about.*

Nothing on the other side and nothing else in the box. TJ dipped a finger in the powder and tentatively tasted it. It was without much taste at all but clearly bitter. TJ had confiscated heroin from soldiers in Iraq on several occasions, and now she almost felt silly for not recognizing it from the start. Of course, it appearing in her apartment, more than a year out of the army, without explanation, reminded her that there was nothing strange about not getting it right away.

This is heroin and this is what it's all about.

It didn't seem like something Strickland would do. He had already put his cards on the table. TJ wasn't sure whether to believe him or not, but he had made his plea. Of course, he could be screwing around to somehow get TJ to buy into his whole conspiracy theory. It was within the realm of possibility, but it didn't seem probable.

If not Strickland, who?

A bag of heroin was a serious calling card, meant to get attention. TJ cursed her fatigue and wished she had a clear head, though even a sharp mind on eight hours of sleep would struggle to figure this out. Mentally, she backed up and tried to put together what had been going on.

The calls warning her of staged military suicides…Strickland's appearance…the warning that the CIA might be after him and TJ…the fear of their relationship with Trent and fear that he had talked too much.

And now the heroin.

TJ walked the box across the room and sat down—actually, almost collapsed—on the bed.

Heroin is what it's all about.

All what's about? TJ thought.

• CHAPTER FORTY-FOUR

Suicide Claims Another Soldier
    Associated Press
    An army corporal recently arrested by Afghani military police for possession of heroin has killed himself. Corporal Wilson LeMoyne was released into US Army custody on Friday and his body was found hanging in his army detention cell Saturday evening.
    The Philadelphia resident was twenty-two.
    LeMoyne was in Afghanistan for just six weeks. It was his second tour. He joined the army right after graduating from Central High in 2007.
    LeMoyne was arrested and charged with possession of narcotics with the intent to sell to a member of the Afghani military. His release to US forces was considered unusually quick and Lt. Colonel William Cantwell, the spokesman for his unit, did not offer an explanation.
    LeMoyne is survived by his parents, Roger and Florence, and a younger brother, Michael.

• CHAPTER FORTY-FIVE

After a few hours of lying on her bed, unable to sleep, TJ dug out the piece of paper on which Strickland had jotted down his number. It dawned on her that she had no idea where he was staying, or much else about him. She reached him a few minutes after nine o'clock.

As soon as he answered, TJ blurted out, "What do you know about the package?"

"Good morning to you too. What the hell are you talking about?" Strickland asked.

"David, I'm done with this bullshit. Tell me what's going on and stop the nonsense."

"Package?"

"I came home from the club late last night and there was a small box on my counter. It was a military issue box."

Strickland remained quiet. TJ waited for a response. It didn't come.

"What was in it?" Strickland asked to break the silence.

"You're telling me you don't know what was in it?"

"I swear I don't know," Strickland said with rising anxiety.

"I don't believe you," TJ said.

"Look, I've been straight with you. When I wanted to talk to you, I found you and I was direct. I haven't been coy with you."

"Really? You've told me everything? Then where are you staying? What money are you living on? And who, exactly, are you connected with?"

Strickland didn't answer.

"Yeah, so much for full disclosure," TJ said.

"I've got money left from over there. I'm at the Residence Inn off Route Seven. I'm not connected to anyone. Haven't been since I got out," he said with a degree of exasperation.

"So, why the secrecy?"

"I feel like a scumbag for telling you what we did over there."

This time it was TJ who got quiet.

She waited until Strickland spoke.

"What was in the box?"

TJ thought for a moment. She had no idea what was going on or who to trust, but she didn't want to be alone in it.

"Heroin. I'm pretty sure it's heroin," TJ said.

"What!"

"Yeah, and you're telling me you have no idea?"

"Was there anything else?"

"There was a note that said, 'This is what it's all about.'" Nothing but silence came through the phone line. "David? Are you still there?"

"Yeah, sure, I'm here. Just thinking." TJ could hear panic in his voice. "I have no idea what it's about. I really don't." He also sounded earnest. "Hey, why don't you meet me. Let's talk this over in person. I'm getting scared about your safety."

TJ didn't respond. She didn't like the way it felt. Still, he was the only connection she had to any of this.

"C'mon, TJ. Come to the Residence Inn. I'm in one-forty. We can talk."

She hesitated for a long moment.

"All right. I'll be there in an hour."

• CHAPTER FORTY-SIX

Something just didn't feel right.

TJ had noticed a distinct change in Strickland's tone as soon as she mentioned heroin. Now she was invited to his hotel room, something that in all the other recent bullshit hadn't happened. Something didn't feel right at all.

At the same time, TJ made up her mind to go. She didn't like shying away from, well, anything. She also wasn't stupid; she knew enough to not get herself killed. She had the feeling that the ante in this game had just been raised. She might have been able to rationalize the hotline calls and Strickland's reappearance in her life, but heroin didn't just magically show up in random kitchens. There was no doubt a serious message was being sent—whatever the hell the message was.

She just didn't buy the whole CIA thing either. It was too Hollywood, too thriller novel bullshit. As much as people liked to fantasize about the bogeymen that made up the CIA, in truth she had had very little contact with them in her military experience. There were several occasions when they had joined troops, given briefings, or showed up unannounced and everyone knew *something* out of the ordinary was going on. But they didn't land in hovercraft, answer shoe telephones, or wield poisonous daggers that unfolded from Bic pens. Those were bullshit like the rest of the government bullshit.

Still, going to see Strickland just didn't sit right. TJ went to her closet and got out her small army duffel, the last remnant of her life in Iraq. She dug around and lifted out fatigues, T-shirts, and berets and got to the bottom of the bag. She took the box out, opened it, and looked at the velvet casing. It was the first time she had looked at a gun since she left. A cold feeling came over her, and her mouth went dry. She had intended to never hold a firearm again in her life.

Things had changed.

She found the clip in a separate compartment in the bag and slid it in. The action heightened the surreal experience, and TJ got that old familiar feeling of leaving behind her individuality and becoming a soldier with duties, duties that she didn't always like but that had to be carried out. The gun was loaded. She was ready to kill if the circumstances called for it.

She wore her fatigues, not out of any intentional symbolism, but because they were cleaner than her jeans and because her running pants wouldn't support the pistol. She slid the gun into her waistband at the small of her back, where the muscles along her spine cradled it. First kickboxing and then stripping had kept those lumbar muscles tight and developed.

The gun wasn't registered. She knew getting caught with it in New York State brought a mandatory prison sentence. It was a risk worth taking when her life was threatened. Even so, she kept the Suzuki at a ridiculously slow speed on the way to the Residence Inn. The bike struggled in the low gear like a hungry tiger being held on a leash. TJ was barely able to keep her attention on driving. The heightened awareness was a rush in some ways, but in other ways, it made her sick. It was either kill or be killed, and the danger sharpened her senses. The high was almost enjoyable except that it was about life or death.

She remembered that the entire complex was just a few hundred yards from the airport. When TJ had ridden on Route 7 in the past, she had more than once been freaked out by commercial airplanes landing so close to the road.

Room 140 was around the back of the place, to the right side of the pool. She walked to the door, a cold feeling coming over her. She rehearsed how she would reach for the gun and how she would roll away from the door if he answered with a pistol. A part of her knew that if she was wrong about Strickland and was walking into an ambush, she was probably already dead.

The window to 140 was right next to the door and a heavy curtain was drawn. A faint TV could be heard a few doors down, but other than that the place seemed deserted. TJ had passed the cleaning crew on the other side of the building, and they still hadn't worked their way around to this side. She looked at the number and noted the door was slightly ajar, less than a quarter inch. She looked left, right, and behind her and took a deep breath. She knocked.

Nothing.

She waited and then knocked again.

Nothing.

She waited, then turned, positioning her back to the window. She extended her left hand and gently pushed the door open. It creaked slightly and opened to a ninety-degree angle to the jamb.

Silence.

She peeked around the corner. The room was a suite, and the door opened to a TV area with a couch, a recliner, and an efficiency kitchen area. There were no signs of occupancy and nothing that would suggest anyone had been there.

Nothing.

Something felt very wrong. TJ's first inclination was to get the hell out. Her second inclination was to do what she always had done as a soldier and as a woman—press on.

She gripped the gun and noticed her hand was damp from the clammy sweat of her anxiety. She clicked the safety off and held it in two hands as she had been trained. She swung her arms through the door, pivoting her head quickly from right to left. If she had been with her team, this was when she would have yelled, "Clear!"

There was no team. She was alone. She felt herself breathe, and she was back in mission mode. She shuffled to the bedroom door and moved to the side of it. She took a deep breath, reached for the knob as best she could, and then twisted it and pushed it open at the same time. She swung her arms into a firing position.

Nothing.

A neatly packed army duffel sat on the edge of a made bed. The bedroom wastebasket contained three empty Budweiser cans, and a pizza box was stacked next to it. Strickland had indeed been in this room. The closet door was open, and except for the usual safe, ironing board, and iron, it was empty.

That left the bathroom.

TJ moved out of the bedroom to the closed bathroom door. The closed door was a warning. People generally left it open in hotel rooms unless they were inside. Otherwise, there was no reason to close it.

She also knew Strickland, and he was a smart soldier. He might not have been many things, but he knew soldiering. There was no question he could remain still and silent. There was no question he had the patience for an ambush.

The silence raised TJ's anxiety. A showdown at point-blank distance would certainly end in at least one death, if not two. Strickland would've heard her by now, and he would be ready. TJ thought she could split right now and not engage in what certainly was a well-crafted ambush. But something kept her there.

Again, she positioned herself to the side of the door. Now her breathing came fast, so fast she concentrated to quiet it. She listened.

Nothing.

She slowly reached for the knob. Just before she touched it, she heard a loud clunk from inside the bathroom.

Startled, she jumped back.

TJ waited and heard nothing but silence.

She reached for the knob again, twisted it, and this time aggressively pushed it open, so hard it slammed against the wall and bounced back. In that instant she saw Strickland, saw him holding a gun.

She rolled toward the cover of the bedroom and sprang up in a shooting stance, flashing back to falling and getting shot that day. She was fast, but even in the flash of that instant, she knew she was a sitting duck.

TJ waited, then stepped cautiously to the bedroom door, peeking around the threshold to look into the bathroom.

Strickland was there.

He was sitting, clothed, on the toilet. The gun was still in his hand but it had fallen to his side and rested awkwardly on the side of the porcelain bathtub.

Blood and tissue covered the wall behind the toilet. It sprayed out in a shower pattern from the back of Strickland's head. The angle told TJ he had been shot through his mouth at an upward angle.

David Strickland had killed himself.

• CHAPTER FORTY-SEVEN

TJ got out of there as fast as she could. She spent a moment covering where she'd been in the room and used a face cloth from the bathroom to wipe down any surface that she had run her fingers across. In the end, she couldn't quite remember what she had touched and didn't want to get crazy paranoid about it so she just took off. The one other thing she did, and she wasn't even sure why, was take Strickland's cell phone, which was on the vanity next to the mirror.

TJ's hands shook.

She had seen dead men before, actually quite a few, but this was different. She hadn't been expecting David Strickland to be dead, and when she saw the blood fanned out on the wall from the gun blast it had rocked her.

Back at her apartment, her mind raced. She worried about her prints; she wondered who had seen her and who could've possibly known she was going to the Residence Inn. She also felt for the first time the acute danger Strickland had warned her of. She knew now, without any doubt, that her life was on the line. She also had no idea what her next step should be.

TJ was due in at the hotline in an hour and a half. She wanted to keep to her routine as much as possible, and even though she wasn't close to being in her right mind, she wanted to keep her shift. She wasn't exactly in a naturally therapeutic state, as the social workers liked to call it, but the rule at Aquarius was that you covered your shift—no matter what.

The day's events kept turning over in her mind. Strickland wasn't the type to kill himself. He was full of shit and selfish as hell. He didn't spend much time in angst over life's inequities; he went out and got his. Now he was dead, and someone had taken the time to make it look like suicide. Whoever they were, the CIA or some other bogeymen, they knew what they were doing. When the police got to the scene, it was clear that they would find another distraught serviceman dead by his own hand—a drifter from out of town, clearly not in his right mind.

He had told her they were in danger. But he had been killed while trying to warn her. As much as TJ tried to be cool and detached, she now knew those threats were real. Knowing it was one thing and doing something about it was another. She needed to take her time to be careful and stay aware—very aware. It was time for TJ to become a full-time soldier again, whether she liked it or not.

TJ knew how to be vigilant. She had spent two tours entering booby-trapped buildings and watching women and children turn themselves into to explosives. In combat mode, TJ knew to suspect everything and everyone and to preserve her life above anything. It was an exhausting state, to be on guard at all times, but it wasn't something you did just when you felt like it. That's how you got dead.

The shaking had mostly stopped or was now at least at a level that she could hide. She changed out of the perspiration-soaked T-shirt and threw on a Yankees T-shirt and her Notre Dame hoodie.

She had to go to Aquarius.

Stay with the routine and be vigilant.

Don't stop being aware, and don't overthink, daydream, or lose concentration.

∗ ∗ ∗

When she headed to the hotline, she brought her gun. The irony of being armed at a suicide hotline wasn't lost on her, but this wasn't a time to wink at cute things. This was a time to be ready. TJ had no idea for what, but it was a time to be ready.

"I've been getting hang-ups all morning. It's, like, so annoying! I mean, if you're going to call a suicide hotline, at least have the courtesy to say something," Heather said right after she said hi to TJ.

Before TJ could even respond, Heather went right back to talking.

"You know, it's been an awful morning. I'm getting my period today and I can't wait. I feel bloated as hell and the cramps are awful."

TJ was doing her best to feign interest without encouraging Heather to talk more. At the same time, she didn't want to hurt Heather's feelings by ignoring her. That wasn't because TJ wanted to be nice; it was because she didn't want to then have to get into a conversation tediously centered on apologies.

"I hate the time just before. My doctor gave me something to relax but it's not helping that much," Heather said.

TJ nodded and did her best to make caring eye contact.

"How many hang-ups did you get?" TJ asked when there was a lull in the period discussion.

"At least six in the last hour."

That was a lot, even by hotline standards.

TJ reviewed the log. A couple of the regulars had called in—June, to talk about going to AA and missing her mom, who had died five years ago, and Roger, a gay guy who was chronically depressed. Maureen, the teen, also with depression, had called, and she was having a bad day. In other words, it was a typical day at the hotline.

When the phone rang and Heather was flossing, TJ picked up.

"Check Strickland's phone," the mechanically disguised voice said.

"Who the hell—"

"Check the phone. Note how many calls to and from Venice, Florida. I doubt there will be a caller ID. There might not even be a reference to Venice."

"Who are you?"

"Let's just say I'm on your side."

"What does that mean?"

"You didn't believe Strickland; that was smart. You know that his death wasn't a suicide. You know something isn't right."

"What do I have to do with it?"

"Association is enough."

"What?"

"You're needed in Florida. You'll have to trust. I can't stay on the line. Get a pen and write this down." The voice paused.

"Bogie's parking lot. Friday night at nine. Corner of US forty-one and Main."

"And you expect me to just show up there. This is an ambush. I'm no fool," TJ said.

"I need your help. I'm on your side. That's all I can tell you. Please trust me. Please, I've been trying to help you."

"Who the hell—" It was too late. The caller had hung up.

TJ slumped in her chair. Heather was running her tongue over her front teeth and looking into a compact mirror. TJ got up and headed toward the front door.

"What was that all about?" Heather asked without looking up from the mirror.

"It was a personal call."

"You got a boyfriend you're not telling me about, don't you?" Heather made her eyebrows go up and down.

TJ thought just briefly about the absurdity and resisted saying anything.

"No, not that. I got a friend with some issues."

"Uh, I know, right? Don't you hate friends with issues? Monica is like that. She calls me every day to complain about Michael. I mean after a while—"

"Heather, I gotta run an errand, sorry," TJ said, stopping the word tsunami that was about to crash down on her. She went out the front door.

• CHAPTER FORTY-EIGHT

"It's done," Forbus said.

"Any problems?" Jordan asked.

"None."

"Did you clean up?"

"Yeah, it was nice and tight."

"Anything of concern?" Jordan asked by way of formality.

"No papers, no ID, no personal possessions other than clothes. I searched his wallet and removed anything that wasn't an ID. I got the credit card you asked for."

"Excellent." Jordan felt himself smile.

"What do I do next?"

"Keep an eye on Dunn and wait until you hear from me. I want to know what she does, where she goes, and who she talks to."

"Should I plan on eliminating her?"

"Eventually, but not yet. I want to get a sense of what she knows and what she's capable of."

"No problem," Forbus said and signed off.

Just as Forbus clicked off the cell phone, Dunn left the hotline and walked around the corner. Forbus let her turn right before starting the ignition and putting the car in gear. It was daylight on a workday, and following her without being identified would not be easy.

Taking a right on State, Dunn became visible halfway down the street leaning on an oak. She looked as if she was checking her cell phone. Then she raised her head and stared straight ahead, as though deep in thought. Dunn was a head case, all right, unpredictable and dangerous. That would be the report Jordan received.

Nothing had come of the Strickland incident yet, and Forbus was confident nothing would. The procedure had been honed down to a science; it was a clear matter of precision. When it came time to do the final act, the victim was almost relieved and easily relented. They all knew Forbus. They knew what was inevitable, and they chose the easier way out.

Forbus drove past Dunn and kept going down State. Dunn was visible in the rearview mirror heading back toward the switchboard. Forbus would circle back around to make sure Dunn made it in, and then get on with the day. There was no point in watching all day long. Dunn was unpredictable, sure, but did not warrant constant surveillance.

When TJ got back inside the Aquarius office, Heather was engaged in a call. Heather was annoyingly self-centered and mostly ineffectual as a counselor, but there was no question that she tried. During this call, she repeatedly interrupted the caller and pleaded that they feel better. She didn't want people to hurt, so she tried to talk them out of their pain. It was the exact opposite of what actually worked.

Strickland's cell phone didn't tell TJ much at first glance; she struggled to understand what the calls meant. There were plenty of calls, at least fifty, but most read "Private Caller," which meant they were untraceable. There were two or three that said "Florida Call" that didn't identify the caller but showed a number. She resisted the urge to call it before she thought it through.

Heather finished up her call ten minutes later. She wrapped up with the line, "Don't forget, tomorrow's another day!" and TJ cringed at the Hallmark therapy. Then TJ braced herself for the babbling.

"He was so, like, hopeless. His mother died six months ago and he just lost a thirty-nine-year-old friend to cancer. I mean, life is so unfair," Heather said. "I can't deal, sometimes."

Heather shook her head like she wanted to clear it of uncomfortable thoughts.

"I need to call Monica." Monica was Heather's best friend, and during shifts they spoke endlessly in between calls about absolutely nothing. It was like neither of them wanted to be alone with what meager thoughts they had.

TJ watched Heather pull out her cell, flip it open, and hit one button with the total economy of motion that came from repeating a physical act thousands of times. TJ marveled at it. She was amused by Heather's relationship with her cell phone. How many people did she actually have on speed dial? How would she categorize them?

Then it dawned on TJ.

She had checked Strickland's call history but she hadn't checked his speed dial contacts. She reached for the phone, flipped it open, and hit the option key until she found the "Speed Dial" folder. Number one was identified as "Jordan."

TJ felt a chill run through her.

Jordan was Trent and Strickland's CO.

The area code was 917.

TJ pulled out the top drawer of the desk to get the phone directory. Nine one seven included Sarasota County, Florida.

That would be Venice, Florida.

CHAPTER FORTY-NINE

Afghanistan Vet Found Dead in Hotel. Suicide Suspected.

David Strickland from Murfreesboro, Tennessee, was found dead from what appears to a self-inflicted gunshot wound. He was staying in the Residence Inn on Route 7 in Latham. The hotel reports he had been there for nearly three weeks.

Strickland served two tours in Operation Enduring Freedom in Afghanistan and had returned stateside eight months ago. He was a captain in the infantry. His brother Edward, from Norfolk, Virginia, identified the body after it was found on Thursday.

Hotel representatives did not know why Strickland was in Latham. His brother said that he had lost contact with him since Strickland returned from Kabul. Edward Strickland did not believe his brother was working in the area and suggested that he might have been drifting.

The Veteran's Administration has identified depression, suicide, and other mental illnesses as common among returning veterans. Services for Strickland will be held in Tennessee.

• CHAPTER FIFTY

TJ went to the public library and signed on to the Internet. She googled Venice, Florida, and tried to find something relevant.

It was the shark tooth capital of the world.

It had a community theater and a restaurant on the pier called Sharkey's and it was near Sarasota. Not so relevant.

She googled "Venice military." She found that there was an antisubmarine airfield built there in World War II. The Kentucky Military Institute had a school there and that made little sense. Searches for "Venice Florida Afghanistan" and "Venice Florida Iraq" yielded nothing.

TJ tried "Venice Florida Jordan" and found a chain of golf equipment outlets.

"Venice Florida Strickland" brought up lots of people named Strickland but nothing that seemed relevant.

When she tried "Venice Florida Heroin," she found a site designed to look like an old-school military dossier that said:

The Office of Homeland Security conducted a 14-month investigation into the pilot training school in Venice, Florida, attended by Mohamed Atta and by two of the three other 9/11 pilots. The investigation discovered that during the same month these men attended school at Kauffman Aviation, federal agents seized over 2,000 pounds of heroin in the school's owner's jet at the Tampa Executive Airport.

And this:

Three days after Mohamed Atta arrived in 2000 to attend the flight school, the owner of the school, Travis Leammons, had his Learjet surrounded by DEA agents on the runway of Tampa Executive Airport.

Agents found over 2,000 pounds of heroin. Everyone on board was arrested and the plane was confiscated. No prosecutor made the obvious connection that Atta's arrival and the heroin shipment were connected; those arrested at the airport were mysteriously released after less than two hours in the county jail and no charges were ever filed. The obvious point to raise is that someone with big clout was buying heroin. Could it be that heroin was being purchased from Bin Laden? And what kind of clout must someone have to make an arrest for possession of 2,000 pounds of heroin go away? It would seem to suggest that one would have to have ties very high up in the US government.

Nothing ever happened. It remains the biggest censored story of the 21st century. You can only read about it here at this website. Apparently, if you have a business at Kauffman Aviation you have a get out of jail free pass from the DEA and all of US law enforcement.

Something is definitely wrong.

TJ swallowed hard. She rationalized. This wasn't the *New York Times*, it was the Internet. And the world loved conspiracies. She knew she had to slow down and not react without thinking this through. That was what a good soldier would do.

Yet, her fiancé was dead by suicide. So was her father, also by suicide. And both men were career military.

She thought about the package of heroin. She thought about the phone calls and she thought about Strickland's warnings. She thought about the fact that she had stopped living since Trent and she didn't care much about what there was left to lose.

Something about Venice, Florida, wasn't right. She didn't know what, but she was determined to find out.

• CHAPTER FIFTY-ONE

TJ called Maria and told her she was going to have to go away for a while. She didn't know for how long. Maria said OK, but asked if she could work that night and maybe the next because she was shorthanded. TJ agreed, both because she had to make some travel arrangements and because she wanted to do right by Maria.

To say she was distracted was an understatement. She knew how to dance when her mind wasn't into it; in fact, her mind was almost never into it. This was different, though, and as she got dressed, she knew it. Still, she was grateful to Maria and she didn't want to let her down.

Gloria and Jenny were in the green room getting ready for the evening shift.

"You OK?" Gloria asked. TJ was quiet but didn't realize she was showing anything out of the ordinary.

"Yeah, why?" she asked.

"You're really quiet. It's like you're not here."

"I have to travel for a few days. I'm not looking forward to it," TJ said.

"What's up?"

"Family stuff." TJ looked away to discourage further discussion.

"You need a ride to the airport or anything?" Jenny asked. "I haven't got anything to do the next couple of days. It would keep me busy."

"You sure? It is a pain in the ass trying to haul the bag on the bike," TJ admitted.

"Like I said, it would give me something to do. Where you headed?" Jenny asked.

"Venice, Florida."

"Florida's nice," Gloria said.

"Yeah, but this isn't for pleasure. Family crap, you know."

Jenny nodded with understanding.

Right after that, Sheila came into the room. She staggered and sat down, actually almost fell, onto the couch. It wasn't seven yet and she was trashed. Maria would be pissed.

Another night at the Taco, and TJ was surprised to find herself sad knowing she was leaving. She had grown comfortable here and felt a part of something. It and Aquarius were the only things since the army that made her feel included.

TJ danced a few uninspired sets and made a few more dollars. She felt like a soldier again and she had a vigilance that stayed with her. Florida was a mission. She recalled how she had felt the night before missions in Iraq: the lack of sleep, the methodical nature to every action she took, and there was something else.

At first TJ couldn't identify it, but after she finished working the floor and she headed to the green room she was able to get at what the other feeling was.

It was the feeling that tomorrow she could die.

• CHAPTER FIFTY-TWO

The next morning TJ booked a flight to Sarasota online at the library for that evening. Printing a boarding pass made the whole thing a little more real, and she started to feel less sure.

She was heading to a city on the direction of anonymous tips from someone who wouldn't identify himself. She certainly was heading into danger, and she was going alone, without any backup or support. The more she thought about it, the more ridiculous she felt. Still, since she had identified this as a mission it had become something she needed to do.

She had time to kill before her flight. TJ did her best not to allow her emotions to run wild, but there was something she felt compelled to do and she didn't know why. It gnawed at her and she couldn't let it go. She wanted to go to the gym before she left, she admitted to herself, to say good-bye, and she felt silly. Still, she had to do it.

She dressed in her sweats, threw her hand wraps and gloves into her duffel, and headed to the gym. She had no idea what to say and just brought her body to the situation, hoping what she should say or do would just come to her.

She went up the stairs to the gym and heard the thudding of someone hitting the heavy bag. TJ felt her heart race and a cold sweat forming on the small of her back. When she came through the door, she was both excited and frightened to see Duffy there, hitting the bag.

The bell ended the round and it wasn't until then that he noticed her. He smiled and wiped his sweat-drenched forehead with his sleeve.

"Hey! What's up?" Clearly he was happy to see her, and TJ was immediately relieved. God, she felt silly. This was a boxing gym, not a middle school dance.

"Nothin', really." TJ got her wraps out and started to do her hands. She tried to act normal but was acutely aware of her body language, and his.

The bell rang for the next round. Duffy ignored it and walked toward her.

"You want to do some more work today?" He nodded his head toward the ring.

TJ swallowed and went to speak. She realized the words were a little choked in her throat.

"Not sure." She paused. "I have to leave town tonight. I might want to take it easy."

"Leave town?"

"Yeah, I gotta go to Florida for some family business." She purposely attended to her hands to avoid eye contact.

"How long are you going to be gone?" Duffy asked. She thought she heard something in his voice.

"I don't know. It could be awhile." She stole a look at him briefly. He was squared up and looking right at her.

He didn't say anything.

"You'll be back though, right?"

She felt a warmth in her chest when he said it. There was something in his voice. There was definitely something in his voice.

"Yeah." That was the best TJ could do.

The bell for the next round rang and Duffy went back to the bag while TJ gloved up. She worked the second bag on the other side of the gym behind him. As she worked her combinations, she looked at him and couldn't believe what she felt. She did what she could to dismiss it, but, rational or not, she couldn't. It felt scary and silly. It also felt like being alive.

She worked out for about forty minutes, but her heart wasn't in the exercise. Duffy finished his workout but stayed awhile to stretch and cool down. TJ paid attention to that and wondered if he was hanging around just for her.

She looked at the clock and realized she had just a couple of hours before her flight. She toweled her face and sat down to undo her wraps. She tried not to look at him as much as she wanted to.

"When you come back, let's do some more work, huh?" he said. TJ allowed herself to look up.

"Yeah, sure," she said.

• CHAPTER FIFTY-THREE

Drifting was what TJ did, but never like this. It had been a slower process before, going from one city to another as circumstances unfolded, but never by plane and not in a hurried way. This was different.

She also knew what she was doing was dangerous. It could be a setup to get her killed as easily as it could be a mission to right some wrongs. TJ didn't really care. She had a penchant for action; doing something always felt better than not doing anything. But as much as she preferred action to patience, unnecessary risk wasn't her favorite thing, and it went against her training and what she believed.

Jenny had given her a ride and insisted on waiting until she checked in at the counter before leaving. It felt nice having a friend, or at least a close approximation of a friend. It had been a long time, maybe since college, since she had had a woman friend. The military and MP service especially were mostly male and it was hard to connect with many of the women in the service. The Sarasota airport was quiet with the shuffle of aging snowbirds coming from the Northeast to their southern homes. The cab ride was thirty minutes and cost fifty dollars, which annoyed TJ, but she really had no choice. She had her tips from the previous week, but eight hundred dollars went quickly living the life of a tourist.

She had the cabbie drive past Bogie's, a typical sports bar loaded with Coors Light, Miller, and Corona neon shining through its windows. Advertisements for the NFL Network and the Tampa Bay Rays filled up the rest of the space. She got out of the cab just before a bridge leading over a causeway, paid the driver, and decided to take a look around before heading into the bar.

The ocean was nearby, and the smell of salt water mixed with the stagnant causeway smell permeated the air by the bridge. A breakfast restaurant named Patches was on her left, there was a gun shop across the street, and a computer repair place was a block up ahead and across the street from Bogie's. It was 8:45, and TJ could feel her heart beat.

She wore her Yankees cap, a V-neck men's T-shirt, and carpenter pants. Her ever-present Notre Dame hoodie was draped between the handles of the duffel that she draped over her back. Walking into a bar with luggage wasn't exactly inconspicuous, and her less-than-casual look didn't exactly match Florida women's fashion. She couldn't do much about her clothes; her wardrobe consisted of stripper gear, workout clothes, and what she had on.

TJ walked past the bar three times. Then she saw a space between the dumpsters and decided to take the chance of leaving her duffel there while she went in. She tucked her money into her front jeans pocket, noting that seven hundreds, a twenty, four fives, and ten ones didn't leave too much of a bulge.

The inside of the place was filled with TV sports noise, baseball games mixing with the NBA and college basketball games and, oddly enough for Florida, NHL games. TJ knew from experience that eventually all the disparate sounds would blend together into sports bar white noise. It was amazing what the mind could drown out when it had to.

She took a bar stool on the corner facing the entrance so she could keep an eye on who came and went. A pair of electronic dartboards was behind her but no one was playing. She ordered a draft of Coors Light, and it came in a ridiculously tall twenty-ounce frosted glass that immediately made TJ feel stupid.

The caller to the suicide hotline had said to meet in the parking lot, but TJ didn't like the idea of standing there exposed. Whoever had called her would figure it out and would eventually come into the bar. TJ's watch said 9:10. Five minutes later the bartender, an early twenties blond with a bare midriff and a diamond stud in her nose, handed her a folded bar napkin.

"Who's this from?" TJ asked, trying not to show emotion.

"I'm not supposed to say." The blond shrugged.

TJ unfolded the napkin.

Thanks for coming. Borrow a cigarette off the bartender and at 9:26 go out the side door to smoke.

TJ looked at the clock. It was 9:23. She felt her heart pound and a chill run through her.

"Excuse me. Do you have a cigarette?" TJ heard herself ask the blond.

"Sure, they're Newports. That OK?"

"Yeah. Thanks," TJ said.

It was 9:25.

TJ didn't smoke and never had. Fiddling with a cigarette didn't come naturally, and she worried about that. She noticed that her senses had sharpened. She headed for the side door with the cigarette in one hand and a pack of Bogie's matches in the other.

She lit the cigarette when she got outside and leaned against the side of the building where she had the ability to see in both directions. It was 9:27 and she was alone. She took a puff from the

Newport without inhaling and, as tense as she was, she wondered how the hell people got addicted to cigarettes. The disgusting taste didn't help her state of mind.

At 9:32 two men came out the same side door. They wore jeans and T-shirts and one had on a Rays' baseball cap while the other had a hunting cap with the Skoal insignia.

They stood ten feet from TJ. The one with the Rays' cap turned and asked TJ for a light. The parking lot lights cast a dark shadow over his face from the cap's brim. She struck the match and held it toward his mouth. The flame illuminated the man's face.

TJ recognized him immediately, and she froze.

She tried to speak but couldn't. She began to tremble. Her mouth went dry and her eyes welled.

She was looking into the eyes of her father.

• CHAPTER FIFTY-FOUR

TJ didn't blink and she barely breathed. Her father stood a foot and half from her. This couldn't be.

Her mouth hung open and she just stared.

The trembling turned into shaking.

Her father reached out for her and held her.

"Jack, I'm going to take a walk around the block," the other man said.

TJ wept uncontrollably. She buried her head in his chest and cried as hard as she ever had cried. He began to cry as well. They stayed like that for a long time. As her body shook, TJ's father instinctively held her tighter. Tears poured from her eyes.

TJ broke from the embrace, stepped back, and looked at her father.

"You wanna tell me what's going on?" She wiped the tears that soaked her face, first with the back of her hand and then with both palms.

"Yeah, of course."

"Does Mom know?" TJ asked. She was returning to reality and now she was starting to get angry.

"No, she doesn't."

"Oh, my God. How—"

"I'll explain. I had no choice. It's why I am here. It's what this is all about." She looked at his face. He had aged, but he looked like the same man. TJ felt surreal.

She exhaled hard but the breathing didn't relax her. Her mind raced and her emotions mixed together with no control. She looked at her father.

"I had to get out of what I was into. I got mixed up into something very big, with a lot of money, a lot of corruption, and I had to get out," he said.

"You're telling me it was you? You left the heroin? You've been doing all of that shit?"

He nodded.

"You need to tell me exactly what's going on. Whatever it is, I'm in it all the way whether I want to be or not. So, no more codes, no more innuendo, I need the truth," TJ said. Now she felt anger, nothing else.

"You're right, that's fair." He took a deep breath. "Heroin; it's all about heroin."

TJ stared at him.

"Over there, in Afghanistan. I got involved because I had to. I was running a covert operation in Afghanistan and we needed to trade drugs for information. We helped the Afghanis traffic it in exchange for their cooperation. We needed to sell it to raise cash for what the goddamn government wouldn't fund." His breathing escalated with his tone.

"You sold heroin?" TJ asked.

"Yeah, a lot of us did. It was part of it. It was part of getting the job done. I didn't like it, but that part I could accept."

"What do you mean—that part?" TJ asked.

"We were trying to get information. We were using it as a means to an end. That's the dirty work of war. I know that and I accept it, even if I hate it. I got trapped in my role and what the powers that be wanted. That's when I had to escape."

"I don't follow," TJ said.

"My CO, Colonel Jordan, engineered everything. He's a military genius, no doubt. He knows the Afghanis; he understands that part of the world, the people and their military. He knew heroin was the way to influence and control them." He took a breath. Telling the story was wearing him out.

"Jordan, that was Trent's CO."

"Yeah, same guy. Around 2000, things changed. We were still doing our covert stuff, chasing down the Taliban and trying to make sense of what they were doing. I saw a huge uptick in transactions that involved heroin. It was obvious something had changed, and changed a lot." He paused to see if TJ was following.

"Yeah, what changed?"

"It became clear to me that things weren't just about military issues anymore."

"Things?"

"The heroin."

"What about it?"

"I began to realize that Jordan wasn't setting up strategy and operations to ferret out terrorism or to identify threats to Americans. He had turned straight into a man making money from heroin. Nothing more than a drug dealer."

TJ did her best to let it all sink in. It wasn't easy.

"I don't get it. So you faked your suicide?"

"It was the only way. Jordan is paranoid. Actually, it isn't paranoia, because if he got caught he would be in a world of trouble. I couldn't quit. I couldn't get reassigned. I knew too much. I was too much of a danger to a man who doesn't think a second about killing someone who presents a threat. It was what made him such a competent soldier."

TJ shook her head as if that would clear her thoughts.

"So how the hell do you fake a suicide? I mean, Mom got your note."

"Look, TJ, I don't know if we should go into all those details now." He looked down at his boots and took a breath.

"Uh, I think you ought to go into a few of them if you think I'm all of a sudden going to start blindly following you." TJ raised her voice enough to let him know how she felt without actually yelling.

"All right. There are ways to disappear. It isn't easy but it can be done if you're careful."

"Go on."

"I had plenty of money from working with Jordan. I cut ties with people, I found an excellent forger, and I got a connection in Canada. One night I made it look like I went off the Afghanistan–Uzbekistan Bridge. Anyway, that's where I left the note." He had his hands in his pockets and wasn't looking at TJ.

"And did you think of what we'd go through?" TJ's voice cracked slightly. She had tried hard to keep it steady.

"Goddamn it, of course I did. It's something I've had to live with all this time, but I couldn't live with myself being part of what was going on."

TJ looked down and scuffed at the gravel.

"American soldiers were getting addicted to heroin. It was a perfect market. Stress, boredom, and a population of young men with no coping skills; Jordan knew all that and thrived on it. I couldn't be a part of it. I had to try to stop it." He heard the volume in his voice increase and he consciously brought it back down.

"So have you stopped it?" TJ asked with just a hint of sarcasm.

"Not yet." He pursed his lips and looked away from TJ.

"And your plans?"

"I need your help. I can't do this alone."

"Why me? Obviously, you've got better military connections than me."

"I needed someone I could trust. There's no one who Jordan can't get to. And after what happened to Trent, I knew you'd help."

"You know about Trent?" TJ asked.

"TJ, I've kept tabs on you as much as I could. His death is what convinced me to take action." He reached out and put a hand on her shoulder. TJ looked down.

He waited and let the silence hang.

"So what are we going to do?" TJ asked.

"We're going to kill Jonathan Jordan."

• CHAPTER FIFTY-FIVE

Despite having lived for a long time in the South, Forbus didn't like the heat and humidity. Like everything else, it was a question of mind over matter and not letting it get in the consciousness. That was what Forbus did, and it was what made for excellence in soldiering.

Dunn was stronger than Forbus had thought. A trip to Florida was unexpected, but frankly, it was welcomed because Albany had grown boring. The new scenery was a change of pace. It couldn't have been a coincidence that Dunn had come to Jordan's hometown, and she certainly wasn't on vacation.

Something was up; there was no question.

"She's in Venice," Forbus told Jordan on the phone. "She just met with two men outside of Bogie's. Actually, there were two men there, but one of the guys left. It seemed like there was some arguing. I didn't get too close." Forbus spoke into a new Trac phone picked up before the trip.

"Any idea what prompted the trip?" Jordan asked. None of his anxiety could be heard in his voice.

"No, sir. She danced last night, went to the gym, and worked at the hotline the day before. She did some errands yesterday, but, other than that, there was nothing to suggest travel."

"She has become a concern, no question. Be ready," Jordan said before hanging up.

Forbus smiled. It was obvious that it was just a matter of time until Jordan ordered Dunn's death.

• CHAPTER FIFTY-SIX

"Jordan is well protected," Jack Dunn said. "He doesn't leave himself vulnerable. He's lived his whole life as a soldier."

"How does he run an Afghanistan drug operation from Venice, Florida?" TJ asked.

They were back at her father's cheap motel room, which he shared with his buddy, Eddie. TJ never got Eddie's last name. They were close to the airport in one of those places built on a cement slab that looked like it had gone up in a weekend. It consisted of two beds, a large window that opened from the side, a chair, a bathroom, and a small efficiency kitchen area.

"This little sleepy retirement community has some dirty secrets." Eddie had fielded the question. He looked to be in his late fifties but had a hard build, like the kind of guy who never let himself get out of shape in his entire life.

"Yeah, I don't know if you remember, but the nine/eleven pilots got trained here. This was the place where they learned to fly, but not land, planes. There's also some evidence of drugs coming through the Venice Airport."

"What do you mean?"

"Look it up on the Internet. I've seen the truth on one of those conspiracy 'Illuminati' bullshit sites, but those guys aren't always screwy," Eddie said. "There's a story out there about a plane being impounded with thousands of pounds of heroin and then, well, nothing."

"What do you mean 'nothing'?" TJ asked. She remembered what she had read on the Internet. Eddie seemed to be confirming that, but the conversation was getting hard to follow.

"The conspiracists say that the plane was impounded, the airport owner was arrested, and then twelve hours later it all went away. No records exist about the incident or the drugs," Jack said.

"I don't know if I get it. What do the airport, the drugs, and all of this have to do with Jordan?" TJ asked.

"We're not sure either. Except the airport owner, Travis Leammons, was Jordan's second-in-command for a period in Afghanistan," Eddie said.

"Hold it. You're saying Jordan not only has a drug operation running out of the US military, you're saying he had something to do with nine/eleven?" TJ asked. She felt silly even thinking of it.

The two men looked at each other for a long moment. TJ shifted her gaze from her father to Eddie and then back.

"Talk to me," TJ said.

"Jordan is originally from Texas. His family's money was tied into the oil business with, let's just say, some influential people. Those same people did a lot of business with the Saudis, who they became quite friendly with," Eddie said.

"I don't understand..." TJ said.

"TJ, Afghanistan and the surrounding region is where heroin comes from. For decades, the CIA and the military have traded cash, secrets, weapons—you name it—for drugs. It might as well be currency," Jack said.

"OK, I think I have some understanding of that," TJ said.

"The Taliban is our arch enemy, right? It's why we were all in Afghanistan, right?" Eddie questioned.

"Yeah…"

"A fundamentalist Muslim sect of people willing to kill all enemies of Allah."

TJ nodded and let Eddie continue.

"The Taliban are devout in their dedication to the Koran and its teachings. They don't eat pork, they pray five times a day, and they don't believe in alcohol and drugs."

TJ listened. When Eddie stopped, she raised her eyebrows to let him know she was following, to keep going. Her father picked it up.

"The Taliban is against drug use. In fact, when they took power in Afghanistan, they eradicated heroin production in the areas of the country where they were in charge. It didn't go to zero, but it went pretty close."

"Hold it. I thought the Taliban produced heroin," TJ said.

"Sometimes they do. It depends how the Koran is interpreted. Some say that the Koran teaches that it is OK to act like the infidel if it means making it possible to kill the infidel," Eddie said.

"So the Taliban produces heroin," TJ said.

"They have when it has served their needs. But make no mistake, when they initially took over, the heroin production collapsed and that made people very nervous," Jack said.

TJ scrunched up her brow and thought for a long moment. "I'm not sure I get it," she admitted.

"Money, TJ," her father said. "No heroin means no money for Jordan and Leammons."

"You mean…"

"And if Jordan and Leammons are not making money, then their close and influential friends aren't making money. Their friends in the government and their friends in Saudi Arabia," Eddie said.

Silence hung in the room.

"So you're saying that Jordan and Leammons…and our government *wanted* the heroin to be produced?" TJ asked.

The two men looked at TJ.

"We're not talking chump change here, TJ. We're talking millions and millions of dollars," Jack said.

"Too many people, too many groups of people, lived off that money flow," Eddie said.

TJ thought for a long time while the two men said nothing. When she decided to say what was on her mind, she felt silly.

"You're saying that nine/eleven created a reason to go to war with the Taliban. That going to war and defeating the Taliban would get heroin production where it needed to be for those involved," TJ said.

Both men nodded.

"The nine/eleven pilots were trained at the Venice Airport, rumored to be a drug hub." TJ paused. The men looked at her. "That it is possible that nine/eleven benefited Jordan and everyone involved in the drug dealing…" TJ's voice trailed off while she thought.

"You're not saying that nine/eleven was engineered just to restore the heroin trade…?"

TJ let the statement hang in the air.

Her father and Eddie just looked at her.

• CHAPTER FIFTY-SEVEN

Jordan didn't like uncertainty. He didn't like not being in control. He also didn't like losing.

TJ Dunn had seemed like a minor annoyance a month ago. He'd thought it would be enough to have Strickland check up on her so that a full report could be made and stowed away. Dunn was supposed to be a nothing, just something to assess, not someone to really worry about.

Now she was within miles and Jordan couldn't dismiss it. She was not on vacation. No, Dunn had stopped being an annoyance and had become something else.

Getting rid of her was going to be more complicated than with the others. Jordan guessed that when a suicide hotline counselor killed herself it called attention. Jordan didn't want attention. Suicide's taboo kept investigators away; everyone felt uncomfortable with veterans killing themselves, even maybe a little responsible. The poor PTSD veterans killing themselves were cause for concern, but the general public really didn't want to know too much.

Getting Dunn might take something else. A disappearance, an accident; something that looked and felt like tragic bad luck. Forbus had the skills and would enjoy killing Dunn, making a game of it.

CNN's anchor blathered on in the background. The American public's approval rate of the Afghanistan war had reached an all-time low. Several congressmen were getting their fifteen minutes of fame by calling for an end to it, saying that the US should just get out, leave, and forget about it. There had even been some discussion with a Taliban leader. *The fucking Taliban*, Jordan thought. *Now, we're talking to the assholes.*

Jordan didn't like impulsivity. He preferred to think, to process, to evaluate, and then to decide. He didn't like over-the-top, he liked strategy and calculation. He knew that anything that called attention was dangerous. He also knew that to not make a big play could be a mistake as well.

Growing dissatisfaction with Afghanistan concerned him. The overzealous Afghani law enforcement issue had grown. An event that would distract the public from a never-ending, seemingly pointless war would make his world stable and predictable again. Jordan didn't think about ethical concerns; he never did. He focused on his goal and went after it. The rest was all bullshit to him, anyway.

He called Leammons.

"How long would it take to put an A-Level action into play?" Jordan asked, speaking in a long-ago-formed code.

"An A? Three or four days, depending. I'd have to see who is available and where they are. Where would you like it to happen?" Leammons asked.

"First quadrant, design one," Jordan said.

"OK. I'll get back to you."

Jordan hung up and felt his heart rate increase. He maintained his focus and did his best not to get emotional. Still, even Jonathan Jordan was flesh and blood.

The first quadrant was the Northeast United States. In this case, it referred to New York City. An A-Level Action was an event, usually a terrorist act, designed to distract, change focus, or motivate. Whenever a terrorist act occurred—a shoe bomber on a plane, an anthrax delivery, a sniper on a highway—the public, and hence the political leaders, became obsessed with safety. They wanted to be assured the government was doing everything possible to end their insecurity. When the public felt this way they didn't mind war so much.

Still, even Jonathan Jordan didn't orchestrate such activity lightly. It required thoughtful assessment. He felt he had evaluated this situation fairly and decided something had to be done.

New York City remained the hub of the free world. It got the most attention.

Blowing up the George Washington Bridge during the morning commute would have just the right effect.

• CHAPTER FIFTY-EIGHT

Forbus let the rented Taurus idle with the air conditioner on. It was hot and humid as hell, but why worry about abusing a rental car? TJ had left the bar with the two older guys, and Forbus followed them south on 41 past the sprawl of strip malls to this single-level motel. It was the type of joint you could rent by the month that came complete with an efficiency kitchen and a small, teardrop-shaped, algae-infested pool next to the office.

Forbus remained nearly invisible sitting with the car running in the strip mall parking lot. Rental cars were a dime a dozen in Florida, so there was no real effort or concern about staying covert. Tailing some bitch in Albany wasn't a problem, and it wouldn't be one in Venice, Florida, either.

Figuring Dunn out wasn't as easy. Forbus didn't have a ton of respect for Strickland, but still knew he wasn't an idiot or careless. He wouldn't have told Dunn what was going on unless he had gotten personally involved with her. To that point, he'd seemed to spend more time with Dunn then he'd needed to, and he had seemed to like to get physical with her. Every time Forbus had seen them they'd seemed to be hugging, crying, or both.

You wouldn't catch Forbus doing either with a subject.

Forbus thought about Strickland's death. None of them ever believed they'd kill themselves until it started with them. Inevitably, they realized there was no way out, and rather than prolong a long, slow, tortuous death they chose escape and ended it themselves. It worked perfectly, every time.

Forbus found Dunn a fascinating quarry. First of all, having an opponent who was a woman was different and presented Forbus with different variables. Second, and maybe this was related to being a woman, Dunn was fired with emotion. It made it difficult to predict her behavior or call her next move. Third, she seemed to have this outdated Hollywood version of honor.

Forbus snickered at the third point. Not that Forbus didn't have a sense of honor. No, it was more the pie-in-the sky view that Dunn seemed to take. The military embodied a cold, mean world, and Forbus just found it logical that after time, all soldiers would see it for what it was and change to adapt. Dunn clung to the premise that it was all about righting wrongs, justice, and the fucking American way. Utter bullshit.

Now, here she was, in Venice and awfully close to the base of operations. Dunn was, indeed, at least an interesting foe, if not a worthy one. The atmosphere charged Forbus's senses, and it felt electric.

Forbus mused on a pursuit-and-capture strategy. It would be best to get her when she was alone, away from the men. Not because Forbus couldn't handle the men; eliminating them would mean two squeezes of a trigger or two well-placed slashes to the neck with a knife. The two men were collateral complications. Three dead was harder to explain than a single suicide. Three dead got attention and headlines like "Serial Killer" and "Multiple Slaying." That kind of attention hurt the operation.

Forbus could wait until Dunn was alone. Dunn would need to go to the drug store, need to go to the mall, or need to get a haircut.

Soldier or not, she was still a rich white girl in Forbus's eyes. Dunn wouldn't see it coming, and it would be easy. The trick would be minimizing the attention from witnesses and, of course, getting things set up so what was done with the others could be completed with Dunn.

The excitement would come with the capture and the subduing of the prey. Forbus fantasized about the idea of making it a fair fight, a showdown, one in the white hat and one with the black hat. But showdowns were for Hollywood, and in real life they just didn't make sense. It was more important to ensure a victory and the safe completion of the mission.

Setting things up and breaking Dunn's spirit until she chose to pull the trigger on her own head would be the easy part. Dunn had never seen, let alone felt, the weapon that had made so much possible for Forbus.

But she would, Forbus thought.

And soon.

• CHAPTER FIFTY-NINE

The call had come from Florida and the powers that be wanted it done fast. What they didn't seem to understand was that in this day and age, pulling off a major explosion wasn't quite as easy as it used to be, especially in or around New York City. People tended to keep an eye out for suspicious activity. They'd been trained.

There were chemicals to get in volume and they had to be procured in ways that wouldn't raise any flags. There were vehicles to rent and personnel to hire. There was a fair amount of research into traffic patterns, police coverage, time of day variability, and other factors to take into consideration.

He had experience with this and knew without a doubt it could be done. He just sometimes wished he was given a little more credit, or at least that they even considered how difficult these projects had become. This wasn't as easy as buying a ton of fertilizer and setting a timer.

The strange part of the whole thing was the ease of finding volunteers to drive the goddamn thing. You would think finding someone willing to die in a fiery blaze would take some doing. He had connections to that world and had learned that they would fight over who got to do it. They actually fought over who got to die. It didn't surprise him anymore, but it did make him wonder.

He placed the call to get that part of the task moving. Now he had to locate the materials he needed and get a truck. His chemical engineering background was an asset, but over the years he had learned the tricks of this trade like inmates learned how to make hooch. Just like they didn't have to be brew masters, he didn't have to be a chemical engineer to create systems that could kill thousands. The bomb makers traded formulas like housewives traded recipes, learning from each other. This particular request, however, did have some precise requirements.

First of all, the way he had it figured, it would take two vehicles. One would have to contain the explosive device to get things going. He scratched some numbers on the yellow pad in front of him just to get his thoughts out on paper. The first truck wouldn't have to be that big, and he might be able to rent a Ryder or U-Haul to get it done.

He would need ammonium nitrate, a fertilizer easy enough to get. Since McVeigh it had been a bit more difficult to get a hold of, but his calculations told him that fifty pounds would be more than enough. Buying large amounts drew attention, but his connections could get him what he needed without raising a single eyebrow.

Next, he would need the nitromethane. It was used, among other things, as a solvent. Dry cleaners, pharmaceutical companies, and those idiots who raced hot rods all used it. It wasn't hard to get, and it was easy to handle. For the longest time no one even suspected it was an explosive until a railroad car filled with it had blown up and left a three-hundred-foot crater in a Kansas train depot.

He only needed 1.2 gallons of nitromethane. That meant, in total, what he needed for this end of the job would be less than sixty pounds. Even though he had been at this type of work for well over twenty years, it still amazed him how very little could do so, so much.

There would also have to be a second vehicle. This one would need to be a fuel trailer, like the kind that came to fill up houses with heating oil. He preferred working with diesel because he felt that it ignited more predictably and burned consistently. Other fuels sometimes didn't catch as well or they burned out too quickly. Diesel was his favorite.

The first vehicle would explode and the second vehicle would provide the fuel to ignite the enormous fire. That would mean that the two trucks would have to drive close together or, at least, wind up in close proximity. When the first one exploded, the second one would catch and be obliterated by flames. That was all that was needed. It wasn't complicated, nor did it require exact measurements or timing.

It would require two drivers and someone to handle the explosion who didn't mind the idea of dying a fiery death.

The fire would be intense. It would rise to a temperature high enough to melt steel. The George Washington was comprised of massive steel beams, and it seemed to the casual observer indestructible by anything short of a nuclear device. Little did they know, this chemical combination in rented trucks obtained from everyday sources had the potential to be every bit as destructive as a nuclear bomb. Joe six-pack was always worried about a nuclear bomb getting into the wrong hands, and he rarely spent any time worrying about chemicals found in most factories getting combined by someone who had flunked high school chemistry lab but knew enough to be dangerous.

Almost three hundred thousand cars went over that bridge every day. There were fourteen lanes, eight on the top and six on the lower level. Three hundred thousand: it was hard to fathom. The trucks would have to be on the lower level in order to comply with regulations. The downside of that was that the explosion would be obscured from a clear shot from the television cameras. Television coverage for such events was important to those who ordered them.

It wouldn't matter, though. Though the explosion and the initial fire might not be clearly seen on television, the results would be. The fire would burn hotter and hotter; the steel would melt. By then the TV traffic helicopters, having heard the news, would be in place. There would be an immense ball of fire and smoke. The gargantuan structure would begin to bend.

And then the George Washington Bridge would fall into the Hudson River.

• CHAPTER SIXTY

"We follow him. We study how he spends his time, trying to evaluate where he's most vulnerable," Jack said. They were at the motel in a tiny room painted bright blue. He sat on the hard-back chair at the small round table with Eddie while TJ sat cross-legged at the end of the full-size bed.

"I would bet that he's never alone or vulnerable for long," Eddie said.

TJ just listened. The last forty-eight hours of her life had left her in shock. Life didn't seem to conform to any of the usual rules of reality. Last night she had been tormented by graphic dreams of Trent repeatedly shooting himself through his mouth. The blood would spray across the wall and it would awaken her. After three dreams, TJ stopped trying to sleep. Now, listening to her back-from-the-dead father and his friend plot an execution, she had difficulty following.

"So we find out what his habits are and what he likes to do. Suppose we discover he likes to go to Starbucks for coffee on his own. You're suggesting we wait and then shoot the man in the parking lot?" TJ asked.

Jack put down his coffee and looked at TJ.

"TJ, this is about killing him. It has to be. He's been killing innocent young men for years and will continue to if no one stops him. This is just like being in Afghanistan; this is still war, maybe more so. This is something I'm fully committed to," Jack said. He didn't ask a question with his words implicitly, but the question of whether TJ was ready to be part of this operation hung in the air.

TJ let it sink in. She thought of Trent.

"I understand. God, I understand and I'm on board," TJ said.

Her father nodded. Eddie looked back and forth between the two of them and didn't say anything, making sure the interaction was over. Then he spoke.

"We should each follow him, splitting up in three vehicles. That way he's less likely to ID any one of us. We lay back and just observe until we find out his patterns."

"We communicate through cell phones, with each of us picking him up and letting him off to the other," Jack said. Eddie nodded.

"So we chart time of day, location, who he's with, that kind of thing?" TJ asked.

"Yeah, and when we get an idea of where he's most vulnerable we end it quickly and get the hell out of here, each of us going in a different direction," Eddie said.

TJ and Jack looked at him. TJ let out a long exhale and puffed out her cheeks.

"I'll be happy to be the one who pulls the trigger," Jack said, looking at the other two and raising his eyebrows.

"I wouldn't mind doing it either," TJ said.

• CHAPTER SIXTY-ONE

Leammons called Jordan as soon as he knew the plane was within two hours of landing. He knew that was the way Jordan liked it.

Four times a year a domestic cache of product was made available. The cost to them was so cheap and the profit potential so steep that they didn't pass up the opportunity. Sure, it put them on the hook for doing favors and looking the other way, but that sort of shit had stopped bothering Jordan a long time ago. It had never bothered Leammons. Not even in 2001, when the four of them had trained at the flight school he owned at his airport.

Jordan insisted on eyeballing shipments. He and Leammons had a strange relationship based on mutual distrust. It was as if both of them knew the other's capacity to double cross and screw others, so they didn't question each other's need to take safety measures.

"How much this time?" Jordan asked.

"Not sure, but I suspect it's close to fifty pounds," Leammons said.

"Hmmm, not bad. All the usual precautions have been made, I'm sure."

"Of course," Leammons said. He smiled to himself and thought of what an obnoxious asshole Jordan was.

"I'll be there by one forty-five," Jordan said.

"See you then."

Leammons hung up and looked out at the blue Gulf sky. He thought about how much money fifty pounds of heroin would make him. At nearly seventy-five thousand dollars per kilo on the street and there being a little more than two kilos per pound, it meant that this fifty-pound package would ultimately bring in somewhere around $1,650,000. The fact that they could get it straight from Afghanistan and reduce all the middlemen meant that he and Jordan would split somewhere around $1,500,000. Of course, Jordan got 75 percent to his 25 percent, but it was hard to get resentful when you were about to pocket that kind of change.

The absolute best part was the almost complete elimination of chance. Jordan could make a phone call and all the rules of air travel, customs, and TSA security just seemed to fade away. Leammons was curious how Jordan was connected, but he certainly never asked. It went beyond military and it went beyond government to something else. Whatever the something else was, he could do anything; he followed no rules and he answered to no one.

Leammons knew Jordan was an important man, since they had served together, but this level of influence was something else. He had no idea why or how it had come about, and he didn't ask. He didn't like the man, but with the money he made, he didn't have to.

• CHAPTER SIXTY-TWO

Forbus still looked at the thing in awe. The Active Denial System that American soldiers worked with in Iraq was amazing enough, but leave it to the Israelis to come up with a hand-held model.

The ADS was marketed by the Department of Defense as a nonlethal weapon used to disperse dangerous crowds without causing any lasting injuries. It shot an invisible beam, a few meters wide, and when it came in contact with human beings, those people felt as if their bare skin was exposed to a blowtorch. The current, or whatever the hell it was, reached nerve endings and caused intense, searing pain. Supposedly, there was no permanent physical damage. Forbus had seen angry mobs in Fallujah turn tail, scatter, and run as the US troops laughed hysterically.

Then Israeli engineers had made it into a hand-held weapon. It looked like a crude, four-inch in diameter lead pipe. It only shot a few centimeters of current, but the searing, burning sensation was the same. When it was over there were no scars, no internal injuries, no cuts, and no bruises. The pain was unbearable; the most anyone was able to deal with it on record was four seconds. In practice, even the toughest badasses succumbed immediately.

Forbus took pride in being tough, but in many ways, it was efficiency that was valued even more. One could possibly lose a fight, but when this perfected procedure was followed the risk was almost nil. First, the ability to surprise the victim was crucial. That meant needing to appear like a person who proposed no threat, either a docile stranger or, even better, a trusted acquaintance. Forbus didn't like friendships, not even fake ones, but sometimes they were necessary.

Next, when in close proximity to the victim, procedure required stabbing them quickly, without warning, with the sodium pentothal hypodermic. The drug made subduing the unsuspecting individual easy. Then the victim would be bound temporarily for the ride back to his motel, apartment, or house. During the drive, several painful Taser darts into the meat of the thigh would let the victim get a glimpse of the world of pain he was about to enter.

In the victim's home, the torture would begin. Jordan had provided Forbus with the electronically controlled manacles, carefully covered in sheepskin to avoid marks. The victim could be securely bound and the manacles could be released from a short distance. That was important.

The drug made everything easy. The victims were relaxed and terrorized at the same time. Most of all, they were compliant, which was what Forbus needed. Early on, Forbus had learned to gag the victims because of the screams. Then it was important to let the victims know that the pain wasn't going to end, that they'd continue to be hit with the current indefinitely until they succumbed.

Forbus would talk to them. Let them know that there was no way out. The victims all knew Jordan so they knew what they were up against. In fact, all of the victims knew Jordan quite well. Forbus would remind them of what they were involved in in the military and how now the assignment was to make sure they didn't endanger the operation for the rest of the group. In other words, the victims were told why they were there and why they were being tortured.

At first it had seemed like a mistake. If they got away then they would know too much and they could screw everything up. But Forbus realized very quickly that imparting to the victims that escape was not even a remote possibility was an excellent idea. The victims knew Jordan was behind it, and most of the time that was enough. They knew the man he was. They knew what he was about and how hardcore he was.

The pain would explode inside their bodies again and they'd see the cold, indifferent eyes of Forbus looking on. They knew the pain and the torture could go on forever. They would have to sense it, and the horrible pain combined with the realization that this was a Jordan operation told them they were doomed.

So when Forbus offered them a chance to escape the excruciating pain they accepted it. They always did. Some almost instantly, while some tried to futilely resist for what ultimately amounted to a very short period of time. It was so simple, it seemed implausible, but it worked just like Jordan had said it would. The man knew human nature and what people would accept, what they would deal with and what their breaking points were.

The torture was crucial, and Forbus had become expert in observing the level of exhaustion and stress in the victims. Humans could only stand so much, and Forbus knew when they would happily end it any way they could.

After several successive blasts, Forbus would approach the victims and calmly, without yelling or any verbal abuse, tell them that the torture would go on as long as it had to. Forbus would tell them that they could end it, escape the pain and never have to feel the pain again.

The pistol, equipped with silencer, would be left with one round in it just outside the grasp of their right hands. Forbus would leave the room quietly, and once behind a wall hit the remote button, freeing the victim's right hand.

Then Forbus would wait and listen.

After the muffled shot, Forbus would go back in, remove the manacles, disassemble the chair, pack away the ADS, and wipe down the place for fingerprints, just in case.

After that, Forbus would simply leave.

• CHAPTER SIXTY-THREE

Jack watched Jordan leave the gate of his development. He let him get a quarter mile ahead before he pulled out of his parking space and began to follow him. The Toyota Sienna rental was as nondescript as you could get, but Jack still did his best to avoid being spotted. He had worked for Jordan, so he knew both his paranoia and his capabilities.

Jordan headed straight down to Route 41 before taking a left. Jack became conscious of his sidearm, and a chill at the thought of committing a cold-blooded, execution-style murder went through him. He didn't like it. It wasn't his style, but he knew it was for the greater good. He believed the man was pure evil, as much as anyone he had ever encountered. Jordan was about greed and exploitation at the expense of others who believed they were doing something patriotic. Killing him was the only way.

Jack called TJ on the cell and told her it was time to pick up the tail. She had fallen in behind her father a half a mile from the beginning of the tail. Eddie was half a mile behind her. The plan was for each to follow Jordan for five miles before calling their backup to be replace them as lead. That way they would reduce the chance of being spotted. After they left the lead position, they would park for five minutes or so and then call to get back into the procession. TJ drove a Taurus and Eddie had a Ford Focus and all were equipped with GPS units.

TJ sped up and got within range of Jordan, just in front of the Publix grocery store on 41 North. Jordan made a left and headed down Jackson toward the gulf. TJ passed that news on to her partners and made sure she stayed four blocks behind. He made another left on Manatee and it looked like he was headed either toward the beach or to the airport.

She followed for another three blocks after he turned and phoned Eddie to replace her as they had planned.

Eddie didn't answer.

She hit the button on the cell phone that displayed the number she had just called and double-checked it. She had called the right number. She called again and got no answer.

She called her father and explained.

"I'll pick him up. You find Eddie. He was supposed to be in the parking lot behind the stores around the middle of Main Street by the restaurant TJ Carney's," Jack said.

They signed off quickly. Jack had to make up four or five miles to catch up with Jordan, and he feared he may have lost him. Eddie was the most reliable man he knew, both in the service and since. He trusted Eddie so much he was the only man he had ever considered calling when he resurfaced.

Jack got to the intersection that led to Casperson's beach in one direction and the airport in the other. He had to make a guess and he knew the airport was the likely choice. No matter how he tried, he just couldn't picture Jonathan Jordan going to the beach. He wasn't the sunbathing type. The airport was just a mile and half straight up Sarasota Boulevard.

TJ got to downtown Venice in ten minutes. It was the middle of the day and the senior citizens who made up 95 percent of the traffic drove incredibly slowly in their Town Cars and Devilles. She made the left behind Venice Avenue and pulled into the parking lot. She scanned for Eddie's Ford Focus and spotted it parked by itself away from the sidewalk and the other cars. TJ slowed down to not draw attention and pulled into the parking spot right next to Eddie.

She looked through her passenger side window and saw Eddie, sunglasses on and leaned back in the reclined driver's seat. The car was running, probably to keep the air conditioning blowing. TJ shook her head. She was surprised her father's friend was such a fuckup. She blew the horn to wake him up. The second time she hit the horn she got a sick feeling in her gut that radiated through her entire body.

She got out of the car and looked in at Eddie. His sunglasses were on and he looked asleep, but he had been shot in the chest. His T-shirt was soaked through with blood and he wasn't breathing. A chill ran through her and instantly she was back in Iraq. War, with its different rules and different reality. There was no question, she was back in it.

She hit the speed dial to reach her father.

The call went immediately to voice mail.

She tried three more times.

No answer.

• CHAPTER SIXTY-FOUR

Getting the nitromethane proved to be easier than he thought; the ammonium, a little harder, but really no trouble. The tanker of diesel fuel they would get at gunpoint in the morning because there really was no practical way of getting a truck filled with diesel any other way.

He actually had to turn down two volunteers for the mission. The two left out were angry and hurt they wouldn't be getting a chance to please Allah. It would be funny if it wasn't so pathetic, he thought. It was a weird world, and he knew he made his living in a strange way, but if it wasn't him it would be somebody else. That was how he rationalized it.

Years in the military had taught him just how fucked everything was. Almost everything that the average guy believed was bullshit. He didn't believe in any god, religion, or spirituality. After what he had been through for so many years, how could he? Life was about getting what you could, when you could, and getting out as intact as possible.

Intact physically, but also psychologically. He knew Jordan and was glad he was an ally. He didn't fool himself: he knew Jordan didn't give a shit about him personally. He did know what he could do was valuable to Jordan. The second he was no longer valuable, Jordan would, at best, write him off completely. At worst, Jordan would kill him for what he knew.

For now, it was a job to be done. A highly dramatic job with global consequences, but to him it was just how he turned a widget. It was the clock he punched and the way he went to work. At least if he was involved in the job, he knew he wouldn't be one of the victims.

So there would be no hand wringing or worry. He'd sleep tonight.

Then, tomorrow morning he'd go to work.

• CHAPTER SIXTY-FIVE

TJ kept trying to reach her father. She got voice mail each time.

Her mind raced as it had in Iraq, and she did her best to focus. She could feel it physically and she fought to keep from breaking down. It was time to disengage from emotion and go into the no-feel zone.

One thing she knew was that she had to get out of this parking lot. There was nothing to do for Eddie but mourn and this wasn't the time nor the place. In Iraq, she had learned to move away from dead bodies and not to waste time or put herself in danger by letting her feelings come over her.

She decided to walk around the block and head down Main Street. She needed to see the area and take note of anything out of the ordinary. With the breakdown of communication with her father she knew nothing about Jordan's whereabouts and it made no sense to drive aimlessly all over Venice.

It was approaching midday and Main Street was filled with tourists and snowbirds buying T-shirts and knickknacks. TJ was dressed in cargo shorts, running shoes, baseball hat, and sunglasses, with her sidearm in the small of her back covered by an oversized T-shirt. She was out of place in the pastel alligator shirt and sport sandal world, but not enough to raise attention.

She walked past TJ Carney's pub, scanning both sides of the street. She was approaching a women's boutique and an ice cream shop when a voice calling her name startled her out of her zone.

"TJ!" She snapped her head around. She looked at the familiar face but it took a full minute to identify the woman talking to her.

"Jenny?" TJ recognized her fellow dancer. "What are you doing here?"

Jenny was all giddy with smiles and ran to hug TJ. Her arms were wide and she giggled as she approached TJ.

"Surprise, girlfriend!" Jenny said. TJ, dumbfounded, returned the hug. Before it could register that Jenny's hug clung just a little too long, she felt the prick to her back. She winced and pulled back.

"What the fuck?" TJ asked. She instinctively reached toward her back. She looked at Jenny's face and watched the smile fade, replaced by a cold, all-business look.

TJ immediately felt a surreal detachment sweep over her. She was there but not there at the same time. She felt Jenny grab her arm and walk her down the path between the ice cream store and the boutique toward the parking lot. To observers, they looked like two close friends on vacation, walking arm in arm.

Jenny helped TJ into an SUV with tinted windows. She cuffed her hands and started the car. The cuffs were just an extra precaution because TJ could barely move.

Jenny said nothing as she pulled out of the lot. TJ fought to concentrate, but it was a useless fight. Before they hit the corner of 41, TJ was unconscious.

• CHAPTER SIXTY-SIX

"Don't move. Put your hands on your head and keep your eyes straight ahead." The voice was calm and quiet. The directions were clear and procedurally professional.

Jack Dunn realized he shouldn't have been surprised. Jordan hadn't gotten to where he was by shoddy work. Everything Jordan did had a surgical precision to it. So when Dunn had parked his car near the fence on the north side of the Venice airport, in close proximity to Leammons's jet, it was only a matter of time until Jordan's men approached him. It seemed simple now, and Dunn felt foolish for making such a basic mistake.

The man held the pistol on him with two hands in strict military style. He spoke clearly into his headpiece and in short order another security officer appeared and removed the rifle from Dunn's front seat. That officer said something into his headpiece about the weapon being secured. When Dunn's cell phone rang, the first officer had Dunn hand it to him. He noted the call and said something else into his headpiece and put the phone into his vest pocket.

The first security officer began to speak into his headpiece as if he had received another call.

"It is secure. There were no issues," he said, and then paused.

"No, sir, he does not appear to be from any of the lists."

Another pause.

"Caucasian, late fifties, I believe ex-military." Pause.

"A sniper's rifle."

"Yes, sir."

Dunn thought about TJ. They had his phone. They now had her number and could probably get her location in no time from the GPS device. He felt his mouth go dry and the rest of his body go cold. It was bad enough if he lost his life by Jordan's hand, but the knowledge that he had dragged his innocent daughter into this was something he couldn't bear.

"Sir, this is what's going to happen," the first security officer said to Dunn. "We're going to walk side by side through the airport gate to that jet." He motioned with his gun in the direction of a Learjet. "We will walk as if we are acquainted. My partner will be twenty paces behind us and he will be armed. If you move toward me or attempt to flee you will be killed immediately. Do you understand?"

Dunn nodded.

"Very good, sir."

Dunn walked with the man toward the barbed-wire gate that said "Authorized Personnel Only." He could not hear the footsteps of the man behind him. They walked in the direction of the jet, and while they walked they watched a black Lincoln Navigator pull up to the plane. A security officer got out of the driver's side and walked around the car to open the passenger door. Jordan got out.

At the same time, a security officer walked down the six-step staircase that folded out of the plane. When he reached the bottom of the stairs, another man, who looked like a civilian, deplaned. Jordan and his security guard moved toward the other man and his security guard.

Dunn and his escorts walked toward the circle of men. Jordan turned and looked at Dunn, squinting, trying to identify him. When they were within five feet, Jordan's eyes went wide and then he grimaced.

"Jack Fucking Dunn. Are you shittin' me?" He half smiled and shook his head. "What the fuck, Jack?"

Dunn glared at Jordan without saying a word.

"You were coming to kill me, weren't you?" Jordan said it without fear or anger. It was more like astonishment.

"You bet your ass I was," Dunn said through his teeth.

"Hold it, now it makes sense. That's your daughter who's been fucking things up. Holy shit. Now it makes sense."

Dunn kept his mouth shut.

"She's probably dead already, you know. If the torture is over." Jordan cracked a smile.

Dunn went to lunge at Jordan but was restrained by the two guards.

"Jack, you're a resourceful and creative man, but did you really think that you could get to *me*?" Jordan asked with genuine disbelief.

"Fuck you, Jordan," Jack said.

Jordan shrugged. He took a breath and let out some air. He looked at the lead security officer.

"Take care of it, with discretion." He nodded. The officer nodded back.

Dunn knew the order for his execution had just been given.

• CHAPTER SIXTY-SEVEN

The Holiday Inn in Fort Lee, New Jersey, was three miles from the George Washington Bridge. Truckers with payloads destined for Manhattan liked it there because they didn't have to get into the city traffic mess and because it was a whole lot cheaper than anything in the city.

He pulled in with his U-Haul. He had left clear instructions for the men joining him not to park near his vehicle. He wanted to make sure that no onlookers could draw conclusions from seeing the two trucks parked next to each other. It was probably an unnecessary precaution, but redundancy in this business was a good thing.

In his room he met the three men who were to carry out tomorrow morning's assignment. Their English was good but he could tell just by looking at them that they were experiencing considerable anxiety. Knowing you were going to die in sixteen or so hours would do that, he supposed. It didn't matter how thrilled Allah was going to be with you.

He went over the important issues. They needed to drive very close to each other. They couldn't let anyone else get in between them. They had to signal each other just before ignition of the explosives so the fuel truck could accelerate right into the back of the detonator truck.

None of it took any expertise or elaborate precision, but there were fundamental things that needed to happen. He always suspected that these guys with their extremist views weren't always rational; they weren't always good listeners and thus weren't always good at carrying out their missions. They got emotional, they forgot a basic principle, or they panicked. He'd seen it happen twice with shoe bombers, with pirate activity, and thwarted plane hijackings that never took place—all because they didn't follow the most basic instructions.

He went over the instructions three times. He made them repeat them back to him, which annoyed the hell out them. They knew what to do. They wanted to do it, he could tell, and these three seemed to have the wherewithal to carry it out.

Tomorrow morning at 8:35 a.m., during the morning commute on the George Washington Bridge, they would certainly get people's attention.

CHAPTER SIXTY-EIGHT

TJ came around slowly. When her faculties returned she was in a handmade wooden chair not unlike the pictures she had seen of electric chairs. Her hands and legs were shackled to it and there were electric wires coming out of the manacle that secured her right hand.

The motel room came into focus and TJ was confused by what she saw in front of her. There was a metal or maybe lead pipe about four inches in diameter mounted on a tripod. It had a crude handle, wiring leading to some sort of electrical control box about the size of an old computer, and a small generator as big as a college dorm refrigerator.

The door to the darkened room opened, forcing a ray of bright light across the bed to flash in TJ's eyes for a moment. A tall female silhouette silently entered the room. TJ tried to shake off the grogginess left over from whatever had knocked her out.

"Hey, Dunn. I gotta ask you. Did you suspect me at all back at the Taco? I mean, were you even a little suspicious?" Jenny Forbus asked.

"Jenny…" TJ's voice trailed off in what came out as half question, half statement.

"I mean, did I pull it off as a dancer?" She had stepped in front of the tripod about four feet from TJ. The soft light from the closed blinds gave her a little gray illumination.

"What the hell?" TJ asked.

Forbus stood straight as a board with her hands on her hips and looked down at TJ.

"You probably want to know what's going on, huh?"

TJ just looked at her.

"I work for Jordan. I was like you, a tough female soldier. He liked me and kept me on after discharge. I got sent to cover you when he lost faith in Strickland. Strickland was just supposed to surveil you, but that suicide hotline stuff started to get weird. Your emotional state was unpredictable."

TJ's head was clearing. But even as her awareness sharpened, the situation didn't become any less confusing.

"What did anyone care about the hotline?" TJ asked.

"The warning calls you were getting. Someone was trying to enlist your support. That probably could've been let go, but your emotional reaction and your unstable state—they just couldn't take a chance," Forbus said.

"I don't have any fucking idea what you're talking about," TJ said.

"The calls were right. The GIs weren't killing themselves; well, technically they were, but not really. I was getting them to the point where they would kill themselves rather that deal with more of…well…this." She nodded toward the tripod.

"Why were you killing GIs? I mean, for what reason?"

"Jordan ordered it, which is enough. But it's about the money. The money in the heroin business is huge. You wouldn't believe what they pay me or what even Strickland's salary was. It's crazy money and it's all tax-free. When there's a threat or even a perceived threat, the situation has to be resolved." Forbus lifted her eyebrows as if to say, "Understand?"

"What do I have to do with it?" TJ asked.

"C'mon, Dunn. You came to Venice. Jordan's here. Why the hell would you come to Venice if not to mess with things?"

TJ swallowed. Not knowing what was going to happen made everything worse. Forbus went behind the tripod and hit a button. A fan sound kicked in like when a computer booted up. She hit another switch, and several LEDs illuminated on the generator.

"Remember those ADSes in Iraq? This is a hand-held model the Israelis came up with. It shoots only a centimeter ray, but it's enough," Forbus said.

"You're going to shoot me with it? I don't get it. I could understand if you were going to kill me and get it over with. Why torture? I don't know anything that you haven't already told me."

Forbus half smiled and exhaled.

"You don't get it, do you?"

TJ squinted and looked at Forbus in confusion.

"Some of the others I could get to the point of suicide through psychological torture. I think some even called you. But then there were some who resisted. This is how I got the others to pull the trigger on themselves."

TJ just looked at her.

"Shit, hang on," Forbus went behind the device and looked through a small scope crudely affixed to the pipe with silver duct tape. She pointed it at TJ's chest. There was a silent pause.

"Agh!" TJ screamed as a searing flame of pain seemed to ignite at her solar plexus and burrow through her and out her back. It was like when she had been shot on the UAH, except the pain remained constant instead of running through her when the bullet exited.

TJ's body convulsed and she vomited. The pain didn't lessen. She felt on fire through her entire midsection.

Suddenly it stopped.

Forbus stepped into the light.

"I'm going to do that to you again and again and again."

TJ felt the vomit on her chin, and the aftermath of the pain was made worse by her inability to move in the chair. She looked at Forbus.

"Still don't get it?"

TJ managed to shake her head.

"I'm going to do this to you, over and over, without relief. Then, I'm going to give you a chance to escape the pain."

TJ looked her in the eyes.

Forbus gave her a humorless smile.

"You want to know how you'll escape the pain?"

TJ looked at her through the tears that had welled in her eyes.

"You will shoot yourself," Forbus said.

CHAPTER SIXTY-NINE

One of Jordan's men grabbed Dunn's elbow and told him to walk. The two men who had escorted him to Jordan began to walk him toward their vehicle just outside the fence.

The escort let go of his arm and the two men followed him from behind, back about five strides.

The gate was no more than two hundred feet ahead. Dunn had a sick feeling of dread in his gut but he forced his mind to problem-solve. If he ran, he'd be shot instantly. If he turned to speak they would raise their weapons and instruct him to turn around. If he failed to do that, he would be executed. They were out of reach for him to engage with his hands.

He resisted the urge to sprint just for the sake of doing something. Once he got into their vehicle, he knew he was dead. He'd be handcuffed, probably blindfolded and bound, maybe even hooded and gagged. He knew the procedure. He had lived in this world. He had completed this procedure himself many times and the knowledge of it sickened him.

When they approached the gate, one of the men walked ahead. He turned and walked backward to keep Jack in his sights. The other escort spoke.

"Stop right there."

The first man unlocked the gate and held it open.

"Walk to the back passenger side of the vehicle with your hands on your head. If you move you will be shot." It was said with force but without emotion.

Dunn had no answers. He had no plan, and though he was expert in a number of fighting arts, if he moved on the man who was about to cuff and gag him, the other would shoot him without hesitation. That was how this worked, and there were no variables. These men were trained at this and they were undoubtedly the best at it. Jordan would have accepted nothing less.

Dunn heard the dangle of handcuffs behind him and in that instant he realized he would be dead shortly.

"Hands behind your back," the first escort said.

Jack hesitated just a second.

"Hands behind your back." This time the intensity in his voice had increased.

As Jack Dunn began to move his hands, he heard the crack and whistle he associated with a long-range rifle. In the following instant, he felt the man behind him bounce into him, then into the fender of the SUV. As the man hit the vehicle, he heard the second shot.

Dunn turned just in time to see an explosion of blood come from the back of the second escort's head. The force of the shot turned the man around, and as he landed on the pavement, he rolled on the ground with the back of his head blown off.

Jack looked at the man as blood poured out the crater in the back of his head. They were both dead.

Dunn reached down and took his first escort's weapon, and then reached into his pocket for the keys to the SUV. He looked up, and as he suspected, the shots had gotten the attention of Jordan, Leammons, and the remaining four security officers. Leammons and Jordan scrambled into the jet with one of the guards while the others aimed at Dunn.

The surprise of the sniper shots gave Dunn enough of an advantage, and he was in the SUV and headed toward US 41 before they could get off a shot.

• CHAPTER SEVENTY

Forbus hit it again.

She had taken a break only to gag TJ to minimize the carry of the screams.

The invisible ray seared into TJ. The spot wasn't even an inch, but the excruciating pain burned like it went right through. TJ screamed into the gag. It was a reflex scream because of the pain; she knew no one was around to help.

Forbus sighed impatiently. This was repetitious and almost tedious for her. She knew in time the procedure would work. It was human nature to give up when there was no escape. In this case, suicide was the only option available.

She knew from the start that Dunn would stretch the boundaries of tolerance.

"You know, this isn't going to let up. By now your father is dead, you already know his buddy Edward Surett is dead. You will endure pain wishing you could die. Or you can die without the pain. To me, it doesn't matter," Forbus said.

She hit the button again. This time she moved the target to TJ's throat. TJ screamed again into the gag. The thinner skin and lack of clothing covering the region intensified the burning pain. She vomited into the gag and then forced herself to swallow it.

Forbus studied the reaction that each shot brought. She sometimes varied the shots to different body parts and other times repeated a shot into the same area. She had learned that the subjects responded differently. This shot to the neck got Dunn's attention.

She hit the button three more times in rapid succession.

TJ's head snapped back violently each time and she vomited again. She had very little to spit up but her stomach contractions forced the reaction.

TJ began to think about dying.

• CHAPTER
SEVENTY-ONE

"Would you like the pistol?" Forbus asked blankly.

"Fuck you," TJ managed, muffled through the gag. She had been hit with the ray at least a dozen times. She was unable to move from it, and each time it hit her she writhed. Not being able to escape a burn like that was something she had never experienced before.

"This will continue indefinitely. You will kill yourself, sooner or later. You can do what you think is brave but you are only subjecting yourself to unnecessary pain." She moved toward TJ. "I'm going to remove the gag so you can talk, but the instant you get loud it goes back on. Understand?" Forbus asked. It was all part of the technique.

Once the gag was removed, TJ managed to look up at Forbus. "Did you kill my fiancé?"

Forbus smiled. She continued to look at TJ.

"Answer me, you bitch!"

"No, I didn't. Your boy actually killed himself, as far as I know. He was a head case too. I'll tell you this, though; he made it easy on the rest of us. He was such a whiner I'm sure he would've been on my list."

Forbus moved the gag back into place. She hit the button.

TJ's entire body spasmed. She felt her eyes bulge and she wretched. She had vomited so many times there was nothing left. She began to hyperventilate.

Forbus smirked.

"Strickland went easy too. That was actually a crude job. He knew what was coming and he just used common sense. He realized what he was in for and was smart about it."

"Fuck you!" TJ said.

"What's that? Fuck me? No, *fuck you, Dunn!*" She hit the button again.

TJ writhed and Forbus smiled. The smile was short-lived.

The sound of shattering glass broke the silence. Forbus looked toward the window next to the room's entrance as a second whistling sound pierced the room. This time the entire window blew out.

Forbus drew her gun, hit the carpet, and went to peer out the window. A hail of fire sprayed the room. From the sound of it, she figured it for a P3.

TJ became aware of what was happening in the room. The latest wave of pain had not yet subsided, but with the hail of fire, her fatigue lifted. She remained immobilized by the manacles.

Forbus slowly lifted her head to peer out the shattered window. Immediately another hail of fire lit up the room. She slid down, her back to the wall, and quickly rolled over, away from the window to the wall behind the door.

"Fuck!" Forbus yelled. TJ looked at her and she could tell from the widening of her eyes and the pace of her movements that Forbus was panicked. Forbus stood with her back to the door and took a deep breath. With her pistol in her right hand held high, she reached for the doorknob with her left. She took another deep breath, grabbed the knob, threw the door open, and ran out of the motel room in a crouched position.

TJ braced for more fire.

It didn't come.

She remained fixed to the chair. The torture was over, for now anyway—at least the physical torture.

• CHAPTER
SEVENTY-TWO

"You didn't secure the fucking area!" Jordan yelled at Leammons. "How many times have I told you!"

"The area was secure. That was goddamn sniper fire. It came from at least a half a mile away. What the hell am I supposed to do with that?" Leammons asked.

"The police will be on their way. What the fuck are we going to do?"

"I can handle them. I'll make a call," Leammons said.

"There are two dead bodies out there by the fence."

Leammons motioned to the two remaining guards.

"Get them out of there right away. Put them in bags and get them to the storage facility with the pilot's luggage." The two men didn't hesitate and ran to get the bodies.

"We have to get out of here. I don't want to lose this product. Can you get the plane out of here?" Jordan asked. He had the rare sound of panic in his voice.

"We'll need about twenty minutes to refuel."

"Do it and get it up in the air," Jordan said.

Leammons radioed the pilot, who was getting lunch at the Cockpit restaurant. He responded immediately and in seconds could be seen running toward the plane.

"Get him up in the air and on his way to New York as fast as possible," Jordan said. "I'm getting the hell out of here."

Jordan motioned to his two security officers and they led him off the plane toward their remaining SUV on the tarmac.

• CHAPTER
SEVENTY-THREE

Jack Dunn headed back to the hotel on 41. He pulled into the parking lot, saw the blown-out window, and felt his stomach turn over. He sprinted through the parking lot, through the open doorway, fearing he was about to see his daughter dead.

"Dad!" Jack saw TJ manacled to a crude wooden chair.

"TJ, my God!"

"I'm all right. Hit that remote and get me out of this thing."

Jack saw the remote device, hit the button, and heard the manacles unlock. TJ bounded out of the chair.

"Get me the hell out of here before the cops come."

Through the excitement, Jack hadn't heard the sirens. The two them ran out of the room to the stolen SUV and Jack floored it out of the parking lot.

"Are you all right?" Jack asked.

"I think so. She kept hitting me with some sort of goddamn portable ADS."

"Oh my God. That fucking Israeli thing?"

"That's how they're getting men to kill themselves. The pain is so bad they choose to end it."

"My God…" Jack said.

"How did you know to shoot out the windows? How did you know where I was in the room?" TJ asked.

Jack looked at her.

"What?"

"The windows," TJ said. "I could've been right behind them."

Jack looked at her.

"I didn't shoot out the windows," he said.

They just looked at each other.

CHAPTER
SEVENTY-FOUR

It took a lot to make Jonathan Jordan panic. This was about as close as he came.

It wasn't the loss of life that concerned him. He had stopped caring about casualties a long time ago. Shots fired at an airport in the middle of the day concerned him. So did a private jet filled with heroin.

Sending the plane to its destination without the proper preparations was risky, but circumstances dictated that he act quickly.

Right now, he had a few more quick decisions to make.

He had ordered the two men to get the dead bodies and dispose of them as discreetly as possible. The other two security men had accompanied the plane. He would head home by himself. He was armed and though it had been some time since he had had to defend himself alone, he still could. The first thing he would do when he got to his house would be to get his sidearm from the bedroom. He'd have it loaded and there'd be a round in the chamber.

It was a ten-minute drive to the gate. He had always made sure he was cordial to the guard. He didn't want him to note anything remarkable if he ever got questioned.

He smiled and nodded as the gate was lifted. He took the right toward his house a quarter mile later and kept to the ridiculously low speed limit. He pulled into the garage and entered the house through the door that put him in the kitchen. He was focused and he had a mental checklist of what he wanted to accomplish. Get the gun, turn off the lights, hunker down, and wait for things to blow over. He'd make a call to his contact who influenced the media and he'd wait.

He moved fast in his home, passed through the kitchen to the great room and headed for the staircase. He heard a metallic sound and whipped his head around.

"Hello, Jonathan," Jack Dunn said. His .38 was aimed at Jordan's chest. "Say hello to my daughter, TJ."

Jordan's eyes went back and forth between Dunn and his daughter. His mind raced.

"You killed the man she was going to marry. A good soldier, a man who didn't deserve to die. You killed a lot of men who didn't deserve to die," Dunn said. His words had almost become hypnotic.

TJ wondered if he would kill Jordan right there, right then. She had drawn the gun her father had given her. It was all so surreal. Jordan was frozen with his hands in the air.

"It ends here, Colonel. Right here and right now."

TJ heard the gunshot and it startled her. Her father screamed in pain and spun around, crashing into and falling over the coffee table. TJ, confused, looked up and saw Jordan run toward her father. Her father had been shot, not Jordan, and her father's gun had dropped out of his hand.

She spun and fired in the direction the shots had come from. A second round of fire came in her direction and the bullet caught her pistol, rocking it violently from her hand.

As she turned, she saw Jenny Forbus emerging from the kitchen. TJ's shot had caused her to jump back and bang into the stainless steel refrigerator. In the process, she had lost her grip on the gun.

Forbus lunged for her gun. TJ stepped toward her, planted her left foot, and threw a jumping front kick that landed squarely on Forbus's chest. TJ heard the rush of air leave Forbus as she fell backward. TJ went to pounce on her but Forbus got her legs up in a squat and pushed TJ back with everything she had. TJ went back against the kitchen island, banging her head violently in the process.

Jordan scrambled for Jack's gun. Jack was able to get his leg between Jordan's legs and he swept him to floor, out of the reach of the pistol. Blood matted the fabric of Jack's T-shirt to his shoulder and he writhed with white-hot pain.

TJ and Forbus both were standing. Forbus dived to tackle TJ around the waist but TJ pivoted to her left and countered with an uppercut. The punch landed flush on Forbus's nose and TJ felt the cartilage crackle under her fist. Forbus's momentum brought her down hard, face-first on the tile floor. Instinctively, Forbus reached for her bloodied nose.

TJ dropped her bent knee with all her body's weight and with all the force she could muster into the center of Forbus's spine. Forbus screamed in pain and TJ felt her struggle to breathe. TJ grabbed her by the back of the neck and began to choke the life out of her. Forbus lapsed into unconsciousness.

Jordan lunged again for the gun and Jack body-blocked him from it. He kept him from the gun but now he was sprawled on his back. Jordan kneed him in the groin, rolled off him in one motion, and came up with the gun.

TJ was reaching for the gun Forbus had dropped. She got to it, but not before she heard Jordan yell, "Freeze!"

Jack Dunn was flat on his back. He had lost a lot of blood and his ability to concentrate had faded. Jordan held Jack's gun in two hands and had it trained on TJ in a shooter's position.

Jack attempted to lunge at Jordan. Jordan stepped back, keeping the gun on TJ.

"Don't do it, Jack. I'll kill her," Jordan said.

"Drop the gun, TJ, or I put a bullet in his head," Jordan said.

TJ's gun wasn't in position to fire. Jordan would kill her if she tried, and then execute her father. She slid the gun across the kitchen floor toward Jordan.

Jordan broke into a half smile and steadied the gun at TJ.

Jack threw a kick with all his might at Jordan's shins. Jordan stepped back easily and re-aimed. The smile came back to his face.

The blast of a gunshot rang through TJ's ears and shook the walls of Jordan's house. She remained standing, feeling nothing. Her eyes had shut and her mind raced. She was in shock. She resisted opening her eyes to see her father dead.

She felt a heavy arm placed on her shoulder from behind. She opened her eyes to see Jordan's body lying over the smashed coffee table. Half his head was gone and his lifeless body was still. The back of Forbus's head was also missing.

TJ felt the arm pull her in close. She was pressed against another body.

She opened her eyes and turned.

And looked directly into Trent's eyes.

• CHAPTER
SEVENTY-FIVE

TJ's mouth hung open and she began to shake.

"Listen to me." Trent held her by the shoulders. "I am so sorry. I had to do this. I didn't mean to hurt you. I had to do this." He held his M4 machine gun, the weapon of the US Special Forces, in his right hand.

TJ's mouth hung open and her eyes went wide.

"I need to get out of here. I am way too exposed. I will find you, but I need to get moving. Know I love you, I have always loved you, and I always will."

He pulled her to him and held her. They broke for an instant and he kissed her long and hard.

"Get your father to the hospital ASAP. He's lost blood. I have to leave now. I only have a few hours to get to New York. You've got to understand."

"But—"

Trent had already turned and headed out of the kitchen and through the garage. TJ ran toward him, tears running down her face, but he started his SUV and put it in reverse.

• CHAPTER SEVENTY-SIX

TJ waited while they performed emergency surgery on her father. She spent the night in the surgical waiting room. She was exhausted physically and emotionally and knew from experience that there was a long road ahead for her.

At ten minutes to nine, a doctor came out to speak to her.

"He lost a lot of blood, and we struggled for a long time to stop the bleeding. Fortunately, he was strong enough to make it through the process and it looks like he's going to be fine. It will be awhile before he can use his arm and shoulder, but he will live."

"Thank you," TJ said. The doctor turned and left, and TJ almost collapsed onto the vinyl couch. She exhaled and began to wonder what new demons she would need to fight. She found it difficult to concentrate and knew it wasn't even close to the time when she would be able to address what had happened.

As she sat in that state, she became distracted by the waiting room television. It was fixed on CNN. There was an overhead shot of the George Washington Bridge and a split screen view of a Ryder truck parked next to an oil truck. The trucks were surrounded by police tape and there were several bodies on the pavement. The anchor's voice came into focus.

The George Washington Bridge remains closed in both directions at this hour, causing massive gridlock going in and out of Manhattan. New York City Police, the FBI, and the Office of Homeland Security can be seen at the site but there has been no official word of what is happening.

So far, this is what we know:

Four Iraqi nationals were found shot dead in a Fort Lee, New Jersey, garage this morning. Two men were apprehended in a rented Ryder van loaded with the explosive nitromethane. Two more men were apprehended in a diesel truck parked directly behind the Ryder vehicle. A driver of a Lyons Fuel diesel truck was found dead earlier this morning in a ditch off the Palisades Parkway. He had been bound and gagged and had a bullet wound to the back of his head.

The Fort Lee garage was rented two weeks ago and the owner reports that it was rented over the Internet and he had not met the men who rented or paid for it. The garage is three miles from the George Washington Bridge.

The men were not employed by any local diesel firms or moving companies. Speculation at this hour is rampant. Some New York City media outlets are claiming that a terrorist attack on the George Washington Bridge was foiled minutes before it was to happen. That has not been confirmed by any source.

Once again, the NYPD, the FBI, and the Office of Homeland Security are not commenting at this hour on the event. The area is secured and no one is allowed into a mile square of the crime scene. An unconfirmed rumor that the four Iraqis were shot and killed with an M4 rifle has not been substantiated. The M4 is the weapon of choice in the US Military Special Forces.

We will continue to report on this story throughout the day as details develop.

TJ sat and watched. She calculated how many hours had elapsed and realized there had been time.

She didn't have to speculate.

CHAPTER SEVENTY-SEVEN

"That is an incredible story," LaMontagne said.

Four weeks had elapsed since the nightmare had come to a close, but it still seemed so fresh. "I'm so sorry you were affected," TJ said. She looked at LaMontagne. Her arm remained in a cast and she had three bandages covering facial wounds.

"They say I'll be fine. It isn't likely that there will be scarring, and my knee will heel without surgery. All in all, I'm lucky," LaMontagne said. "I'm more concerned about you and the piling on of trauma in your life."

"I am not sure how to even process what went on. I mean, getting my father and then Trent back is…" TJ couldn't find the words. She felt the wave of emotion come up again and she started to cry. It had been that way for the last month. Getting back to therapy was going to be a huge help.

"TJ, I don't think it is even close to the time to think about processing this. I know how you like to have the 'take care of business' attitude, but just like before, this won't be easy."

TJ sniffled back tears.

"I don't really have him back, do I?" TJ asked through the tears.

"I can't pretend to have experience with such things. This is just so out of the ordinary. But, I think you're right, you don't have Trent back. It's like you have the worst of both worlds."

TJ looked at LaMontagne. The confusion on her face showed. LaMontagne went on.

"Trent isn't dead but he's still gone. However heroic his motivations are, he has still left you behind. He chose something over you. I'm not placing blame or evaluating right or wrong. But being left behind by your partner is still loss."

TJ looked down at her Nikes. She had no idea what to feel.

"You've been back for a month. How have you been spending your time?" LaMontagne asked. TJ was relieved by the topic change.

"Same stuff as before. I'm dancing and working at Aquarius."

LaMontagne smiled and shook her head.

"I guess I've come to understand you in a slightly different way."

"I don't know if *I* understand," TJ said.

"You need to do. Others need to feel. You've become more willing to feel, but though I didn't approve of it before, I think in a strange way what you do is curative."

TJ looked at her while she paused.

"You need action to help you feel. As you feel, you begin to understand and learn. That's growth," LaMontagne said and smiled.

TJ felt herself blush from the compliment.

"Doctor, what do I do know? I mean, Trent's alive but gone again, with no explanation or plan for the future. I love him, but how do I live my life in limbo?" TJ asked.

LaMontagne took a breath and looked as if she was thinking of the words to use.

"I believe you need to live for now. Someday, Trent may return to your life in something that approaches normalcy. But there's nothing to predict when, how, or if ever. I think you do yourself a disservice by not living your life. You really have no choice."

"I can't let go of him," TJ said, almost pleading.

"You don't have to. At the same time, live your life. Do what makes you feel alive."

TJ let it sink in. It felt almost right. Though she realized nothing felt completely right anymore, and as long as she lived, it might never feel right.

* * *

TJ had three hours before her shift at the Taco. She had worked at Aquarius the night before, and though she was glad to be back around Billy and Heather, she didn't want to spend any more time there today.

She thought about what LaMontagne had said, and in some ways it made sense. The whole experience was just too weird to process. TJ didn't like thinking too much; she'd rather move, *do*. She headed up the stairs and heard the familiar thump and the jarring sound of the round buzzer. She came through the door with a little more anticipation than she had counted on.

He was there, and as she wrapped her hands to get ready, he came over.

"How was Florida?"

"Ah, you know how family stuff can be." TJ smiled at her own irony.

"Well, glad you're back." Duffy walked toward the heavy bag to get ready for the next round of work.

TJ hesitated and then made herself say it.

"Hey, Duffy?"

He turned and raised his eyebrows. "Yeah?"

"Could we do some sparring today?" TJ asked.

• ABOUT THE AUTHOR

Tom Schreck is the author of five novels, including *On the Ropes* and *Out Cold*. He graduated from the University of Notre Dame and has a master's degree in psychology—and a black belt. He previously worked as the director of an inner-city drug clinic and today juggles several jobs: communications director for a program for people with disabilities, adjunct psychology professor, freelance writer, and world championship boxing official. He lives in Albany, New York, with his wife.